It was impossible. She couldn't really be *his* witch…could she?

You idiot, Jack. Less than sixty seconds into the game, and you've terrified her.

The Dark rose inside him in a growling tide. She shouldn't have to be afraid, this little pale-eyed witch who smelled of desperation and sweetness. What had happened to her? Did the green witch know her?

It didn't matter.

She's lucky I'm here. I'm lucky too. More damn luck than I deserve.

The car dropped into gear and started forward, tires shushing though water. She pulled through the empty parking space in front and twisted the wheel hard, deftly turning into the paved aisle leading to the exit. Jack tensed. *Follow, or stay?* There was little in the Watcher codes that covered this situation except the general dictum of protection. If he pursued her too quickly she might sense him and become even more frightened, and he found he wanted to avoid that.

Wanted it, in fact, with an intensity he wasn't used to feeling about anything anymore.

For James, because he asked me to.

Other Books by Lilith Saintcrow

Dark Watcher
Storm Watcher
Fire Watcher
The Society
Hunter, Healer

Coming Soon
Mindhealer
The Demon-Hunting Librarian

Cloud Watcher

***

Lilith Saintcrow

Cloud Watcher
Published by ImaJinn Books

ISBN: 1-933417-18-8

10 9 8 7 6 5 4 3 2 1

PUBLISHER'S NOTE:
This book is a work of fiction. Names, characters, places and incidents are products of the author's imagination or are used fictitiously. Any resemblance to actual events or locales or persons, living or dead, is entirely coincidental.

Books are available at quantity discounts when used to promote products or services. For information please write to: Marketing Division, ImaJinn Books, P.O. Box 545, Canon City, CO 81212, or call toll free 1-877-625-3592.

Cover design by Patricia Lazarus

ImaJinn Books
P.O. Box 545, Canon City, CO 81212
Toll Free: 1-877-625-3592
http://www.imajinnbooks.com

Aegroto, dum anima est, spes esse dicitur.
—Cicero

One

"Got to go potty," Shell reminded her, shifting uncomfortably in his seat.

Anya checked the rearview mirror. Nothing but a blank freeway receding into infinity. "Okay."

She hit her blinker. The rest stop exit appeared like a gift, and she pulled off, headlights slicing the purple dusk in front of the blue Taurus. "But we'll have to be quick, okay, sweetie?"

"Okay," Shell agreed placidly. His round blond face was spectral in the green glow from the dashboard.

Anya's head hurt, both from a nagging headache and from the goose egg under her hair. She'd hit the doorjamb hard, stunned for a moment while the *thing* screeched, before Shell could drag her away.

Don't think about that. Concentrate on what you have in front of you. She hit the brakes. "Good," she murmured, and coasted to a stop.

Shell was almost out of the car before she could cut the engine, and Anya sighed. Her eyes were hot and grainy, her entire body aching with exhaustion, and she had only her car and a pile of clothes to her name. Oh, and the coffeemaker.

The slight thunderous smell of smoke and fury in the car didn't help her headache one bit.

The rest stop was set at the top of a green hill and water rilled in a creek behind it. A concrete path zigzagged up the hill, and the entire place was deserted. It was a good thing. Both she and Shell were exhausted and grimy, dressed in odds and ends.

How am I going to feed and clothe us both this time? She got out of the car and stretched, watching as Shell lumbered up the hill, his huge shoulders hunched under his favorite Green Bay Packers sweatshirt. He ducked into the men's bathroom, and Anya wearily started up the hill herself, her zoris flapping. Wet grass slipped under her feet until she reached the next strip of concrete.

Shell saved me. If it hadn't been for the roof caving in, we wouldn't have gotten away. Anya shivered. The sky was overcast, chill November night falling like a soft cloud. She smelled smoke and wrinkled her nose—it was the scent of her life burning down. Again.

How many times am I going to have to do this? This is the fourth time we've had something attack us, the third time we've been driven out of a city.

She washed her face in the metal sink. There were no paper towels. That was all right. The chill would help keep her awake. Anya didn't dare look into the slice of scratched metal serving as a mirror, either. She came out into the gathering dusk to find Shell waiting for her, his sleepy blue eyes wide and fearful.

"Anya." His voice trembled. "I was afraid."

Me too. But I can't show it or you'll be even more upset. "I know, buddy. Let's go, okay?"

"Okay. Where are we sleeping, Anya? I'm sleepy."

For a single moment she let herself feel the bitterness. *How on earth should I know? I just had my house burned down and my life destroyed by a big, tall fiery shadow nobody else can see. How am I supposed to make this better?*

Why me?

Guilt rose sharp and bitter inside her throat. She straightened her shoulders, taking an accustomed weight of guilt and responsibility. "I know you're tired, buddy. I'm sleepy too. We'll stop in the next city and find a place to sleep, and I'll have to get a job. You'll have to be a very good boy, Shell. All right?"

"Okay, Anya." He tromped back down the hill, almost glowing with happiness. If she said it was going to be all right, it was going to be all right. After all, Anya was his protector, and she had always found them food and shelter before.

I'm going to have to use the Persuasion again. If I don't, we'll starve. Anya picked her way carefully down the hill. *I wish I didn't have to. Why is this happening to me?*

She knew why. Anya could do things other people couldn't; sense things other people couldn't. She was, in the truest sense of the word, psychic. And she had a sneaking suspicion that was why the huge hairy and shadowy things were after her. Not to mention the fanged things, or the clawed things, or the winged things...

I must be insane. I hope I'm insane. I'm wishing I'm insane. Isn't that crazy?

She heaved a sigh as she reached the bottom of the hill. Shell had already folded himself into the car. Her zoris flapped as she crossed to the driver's side, opened the door, and got in, rubbing at her grainy eyes.

"We gonna go, Anya?" Shell asked.

"Sure. Just give me a minute, buddy. Okay?" *Just give me a minute to pull myself together and quit wishing I was batshit nuts.*

"Okay." He waited. "I sure hope they don't follow us."

"I hope so too, Shell. I don't know how many more times I can do this."

"It'll be okay, Anya."

He promptly fell asleep before she pulled back out onto the freeway. The next big town—Santiago City—was fourteen miles away.

It was as good a place as any. After all, it wasn't like they had anywhere else to go.

Two

Jack checked the address again, though he didn't need to—a blind man could have seen the shields resonating over the small shop, its window brightly lit in the gathering dusk. The sawing of pain in his bones was normal, and if the intel was true it was going to get worse soon, so he ignored it.

He rolled his shoulders back, settling the leather weapons-harness more securely, then detached himself from the shadows and glided across the street.

Rowangrove Metaphysical and Occult Supplies, the window's gilt lettering declared proudly. Jack shook his head. He remembered when it was death to admit you were a witch, death to be suspected, and the only thing standing between a Lightbringer and the Inquisition—not to mention the Crusade—was a Watcher's care.

Come to think of it, things weren't all that different nowadays. Watchers were still the best defense for a witch, and the world was still dangerous. Just last night he'd dispatched a *kalak*, his first kill in this new city.

The new city that was like every other damn city on the face of the Earth. And here were Lightbringers announcing their presence to the general public.

I'm not in a good mood tonight. He grinned mirthlessly. It was a good thing no Lightbringer was around to see that grin.

He waited for the shields on the shop to recognize the Power he carried and pushed open the door, the small bell over it tinkling merrily. Immediately the pain spiked, a fresh crescendo of turmoil inside his bones, acid threading through his nerves.

Jack ignored it. The shop was full of Lightbringers, and the Power blazing from them reacted uneasily with the Dark symbiote melded to his body. He set his jaw, his eyes flicking over them. *Well. Would you look at that.*

The leader, a witch with a long fall of dark hair, stood at a bookshelf, her long green dress fluttering around her ankles as she turned toward him, her cheery, "Welcome to the Rowangrove!" ringing out. Beside her, on her knees next to a large cardboard box, was a blue-eyed blonde whose aura bore the unmistakable blue shimmer of a water witch. Behind them, at the curtain closing off another part of the store, a witch with copper-gold hair and a spinning gold-red aura to match raised one hand, crackling static outlining her fingers. The fire witch had something pulsing on a ribbon around her slim white neck—it was a Talisman, he guessed, and decided it would be a good thing to stay where he was.

She can't kill me, he thought, calculating the Power fluxing around her. *But she could make me pretty damn uncomfortable.*

The witch in the green dress smiled. Clear green light radiated from her, the deep serene calm that marked a healer. He'd Watched healers before; they were a challenge, always trying to save the world. He didn't envy the Watcher currently guarding *her*, whoever it was.

"Who the hell are you?" the fire witch snapped.

"Elise," the green witch said. The Power in her voice made Jack's entire body twitch with pain. He stayed still, overriding it.

"Watcher reporting for duty," he replied politely enough, through almost clenched teeth. The rhythm of his native tongue sometimes wore through his English, so he spoke with care, stripping the words down to bone. "Jack Gray, at your service, ma'am."

A silence greeted these words. They stared at him as if he'd just announced the moon was made of cheese. *Not very welcoming, are they? Don't blame them, either.*

The blue and green curtain over the door billowed aside, and a golden-eyed Watcher slid out, closing his broad hand over the fire witch's delicate wrist.

"Elise?" His tone was excessively neutral, and his eyes flicked over Jack once.

Good kid, keeping contact with her. She looks like a spitfire.

Then Jack noticed the golden-eyed Watcher wasn't flinching from the contact with the Lightbringer's skin. In fact, their auras—the bright clarity of the fire witch's and the red-black bruise of the Watcher's—melded together at the edges, the Watcher's darkness seeking to veil the witch's glow.

Lucky bastard. He'd bonded.

"It's all right," the green witch said firmly. "Dante?"

Another Watcher, this one dark-haired and black-eyed, shouldered the golden-eyed man aside. This was a familiar face, and Jack nodded in recognition.

"Well, I'll be damned." Dante said, his broad shoulders filling the doorway. "Honor, brother."

"Duty, brother." Jack was hard-pressed not to sound relieved. He could talk to the Watchers much more easily than the witches.

"Sorry," the golden-eyed man said. "Honor, brother."

"Duty, brother." *Where's the third one?*

The water witch pushed herself up to her feet, yawning and dusting off her knees. "Hanson should be back with the pizza soon," she said to Jack, who felt his stomach turn over at the sound of a Lightbringer speaking directly to him. "Come on in, if you can stand it. Elise won't hurt you; she's just set on 'stun.' We've had a bad time with something called the Brotherhood lately."

I know about that. Jack had been briefed on the Brotherhood presence in town. They had tried to take the fire witch three months ago—and almost succeeded. No wonder she was still nervous.

Jack had to move aside as the door opened behind him. He sensed the red-black stain of Watcher power and relaxed slightly. Another Watcher, this one blue-eyed, pale-haired, and sharp-faced, ducked in carrying four large pizza boxes. It was Hanson, the bane of the Crusade.

"Honor, brother." Jack jumped in, not wanting to say 'duty' again.

Hanson's immediate smile was slightly unsettling. Precious little of it reached his pale eyes. "Duty. It's the famous Jack Gray. You like pizza?"

This instantaneous welcome almost made him doubt his ears. *Don't they know why I'm here? Just tell me what to do and let me get to work.* "I thought you'd tell me which quadrant needs the first sweep."

"Oh, for heaven's sake." The green witch touched Dante's hand. The black-eyed Watcher drew himself up a little taller, and Jack noted with faint, pleasant surprise the soft rounding of the green witch's belly. The gods were kind—hopefully, another Lightbringer in the world.

So. They were a pair, Dante and this witch. He'd heard it was true—three powerful Lightbringers, bonding with three separate Watchers, in a little under two years. He hadn't believed it.

Getting suspicious in your old age, Jack. He moved aside until he stood next to the glassed-in counter and the cash register. Hanson handed the pizzas to the fire witch, whose golden-eyed Watcher touched her shoulder and disappeared into the back room again. Then Hanson slid his arm over the water witch's shoulders, and she smiled up at him.

"Come in and have some pizza, you're probably hungry,"

the green witch continued. "I'm Theo. That's Mari, and that's Elise. You obviously know Hanson and Dante; the big lug who just vanished into the kitchen is Remy. He's in a mood because Elise was attacked last night."

"I wasn't *attacked*," the fire witch immediately objected. "I just had a bit of trouble with a mugger. Remy handled it without even breaking a sweat."

"If you didn't wander around the city late at night, you wouldn't be at risk." Dante's voice rumbled in his chest. His hands found Theo's shoulders, an unconscious, tender gesture.

Jack looked down at the wood floor, old dark pain rising from his backbone. The air in the shop swirled with Power, drenching the floorboards, taunting the Dark that lived in Jack's bones.

Duty, Watcher. He set his jaw. *It's only what you deserve.*

"When I want your opinion, Stoneface, I'll rattle your cage," the fire witch replied acidly. "Come on in, Mr. Gray. Nice to finally meet a Watcher with a real name."

"I was sent to do patrol and—" He wasn't used to floundering.

"Yes, yes." Theo's eyes lit up. Beautiful eyes, full of light— a calm deep green the color of sunlight shining through mossy water. "But you can have something to eat first. You're the first Watcher we've let into the city." Here she glanced at the fire witch, Elise, who raised her coppery eyebrows in a gesture of magnificent disdain. "And we're very curious about you, of course. If you don't mind."

"Of course not, ma'am," he replied automatically, and glanced over his shoulder at the front of the store.

"Don't worry." The green witch's lips curved into a merry smile. Her light made Jack's bones burn as if acid was leaking through the marrow. "We're safe enough. Four Watchers and three Guardians, what can go wrong?"

Jack almost flinched. *I wish she hadn't said that.* "Yes ma'am."

"Call me Theo. We're glad you're here."

That's funny. Most people hate to be in a room with me. Especially Lightbringers. He obediently moved forward, letting the light of the shop close around him. "Pizza sounds good," he agreed cautiously, wishing the presence of the Lightbringers didn't make his entire body burn with acid etching.

"That's the spirit!" Theo said, and her smile was almost enough to make up for the pain.

Three

It took a chunk of their waning money to get a hotel room, but at least they could stay for a week or two. By then, Anya was sure she could get a job and maybe find them somewhere else to live. If all else failed, she could use the Persuasion at a bank—though she didn't want to. It wasn't a good thing to do.

Then again, what choice do I have? She sat at the table and stared bleakly at the newspaper she'd bought. Shell was still asleep, gently snoring, his round, pale face open and trusting as a child's. *I have to feed us. It's not like I'm using it to get rich, is it? And I don't take enough for it to be serious, I take an amount insurance will cover, don't I?*

It doesn't matter, her conscience replied as it always did. *Taking money is thievery. You're using your freakish talent improperly. No matter how desperate you get it's wrong. Nothing changes that fact.*

She shook her head and glanced at the window. Morning light seeped through the curtain-edges. Another night survived.

It was odd, but this city—Santiago, what a pretty name—felt a little safer than the last town they'd lived in. For some reason her chest was lighter, and she felt none of the dread she associated with a new place. Instead, she felt vaguely hopeful.

Though even my optimism is taking a beating lately. Having one's house torn down and burned can do that, I suppose.

The coffeemaker from her old house gurgled quietly, and the rich scent of coffee began to dispel some of her morning cobwebs. She missed her neat yellow-and-white kitchen with its stripped pine cupboards—that had been two cities ago, the house with the grand curving staircase Shell had loved to sit on while playing cards. That house had been reduced to matchsticks as something huge and dark, smelling of violence and burning blood, had torn through it looking for her.

She hauled herself up and stretched, walking across the room to pour a cup of coffee. It had become habit to take her coffeemaker with her, and to stick two extra mugs in the car just in case. *I must be crazy. Nobody else is pursued by big, dark, burning things. Maybe I belong in a mental institution.*

The fact that Shell saw the same things she did was little comfort. He had the mind of a five-year-old in the hulking body of a linebacker; he wasn't qualified to judge her sanity.

Then again, Shell knew things he had no business knowing, too. Maybe he was just more observant than most.

Anya sighed, pouring her coffee into the cracked white mug. Then she crossed back to the table and opened the paper. Time to find a job.

She lingered for a moment over the professional section— she had a teaching degree, after all—and shook her head again, sighing. She'd disappeared from her last three jobs. Nobody was going to hire her with that kind of record. Besides, who could tell when she would have to flee again? No, she'd take something like waitressing. That would give her cash tips immediately. She'd worked as a cocktail waitress in college. The money was good and she could work at night while Shell slept. It was a good idea.

Hell, I've tried everything else, haven't I?

She leafed through the classifieds and stopped, her eyes drawn to a particular ad.

Help Wanted: Rowangrove Metaphysical is hiring. Must be over 21, good sense of humor, literate, and open-minded. Pay negotiable. Hours negotiable. Perfect for caretakers.

Now what did that mean, perfect for caretakers?

Anya's fingers tingled, prickling with heat. The feeling was impossible to ignore.

She circled a few more ads for waitresses and returned to the Rowangrove ad, impelled by instinct. The tingling in her fingers had never led her wrong before.

It can't hurt. I suppose. I'll just take a look and maybe turn in an application. After I apply at the others.

With her day's work cut out for her, Anya settled back in the chair and sipped at her coffee. She hoped she'd brought some decent clothes, and she hoped she could find a job as soon as possible. And she hoped the darkness wouldn't find her again.

She *could* hope, couldn't she?

Four

It was a boring day, but Jack didn't mind. Learning the geography of any new city was a challenge. Sooner or later they all started to look the same. When he finished his rotation here he'd be sent somewhere else, a new city to learn. Repeat *ad nauseam* until maybe he had done enough penance.

Yeah. As if anything could erase the stain on *his* soul.

Jack leaned against a brick wall, watching the street as Hanson separated from the shadows farther back. "See?" the blond Watcher said. "Easy little pass-through."

Despite himself, Jack was impressed. The rapier-quick younger man had a good grasp on the city's shadow-side and was introducing Jack to some of his more useful shortcuts and contacts. Not all of them, Jack suspected—the boy was no fool— but enough to make Jack's job easier.

"Good work," Jack said mildly, and watched the boy grin. Jack hadn't seen him in combat yet, but he suspected Hanson was sharp and vicious—especially when defending the water witch. He had that look. "So, what part of the city is the worst?"

"Oh, the docks and that entire area. Near the water, lots of transients, and the Lightbringers don't often go there, so we kind of keep it as a pressure zone. Some nasty shit comes out to play sometimes, keeps us on our toes." Hanson blinked at the gunmetal-gray sky and glanced out onto the street. Traffic was light today, downtown in the financial district—something that didn't happen often in cities this size. "Let's work back uptown a bit. I've got to be back to the Rowangrove in a few hours to take Mari to the library."

After settling his long black leather coat more securely, Jack followed the younger Watcher out onto the sidewalk, both of them sending out invisible waves of awareness, cataloguing, moving, weighing, measuring. Being a Watcher demanded constant scrutiny, constant alertness. You could never tell when danger might rear its ugly head and streak straight for a Lightbringer. "So you're all three bonded." He drew level with the blue-eyed man.

"Oh, yeah," Hanson replied, deftly flaring his aura to make a small knot of chattering kids separate around the two of them. "It's a helluva coincidence—if it *is* one."

"There's three of them—fire, earth, water." Jack didn't have to put any inflection in his words, the sentence was question enough. He even managed to sound normal instead of stilted and foreign.

"There was a fourth—the Teacher, the one that trained them. She was an air witch. She's on the other side of the Veil now, one of the Guardians."

Interesting. Their boots resounded against pavement. It was a breathlessly muggy day, clouds gathering close, desultory splatters of rain decorating the sidewalk. A twist of paper ruffled in the uncertain wind, and cars zoomed by. Jack checked the street again. Why was he nervous? He was *never* nervous, hadn't been for a good seven or eight decades.

"Still," said Hanson, "it boggles the mind. We've discussed it a little, and all three of us are uneasy. The gods don't set up things like this for nothing."

"True." Jack noticed a low brick church with the unmistakable odor of Dark clinging to it. "That's a nest over there. Probably *s'lin.*"

"It is, but we don't have the firepower to clean it. Trying to get those three to stay undercover while we work is like herding cats."

"You should enforce their safety." *You should tie them up in the basement if you have to, kid. Leaving nests in a city is asking for trouble.*

"You try it. They're *Lightbringers.*"

At least the young man knew where his duty lay. "So they're foolhardy." That was valuable information. Then again, when were Lightbringers *ever* conscious of their safety? They just wandered through the world, trusting in their gods.

"Wait 'til you bond, old man," Hanson snorted. "Then *you* try getting your witch to do anything for her own safety."

"I haven't bonded yet." *Shut up, kid. No witch for me.*

"Well, why else are you here?" the other Watcher returned reasonably enough, turning to his left and waiting to cross the street, the weak sunlight light glinting in his pale hair. Jack followed, his boots silent against pavement. "Seems like you'll be in the same boat with us before long. Remy wasn't here twenty-four hours before lightning struck *him.*"

"Wouldn't count on it." *There's no witch for me. Ever.* "If it hasn't happened by now, it's not likely to."

"How old are you, anyway?" Hanson started across the street when the light changed. "Seems like you've been around forever."

"Old enough to know better." Jack's hand touched one of his knife hilts. Reassured, he followed the younger Watcher. Soon enough he'd learn this city, and he'd begin cleaning out the Dark, one methodical step at a time. If he focused on that, he wouldn't have to think about the raw aching wound inside his chest. Seeing the three Lightbringers and the lucky bastards bonding with them, seeing what he could never have—

Well, that's why he was doing this, wasn't it? Paying his dues.

Performing a penance. Blood and steel instead of Hail Marys and Our Fathers. *Change the subject, dammit.* "So this is a major artery, this Fifth Street?"

Hanson shrugged. "Yeah, that and the Ave, where the Lightbringers tend to congregate."

The lunchtime crowd swirled instinctively away from both Watchers, sensing predators in their midst. *At least the normals know enough to get out of the way,* Jack thought sourly, and checked the perimeter again.

"Hey, you've got a good sword there," Hanson continued. "Dante says you're the only Watcher who's ever faced down two *belrakan* at once."

For a moment Jack's breathing halted. The memory rose— dirty water dripping, concrete, the witch he'd been guarding screaming as he shoved her against the wall and prepared to make his last stand—and he wrestled it down. His skin roughened with instinctive gooseflesh. No matter how old or dangerous he got, he still didn't like almost dying. "I hear you've faced a Bane yourself, brother." He caught himself almost thinking in his native language again, stopped with an effort, and forced the words back into English.

"Last year. Nasty fuckers. Here, we can cut through this restaurant. They've got a back door and hardly notice us." The younger Watcher seemed to realize he was being rude, speaking of *belrakan* when Jack obviously didn't want to talk about it, and led him through a Chinese restaurant and out into a small alley. "Sorry. I'm used to Dante, we've worked together for so long."

"Well, I'll only be here to finish my rotation," Jack replied harshly. "So don't get used to me."

"Heard and understood." Hanson glanced back over his shoulder, a flash of blue eyes in the gray day. "You hungry?"

Jack's stomach flipped. He was starving, despite the fight with the *kalak* last night and its attendant cargo of useful bloodlust—but hunger was a weakness. The older he got, the less he liked living on the energetic charge of violence. "No," he replied, and the other man mercifully shut up.

Five

"Stay here," Anya told Shell. "I'm just going to get another application."

"I'm *hungry*." He pushed his lower lip out. His heavy-lidded eyes drooped even further.

Anya took a firm hold on her frustration just as a smattering of rain kissed the windshield. *He can't help it; he's not responsible. Don't take it out on him.*

Shell was having a bad day. His old teddy bear was gone in the fire, and she knew she wasn't her usual calm self. Instead, she was snappish and her mood had infected him. She considered scrapping the whole idea and going back to the hotel for another long sleep—but she was near the Rowangrove, and she would be a fool to let the intuition she'd received slip past her. Even if they only paid minimum wage, she might be able to stave off the inevitable for another few weeks.

Anya gathered her waning patience, her fingers knotting together around her car keys. Metal bit into her palm. "I know you're hungry. I'm hungry too. Look, as soon as we finish here, I'll get you some chicken strips. How about that?"

Shell's round face lit up. He loved chicken strips. And french fries. "You promise?"

"I promise," she replied just as seriously, holding up her fist with the pinkie free. He clasped pinkies with her. "Now, just wait for me, all right? This won't take long, and I *need* a job."

"Okay, Anya." Supremely confident now, Shell leaned back in his seat and closed his eyes. "I'll be good."

"You've been good all morning, Shell," she had to admit. "I'll be right back. Wait right here."

"I'll wait."

Anya closed him in the car with a little trepidation. It was like having a child, Shell required almost constant supervision. She'd always been able to find something that let her look after him, but a nagging unease began under the surface of her thoughts and wouldn't let go. When would she have to put him in a home? When would he become unmanageable, or when would she no longer be able to care for him?

Don't borrow trouble, as Granmama used to say. Deal with the current crisis and let tomorrow take care of itself.

She waved to him before she turned the corner. She'd parked in a grocery store lot, so he would be safe enough for ten minutes while she went to collect an application from the shop. The grocery store beckoned with warm yellow light and the promise of food, but Anya squared her shoulders and walked away, threading through parked cars. Clouds were overhead, and a chill raindrop kissed her cheek. She hoped it wouldn't start pouring until she finished getting the application.

She walked down the pavement, head down, almost lost in thought. The shop was on a major street, University Avenue, and she'd managed to spot its front window while driving past, looking for a parking space. *I wonder what they sell. Metaphysical? What does that mean?*

She smoothed her gray wool skirt and adjusted the matching blazer. It was the only unwrinkled outfit she'd found suitable for job hunting in the mess of her car. She was going to have to be careful not to wrinkle anything else until she could find a Laundromat.

The hair on the back of her neck stood straight up. Anya stopped in the middle of the sidewalk and glanced around, just as a bolt of lightning lanced the sky. Thunder pealed a few moments later, and rain started pattering down in earnest.

She was half a block from the Rowangrove.

For a moment she hesitated, torn. Shell hated thunderstorms. He would be frightened, and by the time she got back, he'd be unwilling to be placated even by chicken strips. But she *needed* a job and the intuitive tingling in her fingers had never led her wrong. Her instincts all but demanded she take a look at this place—and her intuition had saved their lives before. "I'll just get an application." She put her head down, determined to ignore the rain and the growing sense of unease. "I need a job, after all." *Talking to myself. Maybe I am crazy.*

The unfairness of the whole thing was almost laughable. She had never knowingly done anything to hurt anyone in her life, and yet she was driven out of city after city, pushed from place to place, hunted by things nobody else could see.

Maybe she *was* crazy. But if she was crazy, had she burned her own houses down? It was impossible for her to cause that sort of destruction, reducing a house to splinters in fifteen minutes.

She shook herself out of woolgathering. There was work to be done.

Rowangrove Metaphysical and Occult Supplies, the gilt lettering on the widow read. Anya nervously pushed her fingers through her hair, hoping she didn't look too shabby. *Please, God, let there be something here for me.* She ignored the prickling against her nape as she pushed through air suddenly gone syrupy-thick to step up to the door.

The bell jangled and Anya stepped inside, suddenly enfolded by a feeling of warmth and safety she had never known before. She blinked, running her fingers back through her recalcitrant hair, trying to pat the shaggy black strands into place. She wished for the hundredth time that she could have found a hairdresser this morning to cut the charred bits, instead of doing it herself.

"Welcome to the Rowangrove," a deep, calm female voice greeted her. "You must be here about the ad."

Anya blinked.

The store was full of books and healthy green houseplants, and all along the wall behind the cash register were glass-fronted shelves of other, probably more valuable books, each shelf neatly labeled in a beautiful clear script on white stickers. Racks of clothing stood arranged to Anya's right, and stretching back toward the rear of the store was a section of candles and other things Anya knew nothing about.

I'm in the wrong place. She would have turned to go if not for the pair of dark green eyes beaming at her from behind the register.

"I—I'm sorry," Anya managed.

The woman was tall and had a long fall of dark sandalwood hair. She was also beautiful, a kind of cool impenetrable beauty that made Anya want to check for loose threads or holes in her own clothing. Perfectly balanced cheekbones, a sculpted mouth, and those eyes—Anya blinked. The woman's eyes seemed to glow in the wash of golden light from the store's ceiling fixtures.

"No need," the woman said. "I'm Theo. You are...?"

Confused and at the end of my rope, thank you. "Anya. Anya Harris. I came to apply for the—"

The woman's dark eyebrows drew together briefly. Then her entire face broke into a smile like sunlight. "Of course. You'd prefer morning hours or evening?"

"E-evening. I have someone I have to take care of." The air in here seemed richer, full of the scent of growing things. There was a red blooming orchid next to the woman, and it stretched toward her, as if drinking in her heady light.

She glows. Anya shivered. *She glows like I do, but a different color.*

"Perfect," the woman said. "Tomorrow, at three o'clock. You're hired. I know the pay may not be all you'd hoped for, but it's steady work and we're nice people, I swear."

Anya's jaw dropped. She stood dripping on the Rowangrove's 'Welcome' mat and gaping at the dark-haired woman, who wore a green sweater that brought out the best of her eyes and creamy complexion.

I'll bet she's never had a pimple in her life, Anya thought with a nastiness that both surprised her and slapped her back into an almost normal thought process. "You're hiring me? Just like that?"

"Of course." The woman laughed, but the laughter was so good-natured it was impossible to take offense. "I know what I'm doing or I wouldn't be running this place. You need the job, don't you?"

Anya nodded. She couldn't lie. She needed something—and she might be able to find some way to take care of Shell too.

The bell over the door jangled sweetly, and Anya flinched.

"Come back tomorrow," the woman told her. "Three p.m. Don't be late. And you can bring your little boy with you."

I didn't say anything about a little boy. Anya backed up instinctively. The woman smiled, kindly enough, but Anya's entire body went cold and prickly with foreboding. Something was going on here. She was backing up so fast she almost tripped, and she braced herself to hit the door.

Great. I'm going to klutz myself out in the first five minutes.

She ran into someone, the breath driven out of her in a whoosh.

Oh, no. Anya whirled, breaking away from a pair of hands that had closed around her shoulders and steadied her—and found herself face to face with two men.

One was tall, blue-eyed, and white-haired. The one that had steadied her was slightly taller, but his eyes were gray like her own. Straight eyebrows, high cheekbones, a thin no-nonsense mouth, and a thatch of dark hair.

No, his eyes weren't like hers. They were cold and flat, nothing soft or forgiving on their icy surface. He looked furious, and not particularly upset about the fact, either.

"Oh, God," she said immediately, through a sudden frozen

lump in her throat. "I'm sorry."

The gray-eyed man wore a long black leather coat—both of them did, but Anya didn't want to look at the blond man. They both had broad shoulders, taking up too much space. The remainder of Anya's breath left her in a shocked gasp. Her eyes were drawn irresistibly to the gray-eyed man's face. He hadn't shaved—charcoal stubble spread up his cheeks, but it didn't make him look scruffy. Instead, every single shadow on his face looked planned. He stared at her from eyes infinitely gray as a snowy sky, and Anya's heart leapt into her throat, pounding as if it wanted to burst out and run merrily around the block.

Both men looked dangerous and too big for the space they found themselves in. Anya backed up, and the gray-eyed man's gaze fastened on her throat.

The bottom dropped out of Anya's stomach again. "I have to go," she said breathlessly, and tore her gaze away from the man to look at the woman behind the counter, who'd said something Anya hadn't heard.

"I'm sorry?" *Great, now I sound like an idiot as well as a klutz. Get a grip, Anya!*

"Come back at three o'clock tomorrow, Anya. Please." Now the woman looked puzzled. The air filled with the smell of green growing things, as if she'd just watered the plants in the shop.

Anya slipped between the two men as thunder roiled the sky again. A crackle of heat slid over her skin. Maybe it was fear. They were both so *tall*. She caught a flicker of movement out of the corner of her eye. The blue-eyed man stepped quickly away, but the other one stood where he was so she had to squeeze past him, holding her breath in case she brushed against him.

Just as she hit the door, hearing the little bell tinkle again, she heard another female voice, clear and sweet with a breath of salt to it. "What's all the—oh, hi, Hanson. Theo?"

"Mari, there's our new—" But Anya didn't hear the rest. She was too busy scrambling out into the rain and running back toward the dubious safety of her car. Oddly enough, it wasn't the green-glowing woman or the shop itself that made her flee.

It was the gray-eyed man. Because he'd looked at Anya as if he knew her.

And the shadow of something dark seemed to hang around him, perfuming the air with the scent of the nasty things that had driven Anya from all her homes.

Six

Jack's eyes followed the witch as she ducked out the door and into the stinging rain. He catalogued her automatically: fragile and small, her black hair cut haphazardly, as if she'd trimmed it herself, her gray eyes wide and fearful.

She had flinched away as she squeezed past, Jack's feet all but nailed to the floor. It was a sheer impossibility, one he was having a little trouble processing.

The glow coming from her hadn't hurt him.

What the hell?

"What the hell was that?" Mari put her hands on her hips, her eyes burning blue. She shook her tumbled golden curls back, and the light flaring from her made Jack's bones twitch yet again. The spike of pain shocked him back into rational thought. Nothing was wrong with him; the other Lightbringers still made him hurt.

"Our new employee," Theo replied softly. "I think she's a witch, Mari. And I think she's in trouble."

"Well, *that's* par for the course." Mari pulled her blue sweater up on her shoulder. "What's he doing?"

"I'm going after her," Jack told Hanson. "Take care of your witch, Watcher."

"Honor, brother." Something like mischief sparkled in Hanson's blue eyes.

Jack didn't waste time, just yanked the door open and followed the black-haired witch.

The smell of jasmine hung on the air—her perfume. His heart pounded, red rising up behind his eyes. Was it true?

Of course not. You're just following standard Watcher codes. You see a Lightbringer in distress, you help her. She's radiating enough fear to bring all sorts of Dark out, even during the day.

The witch pelted down the wet street away from him, leaving a crystalline trail of Power glowing like sun-fired amber in the rainy air. She was unshielded, heedless, fleeing without even bothering to mute the wild beacon of her distress. Had he frightened her that much?

I didn't say anything to her, so why is she running? I shouldn't have touched her. But what else could he have done? If he hadn't grabbed her shoulders, she'd have fallen on him.

The spike of sensation tearing through him at the thought

almost made him stumble. It wasn't pain.

But if it isn't pain, what the hell is it?

She rounded a corner and bolted into a grocery store parking lot, awkward because of the low black heels she wore, but still beautiful, her short glossy black hair flying on the wind, that trailing perfume of flowers and sweetness as wide as a highway. She was short and slim, and she ran as if the hounds of hell were after her.

Calm down, he thought fiercely. *Slow down. I'm trying to help!*

He heard her gasp, even through the falling water and rattling thunder. She made for a car—a blue Taurus, low-slung and full of something that pulsed in the unnaturally dark afternoon. Her footsteps clicked and splashed. He could almost taste her fear, a metallic tang riding through the jasmine smell.

Does she have another witch in there? He scanned the area. No, no Dark, and no other witch but her, but what *was* in the car? She almost tripped on her own feet, she was moving so quickly. *Slow down. You'll hurt yourself.*

She reached the Taurus and tore the driver's side door open, flinging herself inside so fast she almost hit her head. Jack took cover behind a red Jeep and decided to think things over a bit.

The shock of *contact* when her eyes met his had been instantaneous—inescapable. For a single moment he'd been nailed to the ground, incapable of reacting even when she'd brushed by him and run out into the rain. For that moment he'd forgotten all about his failure, and his penance, and the bitter acidic pain twisting inside his bones. The single moment stalled, turning over in his memory, and his breath came short and harsh, tearing inside his chest.

I don't even know your name, little witch. Come on, show that pretty face again, hmmm? It took a conscious effort to calm himself down, to bring his heartbeat back under control and take a deep breath tainted with the iron scent of falling rain.

The car's engine came to life with a sweet, soft purr. *Damn. Am I going to have to chase her car all the way through the city?*

The Taurus kept purring, motionless. He saw someone else inside, moving with her. One of the windows was down slightly despite the rain.

Her voice reached him, not raised but firm. "Stop it." For some reason, that voice—husky and light, touched with jasmine sweetness—nailed him in place again. "It's just thunder, Shell. I'm here."

Shell? What? Falling rain coated Jack's face as he tried to decide whether to break cover and run for her, or keep his distance and wait.

Keeping his distance won—but only barely, and only because he'd seen how frightened she was. The Lightbringer? No, she wouldn't be scared of Theo. It was his clumsiness she was scared of.

You idiot, Jack. Less than sixty seconds into the game, and you've terrified her.

The Dark rose inside him in a growling tide. She shouldn't have to be afraid, this little pale-eyed witch who smelled of desperation and sweetness. What had happened to her? Did the green witch know her?

It didn't matter.

She's lucky I'm here. I'm lucky too. More damn luck than I deserve.

The car dropped into gear and started forward, tires shushing though water. She pulled through the empty parking space in front and twisted the wheel hard, deftly turning into the paved aisle leading to the exit. Jack tensed. *Follow, or stay?* There was little in the Watcher codes that covered this situation except the general dictum of protection. If he pursued her too quickly she might sense him and become even more frightened, and he found he wanted to avoid that.

Wanted it, in fact, with an intensity he wasn't used to feeling about anything anymore.

The blue Taurus rolled to a stop at the exit. The left-turn blinker came on. She pulled out across four empty lanes and took to the far right, vanishing in an instant. He could follow, he realized—her scent hung on the air, blurring into his head, a lodestone to his heightened senses. He was a Watcher, had been one for far longer than most of the new Watchers could remember. He knew the dangers and had brought many witches into the safe fold of Circle Lightfall. But he'd never, ever, in his unnaturally long life, *ever* come across a witch who had this effect on him.

He was a Watcher, and she was his witch. And he'd let her get away. Even as he watched from behind the red Jeep, his chest tore in half as she passed out of his new sensing range, leaving nothing behind but a weak tugging to tell him what direction she was heading.

He swore viciously, a curse in old, pure Italian that made water splash up from the pavement at his feet. Then he hesitated, suddenly indecisive. Did he go back to the shop and wait for her to come back—or did he go a-hunting and hope to find her before the Dark crawling this city did?

Seven

Anya's hands trembled, so she clamped them around the steering wheel. Her knuckles were white, and the shaking spread up her arms and spilled through her chest. Gooseflesh prickled painfully all over her body.

"Do we get chicken strips now?" Shell asked plaintively, fiddling with his seat belt.

"Sure." Her voice shook. "Just hang on and let me find a place."

He pointed at a fast-food restaurant, and Anya stood on the brakes and turned into the parking lot, water sloshing up from the tires. Her hands shook even more. What was *wrong* with her? It should have been a coup. The woman had hired her off the street. But still, her heart thudded behind her ribs.

It wasn't the woman, or the way the store had felt so warm and welcoming. It was the gray-eyed man and the way he'd looked at her, as if everything else in the world had fallen away and they were standing alone on a lonely mountaintop.

Try as she might, she couldn't shake the vision out of her head.

It's not fair. Why do these things happen to me? Anya felt unfamiliar anger bubbling up inside her chest and took a deep breath. The last time she'd gotten truly angry, she'd wished very hard for a schoolgirl chum to come to some grief. Four days later, the girl had died in a car accident along with her mother and brother. The night before Cybil's death, Anya had dreamed of screeching tires and shattered glass.

She'd never allowed herself true anger since. Instead, she shoved it away, bottled it, pushed it down.

Sometimes she wondered what would happen if it ever broke loose. The thought was enough to cause nightmares of its own.

"Chicken strips!" Shell crowed.

Anya forced herself back into the present, turning the defroster to "max" so the windshield wouldn't fog up. It was really raining out there, the sky unnaturally dark and lanced with diamond veins of lightning. This city was on a bay and weather was moving in from the sea. She supposed it rained a lot here.

Not that I'm sticking around in one place long enough to

get used to any weather. "Chicken strips," she agreed, and pulled up to the drive-through.

Ten minutes later she navigated unfamiliar streets, winding her way back toward the hotel. Her heart still thudded so hard she couldn't eat, though Shell munched happily, slurping at his 7-Up and occasionally rustling the plastic sheath the kid's-meal toy came in. "Thanks, Anya," he repeated. "Anya, thanks. Chicken strips."

An unwilling smile tilted up Anya's lips. He really was a good-natured boy. "You're welcome, sweetie. I'll open up the toy when we get back to the room." She took a deep breath, turned right on Mango Street, and the hotel rose up dark in the rain. There was even—thank goodness—a parking spot right by the stairs. "Let's go up and dry off, all right?"

"All right." Shell managed to extricate himself from the car with no trouble while Anya struggled free of her seat belt. She led him up the stairs and settled him at the table with the remainder of his lunch and the toy. Then she went back downstairs, carrying the room key with her, to sort through some of the clothes and things she'd jammed higgledy-piggledy into the car. Rain drummed against the car's metal roof while she swore and struggled, getting soaked to the skin in the process.

She found a few outfits that weren't too shabby and carried them upstairs, ducking her head against the rain. Halfway up the stairs thunder rattled and she hunched her shoulders, hair rising on her nape. She still felt uneasy.

Not exactly uneasy, more like frantically paranoid. Almost as if she was being watched.

She hurried up the remainder of the stairs, almost tripping, and made it to the safety of the propped-open hotel door. She ducked inside and slammed the door, her arms full of clothes, her chest heaving, and the car keys clenched in her fist.

Shell glanced up, his heavy-lidded eyes wide and fearful. The toy, a figurine of a comic-book superhero, perched absurdly small in his large hand.

"It's all right," she said, more to soothe herself than him. She tossed the clothes on the bed with her purse and walked to the window, peering out into the stormy dark. It was only two in the afternoon, but already streetlamps were flickering on. Anya shivered, gooseflesh rising on her damp skin. She was soaked, her gray skirt and blazer sopping wet, her hair trickling thin, cold streams down her face and neck.

Shell went back to his chicken, but he ate furtively now, hunched over. Anya sighed, took another deep breath, and tried to calm herself. If she lost control of her emotions, Shell would become unstable. And the *last* thing she needed was Shell having a fit and possibly attracting the wrong kind of attention.

The room smelled musty. She wished she could have left the door propped open a little to let in the freshness of rain-washed air. On the other hand, the beds were made, and there were extra towels in the bathroom. Maybe she could take a long, hot bath and try to figure this all out.

The vision of dark hair and icy gray eyes rose again. Anya shoved it away. *I acted like a fool.* She reached up, scrubbing at her wet hair with her fingertips. *I should go tomorrow and apologize, see if she really meant it about the job. If I can find something for Shell. I can't leave him here all day.*

She sighed again.

"What's wrong, Anya?" Shell's blue eyes were dark now, with suspicion and something like fear. He counted on her to make everything all right.

"I'm just jumping at shadows, buddy." *And I think I just may have crossed the border into "paranoid." Of course, with what's happened to us, I suppose I have a reason to.* "Finish your food."

"You want some?"

"No, thanks." Anya couldn't help smiling. It was a mark of his affection for her that Shell would think to share his beloved chicken. "I think I'm going to take a bath, buddy. You can watch the TV."

He wriggled in delight. She patted his head as she passed him to close the drapes, wondering again at such a small boy's mind in such a large body. Shell was strong and well-nigh unrestrainable when he had a fit. The only thing that calmed him down was Anya's touch—and sometimes, a little Persuasion. She felt awful using it on him, tried not to—but sometimes, she had no choice.

Anya locked the door securely, put the chain on, and shivered as something brushed the edges of her awareness. Something dark and soft, like velvet wrapping around her, an almost physical weight against her shoulders and back.

She whirled, her eyes searching the hotel room. Two twin beds, one chair, one cheap table, the TV on the dresser, the low

counter with a sink and the coffeemaker, the hotel-provided
iron hung on a rack above.

Shell, sipping his 7-Up, watched her carefully, waiting to
see what she'd do next.

Anya turned on the television, found some cartoons, and
adjusted the volume. "I'm going to go take a bath." *And try to
calm down a bit. This is just the last straw.* She wished her
voice wouldn't shake. "Okay?"

"Okay, Anya." But he looked a little worried now, too.

"Don't worry," Anya told him. "I'll take care of us, Shell.
Don't you worry."

"Okay, Anya. I won't worry." But the look in his eyes told
her differently. He knew as well as she did that they were at the
end of their rope.

Eight

Morning dawned cool and gray, the storm having blown itself out. Jack, his leather coat imbued with a turn-aside charm to shed water like a duck's back, crouched in the lee of a juniper hedge and watched as his witch came down the motel stairs, yawning. She wore gray again today, a V-neck sweater and wool slacks, the same low black heels. The young man shambled behind her, his gait odd and his shoulders hulked, a weak glimmer around him.

Well. I haven't seen this before. Her son? No, too old. Brother? Not likely. Then what? Boyfriend?

The thought made a thread of rage slide through Jack's spine, but he buried it. There was no tang of intimate companionship between these two. Or at least, he hoped not.

Lightbringers sometimes accumulated hangers-on, those drawn to their glow. This witch was certainly powerful enough—she burned with clear golden light, her aura stretching and fringing in a way that told him she had no training whatsoever. How had she survived this long?

She certainly hadn't had an easy time of it. Her car was full of hastily packed suitcases and a pile of clothes, and the smell of smoke clung imperceptibly to the vehicle and everything it contained.

Smoke—and Dark, the smell of a night-hunting predator. Something Dark had marked this car. He inhaled deeply, cataloging the familiar scent. It explained a lot—if she'd managed to run before something nasty found her, she could have conceivably survived. Hiding and running; running and hiding.

Not any more, he promised silently. *It's over now. You're safe, I've found you.*

He'd dutifully checked in at the Rowangrove, ignoring Hanson's smirk and the green witch's worried gaze. He simply reported that he was following the black-haired Lightbringer to make sure she didn't come to harm, then disappeared . The streets around the hotel were laid with traps and defenses that would alert him if anything Dark approached her, and he had spent precious time yesterday sliding around the hotel, checking possible escape routes, feeling the lodestone of his witch glow up above on the second floor. Now he was free to do what he was meant to do—watch over her, whoever she was. And maybe, possibly, insinuate himself into her life.

He knew how to bring a witch into Circle Lightfall, of course. But this was different. The three Guardians had barred the Circle from operating inside the city's limits. That meant no Lightfall safehouse, and Jack, as the only Watcher the Guardians had grudgingly allowed in, had to make sure he didn't muck it up for the next poor soul.

He continued to watch the witch. She ran her fingers back through her shaggy shoulder-length black hair and turned, watching as the man shambled down the steps.

"—late," she said, the nervous worry in her tone reaching Jack's acute ears.

He wanted to reach out and close her clear glow in his own red-black aura to warn off any predators. He wanted to get her to a safehouse, and he wanted to ease the obvious tension in her shoulders. What was she late for? She was driving a car, even with Jack's speed and strength she could temporarily distance herself far enough from him to do some harm. He might not be able to reach her in time if she was attacked.

He watched as she closed the young man in the car the same way she would a child, her heels clicking against concrete as she walked to the driver's side. *Today. It's going to have to be today, or tonight at the latest. I'm going to have to meet you, witch, and see what I can do to get close to you. You need some looking after.*

The car's engine roused. He wished he knew where she was going. She wasn't due at the Rowangrove until three in the afternoon; where could she be headed?

Logic, Watcher. Logic. She's been chased by the Dark, is living in a hotel, and has a companion who can't even close his own door or *buy his own food. Ergo, she's looking for work.*

He was lucky. She didn't go beyond the Avenue. She visited three bars on the south end of the thoroughfare, each seedier than the last. The young man stayed in the car except for a quick lunch, both of them eating at a fast-food restaurant. Jack watched uneasily as the witch didn't finish her salad. She was under stress and too tense, a recipe for disaster—and drawing the Dark.

When she came out of the last bar, her hair glimmering in the overcast day, he could see her frown all the way from where he was hidden across the street, in an alley next to a French

---

restaurant. The odor of some long-ago violence hung in the alley, making the Dark symbiote stretch and vibrate under his skin.

She cut through another alley to where she had parked her car, shivering. The thin sweater probably did nothing to ward off the chill in the shade. *You shouldn't be here.* Jack watched her fragile shoulders under the gray cashmere. She ran her fingers back through her gleaming hair, blue highlights standing out even in the cloudy day. *You should be in a safehouse, Lightbringer. With me standing guard at the door.*

He saw it then, a drifting patch of shadow looking very much like a dark cloud clinging to the side of a building. The witch shuddered, paling, and put her head down, her heels cracking against pavement as her stride lengthened. She still frowned, but this time at the sidewalk, her shoulders coming up until she looked very much like she was fleeing.

Jack watched.

The *kalak*—a Dark predator capable of eating people from the inside out—floated a little closer, as if uncertain. She was bound to be powerfully tempting to any slice of Dark. She was unshielded, her Power scattering in random bursts. Jack's entire body tensed, his hand curling around a knife hilt. The black-bladed, rune-chased knife would damage the *kalak*, tear it free of its mooring in the physical world, and he could disperse any lingering whispers left. But if he moved now, she would sense it. It would frighten her even more.

She reached the car, unlocking the door and ducking in. The young man greeted her with a cry, clapping his hands.

Just like a child, again.

Jack dropped the very outer layers of his own shields, the red-black stain of a Watcher spreading out from the chill shade of the alley. The *kalak* wheeled and fled against the wind, almost dropping its cloud disguise in its haste to escape.

Small fry. Lucky it's daylight. It would have been another story at night. I don't like these clouds, makes it easier for the Dark to come out.

He dropped his gaze and saw the witch sitting in her car, clutching the steering wheel in white-knuckled hands. Jack melded even deeper into the alley's shadow. *Did she feel that?* His eyes narrowed slightly as he weighed his options.

She shook her head as if to clear away an unpleasant

thought, put the car in gear, and pulled out.

Jack rolled his shoulders back, trying to dispel the persistent nagging ache in his neck. He climbed up the side of the building, his preternatural speed and strength good for something. It allowed him to keep her in range as he blurred across rooftops, his boots silent and his heart speeding up, the scent of her boiling through the flat monotone of the day. She parked in the small lot behind the Rowangrove, and he stayed out of sight, crouched on top of the building that housed the shop. He sensed the wave of calm emerald Power inside the layers of careful shielding— the green witch would know he was here. As he watched, the store's back door opened and Theo came out into the rain, skirting the Dumpster set along the back wall.

Where's the Guardian's Watcher?

For a moment Jack's skin went cold. Then Dante arrived on the roof right next to him, crouching down. The black-eyed Watcher was built like a linebacker, wide-shouldered but oddly graceful nonetheless.

"Theo's going to calm her down," Dante said. "Want to come in? We've been strategizing."

Jack took another look over the side. The green witch tapped on the car-window. A flood of worry and another just as powerful wave of fear poured out of *his* witch. He flinched. It was like being bathed in crackling honey. Never, in all his experience of protecting Lightbringers, had he ever felt anything like this.

"We have *got* to get her under wraps," Dante murmured. "Every predator in the city will be knocking at her door before long."

"I think she's a flyer," Jack's mouth said independently of his brain. Thank the gods it chose English to mutter in. "Her car smells like smoke and Dark. Something nasty. Want to bet it *hasn't* followed her?"

"Gods above." Dante grinned. It was a lopsided smile, and Jack was startled into a very slight smile in exchange. "Well, you're going to have to Watch carefully. She's skittish. Not even the fire witch was this bad."

Jack watched as Theo leaned down to talk to her. "What's her name?"

"Anya. You missed it?" Dante sounded amused.

He didn't reply. *Anya.* It suited her.

She rolled up her window and got out of the car while Theo waited patiently. Then the young man got out too. Dante whistled out through his teeth. Anya's companion was a big man, but he moved strangely, as if his joints didn't work quite right. Jack was still mulling this over.

"—sorry," Jack heard her say, and strained his sharper-than-human senses to catch the sound of her voice again.

"No need," Theo replied. "The more the merrier. Come on in. We'll have a nice long chat. You need a cup of tea."

The women disappeared inside the back door, and Jack heard the deadbolt thud home. His shoulders relaxed slightly.

"Come on, brother." Dante clapped him on the shoulder gingerly. "Let's get inside. I'll show you the escape hatch."

For the first time in years, Jack's palms were damp. He was going to meet her, face to face, for the second time.

Nine

I shouldn't have brought him inside. Anya accepted the mug with trembling hands. *But he was so upset.*

Shell, contentedly perched on a stool behind the counter, slurped at a cup of hot chocolate. He beamed at the green-eyed woman, and Anya's chest was suddenly hot and tight with something she didn't want to name even to herself.

Stop it. The more friends Shell has, the better. And she's good. It was impossible to doubt Theo's essential goodness, even if Anya had only known her for ten minutes.

"Now." Theo leaned against the counter. "Drink up. That's got lemon balm in it, good for the nerves. So you and Shell are new in town, no friends, precious little resources, and you need a job rather desperately. A job where you can look after him."

Anya bit the inside of her cheek and looked down at the glassed-in counter. A display of double-bladed knives with different hilts glinted back at her, along with two sets of nesting cauldrons, a neat little card proclaiming them to be *Cast Iron— Great for Camping!* A fall of red silk artistically highlighted decks of brightly-colored tarot cards, arranged for maximum effect. There was a huge mass of quartz crystal too, with a card that said *Not For Sale.*

The crystal hummed inside the glass casing, and Anya had to shake her head. *What is wrong with me? I can't afford to be distracted.*

"Y-yes." She brought herself back to full alertness with an almost physical effort. "He's no trouble. Sometimes he waits in the car, but I—"

"He can hang out inside the store with us," Theo said immediately. "At least until we find something he can do. You like to help, don't you, Shell?" The dark-haired woman beamed at him. Her expression was so genuine most of Anya's nervousness drained away, leaving only the regular soft hum of tension. Most people either baby-talked to him or almost-yelled, thinking that if they turned up the volume he would understand. Theo didn't do that, she simply *spoke* to him, which raised her several points in Anya's book.

Shell nodded enthusiastically. His nose needed wiping. Anya cringed inwardly, ashamed of herself. He couldn't help it.

"I can clean real good," he said. "I used to sort bottles for Mr. D'Amato."

Theo's smile grew even wider. "I think we might find something for you to do. If it's all right with Anya." Her green gaze came up, and Anya had to take a deep breath.

I'd give anything to be that calm. She felt her shoulders slump even further. *I wonder what she wants from me. This can't be happening, I've never been this lucky.*

But her fingers had tingled when she'd looked at the ad. Maybe her weird talents had finally worked to her advantage for once.

The shop was bigger than it looked from outside, and full of bookshelves. There was a sun and moon painted on the ceiling, full of baroque curlicues. The paint glowed under warm electric light. Racks of robes and hemp clothing went up the right side, and shelves of books and knickknacks were on each wall. There were racks of candles in glass sleeves—novenas—in every possible color, other candles shaped like black cats or human figures, or funny knobbed candles and other shapes. There was even a collection of crystal balls in one glass case in the back corner next to another display of tarot cards taking up a whole bookshelf. A blue and green curtain hung over the door to a small space that held a sink and counter with a microwave and a coffeemaker sitting on it, and there were a few cabinets of dishes and other things.

"Now," Theo said briskly, "where are you staying?"

Anya blinked. This was not going as she had expected, after a morning of more failed job applications at a handful of sleazy bars. "In a h-hotel."

A door set in the left-hand wall marked *Employees Only* squeaked open, and the sound of boots tromped through the Rowangrove. Anya's fingers spasmed around her cup.

Theo glanced over her shoulder. She leaned against the counter next to the ancient cash register. "Oh, good." Her smile widened. Anya noticed Theo's belly was softly rounded, and she let out a short breath between her teeth. The woman was pregnant. Was she having some sort of maternal hormone surge? Was that why she was so nice?

"Anya, meet Dante and Jack," Theo said. "Store security. Dante's my partner; he's the one carrying the box. You already met Jack. Boys, I'd like you to meet Anya, our new night manager."

Anya's heart leapt like a startled rabbit.

"Charmed," the black-eyed hulk of a man said. They both wore long black leather trench coats, and Anya's nostrils flared, taking in the smell of something dark and violent. Her stomach fluttered, tea slopping against the sides of her mug. "Hello, Miss Anya. Theo, we brought up that overstock. Want me to unpack it?"

"If you would. Jack, please come over and meet Anya." Theo's eyebrows arched. She seemed to be signaling to the silver-eyed man, who stood with his hands in his pockets, his hair damp and sticking to his forehead.

Anya blinked. Her vision blurred, and she saw a swirling, red-black stain, like a bruise, spreading over both men.

No, not another bloody vision! Go away, not now, I can't handle this. Anya concentrated desperately and tried to make the image go away. The *last* thing she needed was to start hallucinating again, seeing colors and hearing people shout their most intimate thoughts in her mental ears.

Theo's soft hand clamped around Anya's wrist. Shell stared at the men, his sleepy eyes suddenly wide.

The woman's touch sent a wave of calm flooding through Anya's entire body. Her stomach unknotted, her neck stopped hurting, and she blinked at Theo in amazement. "You—how did you do that?"

"It's all right, Anya," Theo said, as the tall, silver-eyed man—Jack—approached cautiously. "You didn't think you were the only one in the world, did you?"

Anya's heart flipped and splashed into her stomach. Precious little sleep, unremitting tension, and the smell of the red-black haze covering the two men all conspired to make her wish she'd never come here.

"She's going to be sick." The gray-eyed man had a nice voice, pleasant and deep, even if it was strangely flat, as if he grudged every word. The ghost of an accent haunted the words, a slightly different rhythm teasing at the sentences. "Reaction. You flushed her with too much Power."

"I know what I'm doing. I *am* the resident healer." Theo didn't look frightened at all. "Take a deep breath, Anya. You're among friends."

I have no friends. My last friend died three houses ago, when something that looked like a Hollywood nightmare tore open my front door and sucked her dry like an orange slice.

Anya's stomach abruptly settled. She took a deep breath.

"Anya?" Shell's voice was plaintive.

I don't have any choice, she realized miserably. *If they want to hurt me, I'm trapped in here. There's no way I can get out.*

"Anya?" Shell repeated, and the stool creaked as he shifted his weight.

Anya let out a long sigh and looked up at Theo's worried green eyes. "It's okay, buddy." Her voice was a croak. "Drink your hot chocolate."

"He looks funny, Anya. I don't like him."

Hot acid embarrassment flooded Anya's belly and made her cheeks go hot. "Be *quiet*, Shell!" She met the man's eyes squarely, the little betraying flutter in her stomach more pronounced than ever. "I'm sorry. He doesn't mean it."

"No offense taken. Really." It sounded, oddly enough, like he was trying to put her at ease. He watched her intently, his eyes flat and reflective.

Anya blinked. For a moment it looked as if he had something sticking up over his shoulder, something long and thin.

The bell over the door jingled sweetly. She pulled her wrist away from Theo's hand, tea slopping in her mug. *I don't think I want to stay here.*

"Hi, everyone." A clear contralto voice sailed into the shop. "Stoneface, just the man I wanted to see. Remy's taking the van around back. Can you open the door for him? I'm sure he'll find something for you to carry."

"Sure," the black-eyed man replied amicably.

Anya twisted around to see a tall, porcelain-skinned redhead, dressed in a skintight, torn *Slav Ticklers* T-shirt and soft hip-hugging jeans, come to a halt and lay one elegant finger alongside her aristocratic nose. "Hey. Looks like you've already met the resident gorillas. I'm Elise. I hear you're going to save me from working nights in this place. Thanks—and my condolences. Wow, Theo's already dosing you with tea, huh? And who are you, cutie?" This last was delivered to Shell, who stared gape-mouthed at the woman.

She hung her purse on the antique iron coat rack and proceeded to climb behind the counter, sliding past the gray-eyed man as if he wasn't even there. A silver nose-stud with a red gem winked at Anya. The tall redhead stuck out her hand, thin silver bangles sliding musically down her perfect wrist.

"I'm the tough one. Theo's the nice one, and Mari's the cute one. You think you can handle being the brains of this operation?"

Anya opened her mouth with no idea of what she was going to say—and, embarrassingly enough, burst into tears.

Ten

Jack held himself very still, keeping his aura close and contained. Anya looked dazed. Who wouldn't, with two Lightbringers and two Watchers hanging on her every word? Haltingly, obviously not telling the whole story, she told them enough about her last home to make Jack's heart turn to stone inside his chest, enough to make his entire body go cold at the thought of what *could* have happened to her. She'd recently escaped the Dark by the narrowest of margins—and if she hadn't, he would never have met her.

Although I haven't really met her at all. He noticed how she glanced at him and quickly away, flinching every time he moved. Jack settled down, pulling his aura even closer to his skin, trying not to remind her he was present. The last thing he wanted was to make her any more upset.

Remy stayed tactfully by the front door, his attention palpable. Jack glanced at the other Watcher, hoping his presence wouldn't disturb Anya further.

"I'm s-s-sorry," she said, sopping at her cheeks with an already defunct tissue, the sweet huskiness of her voice tightening around his entire body. Theo had produced some silken cushions, all the women and Shell sat on the floor behind the counter. Jack had lowered himself into an easy crouch by the step leading up to the closed-off area, unwilling to loom over them. The presence of the two Lightbringers rubbed pain into his nerves, just as Anya's nearness spread a crackling balm over him. It was an entirely new sensation, and that was another reason to stay very still—he was afraid if he moved, he would disturb some vital current of air and lose the connection.

"I'm sorry," she said again. "I j-j-just—"

"Nonsense." Theo's tone was firm. "Anyone would be upset by what you've had to deal with."

Elise, patting Shell's shoulder, shook her head. "Jeez. That's really rough, sweetie. You must feel like the low end of the pool right about now."

"I'm n-normally v-very calm," she said defiantly. Her chin tilted up, vulnerable, her dark hair falling away from her face. Jack's heart cracked. "I don't usually go to pieces like this."

"Of course not," Theo soothed. "It must have been awful to lose everything like that."

The green witch's eyes met the redhead's, and the redhead shook her head slightly.

No, Jack agreed silently, *now's not the time to ask her about anything else. Just calm her down, that's all.*

"I don't want to be different." Anya crumpled up the Kleenex in her fist. "I just want to be left alone. Is that too much to ask?"

"Sounds reasonable to me." Elise took up the thread. "Hey, Theo, I bet I could get Shell a job bussing tables at the Widmore while I tend bar. What do you think? That way I'd be close and could keep an eye on things, make sure everyone tips him in."

The look of amazed gratitude Jack's witch gave Elise made Jack wish he could thank the fire witch. He glanced up. Remy stood guard just inside the front door, watching the street. Peculiar gray storm-light poured through the glass windows, glowing in the younger Watcher's golden eyes. Remy smoothed his fingers over a knife hilt, his face set in the alert calm of a man on guard. Dante wasn't in sight, but Jack sensed him up on the roof, watching the back of the store. It was for the best; Watchers tended to make Lightbringers nervous.

We have a wounded Lightbringer here, emitting all over the spectrum. I can't let her out of here without me. I won't let her out of here without me.

His eyes met Theo's for a moment. The green witch studied him measuringly, and he dropped his gaze.

"I c-couldn't ask you to do that." Anya's voice trembled. "The trouble—"

"Oh, no trouble," Elise interrupted, and Shell nodded vigorously. "Shell would love to help, and I bet he'd be a great busser. And I'll watch out for him."

"I can do tables." Shell's eyes lit up. "I did tables when we worked for Mr. Macklin. Remember, Anya?"

Anya blinked again. "But I can't—"

"The next item of business," Theo said briskly, "is to find you a decent place to stay."

Whatever Anya said next was lost on Jack, because he sensed Remy stiffen slightly. Jack looked up, casting his senses out—and smelled the sharp, dissonant stink of Dark.

The curse stayed locked in his throat. *It's coming in fast, whatever it is.*

He looked back at the trembling Anya. "Excuse me," he said softly, and rose to his feet.

She flinched again, her eyes wide, glimmering with tears. "What's going on?"

"Don't worry." The Power humming through the green witch spread a soft blanket over Anya's wildly blinking aura. "I think he and Remy have seen something. It's all right."

Jack barely paused, stalking away and sweeping the door open. The bell jangled thinly.

"Do you think—" Remy began, but Jack shook his head.

"Stand guard." The low tremor of Dark in his voice made the glass rattle in the shop windows. "I'll be back."

"What's he doing?" The note of terror in Anya's voice almost made him turn back.

Do your duty, Watcher. Something's coming in, and if it hits the shields on the shop there's going to be a huge noise and a very frightened witch in there. My *witch.*

Rage prickled under his skin, his coat flapped, and the street was oddly clear of people. That was good. He dropped the weak shimmering glamour that kept his weapons hidden from normal eyes and sent up a flare of Power strong and sharp enough to almost drown out the psychic noise of Anya's fear.

The *s'lin*—a huge, voracious psychic vampire shaped like a manta ray—dropped out of the sky, and Jack dove to the side.

Need some altitude. He reached the alley and went straight up the brick wall, a trick most Watchers learned early. Getting height was often the decisive factor in a fight. *What's this thing doing out during the day? Even cloud cover doesn't account for it.*

Dark didn't usually come out by day, even with weak sunlight and heavy clouds. Sunlight made the Dark vulnerable just as night made it stronger.

The flare of amber light from inside the Rowangrove's shields sent out waves of distress even through the protective layers. The woman had no training at *all*, she shone out like a lighthouse. No wonder she was luring everything nasty in range out of its hidey hole.

He reached the top of the wall and hauled himself up onto the roof, gathering himself as the *s'lin* glided through storm-darkened air, seeking whatever predator had dared to interrupt its feeding.

In other words, just looking to take a chunk out of a Watcher.

The *s'lin* screamed as Jack launched himself toward it, Power flaring and conscious thought fading as he moved on instinct, both knives out. The blades, black and running with livid reddish flame twisting into runes, tore through Dark unflesh.

Manta-ray wings flapped, and pain scored the left side of his face, sticky phantom blood raining down. He ignored it, driving the knives in and ripping one free, smoke roiling up from the *s'lin's* insubstantial skin.

The easiest way to kill a *s'lin* was to ground it, but this one was too big. Jack twisted, driving the second knife home and using it for leverage, ripping and tearing. If he could reach the underspine he would be able to tear the flying psychic vampire free of its mooring in the physical world and disperse it into death.

He landed with stunning force on the rooftop, breath driven sharply out of his lungs. The *s'lin*, wounded, flapped again, trying to regain altitude.

Jack's hand flicked. The slim flat *flechette* split air, a single harsh gleam splintering from its razor edges, and buried itself at the juncture between the underspine and the secondary nerve bundle. The *s'lin* fell, screeching, the little weapon shaken free.

The left side of Jack's face was coated with his own blood, not just its invisible miasma. It had been more than a psychic strike, then. The thing had actually been strong enough to split his flesh.

A moment's worth of work, flaring the edges of his aura, cleansed the air of the stink of Dark and death. The fight was over. Jack's shoulders dropped. He would have to collect the *flechette*. The knives flicked back into their sheaths, and he scanned his surroundings again.

Quick and messy. But I've put up a sign here, I guess. The next creature will think twice before going after her.

Then again, the Dark's not known for intelligence.

"Nice," Dante said. "A bit loud, but nice."

Jack dropped his hand away from the knife hilt. The other Watcher stood on the roof, holding up the dropped *flechette*, admiring its razor-sharp gleam.

"Thanks." Jack's heart pounded, coming down from the redline of combat. The glow of his Lightbringer under shields seemed curiously muted, but he merely noted she was still alive and took a deep breath, easing himself down. He was just keyed up enough to leap on anything that moved.

But Watchers did *not* attack other Watchers.

"Here." Dante approached cautiously and held out the sliver of metal. Jack took it, his nose wrinkling at the smell of Dark and cold steel leftover from the fight. "We'd better get back. It'd be a miracle if the air witch didn't feel that, and she's just frightened enough to bolt."

"Is that a professional opinion?" He had to work to make it a mild question, his temper strained. *Make it a joke. You're being an idiot. She's your witch. He has his own to worry about.*

Dante shrugged, his black eyes gone cool and flat. "You know what you're doing, but this witch is practically a civilian. Be careful."

I deserved that. "Duly noted. I'd better clean up before she sees me again."

"You'd better." Dante shut his mouth, his lips turning into a thin line. Familiar worry spread between both of them, the worry of Watchers under fire with Lightbringers to protect.

The first rumble of thunder shook the air over the city. Jack hunched his shoulders. He'd just done his duty, killed a predator before it could reach his witch.

So why was the guilt still tearing a hole in his stomach? Guilt and another, blacker emotion. Something like fear, maybe.

Don't worry, he told her silently, though she couldn't possibly hear him. *I've taken care of it. No more fear; no more hiding. I promise you're safe now. I swear it.*

Why were his hands shaking? He'd killed it. The danger was past, for now.

It was a moment's worth of work to close the slash on his hairline, another moment's worth of work and Power to wipe off the blood.

He followed Dante across the roofs until they reached the Rowangrove again, but Jack stopped on the roof, his heart suddenly pounding again as the curious tugging started in the middle of his chest. "Gods above," he hissed out through his teeth, *"Where is she?"*

"I don't know." Dante looked over the back wall. "Her car's gone. Maybe we should ask Theo—"

Jack didn't hear the rest of it, because he was already moving.

Eleven

"I like them," Shell said stubbornly. "Nice ladies. I don't want to leave."

"Shell." Anya pulled into the parking spot. "Please. I don't want to go over this again. We're leaving. We're going somewhere else."

"Why?" His lower lip pooched out.

"I felt the bad things again, Shell." Her knuckles were white against the steering wheel, her bitten fingernails turned bloodless-pale. She'd scrambled out of the Rowangrove with Shell anxiously following, despite Theo's calm pleading, Elise's quizzical look, and Elise's boyfriend saying something too low to be heard, making Elise turn on him furiously. Whatever game they were playing, she wanted no part of it. Not when the men smelled like the awful razor-teethed things that had driven her from her homes.

Rain spatted dully on the windshield. Thunder boomed and rattled. The hotel rose up in front of them. Anya sighed. It was a wonder they'd gotten here alive. She barely remembered driving. "We'll leave tomorrow. We'll find something. We always do."

I'm going to have to use the Persuasion. A shiver ran through her, lifting the hair on her scalp. Rain drummed the car roof. *I'm going to have to be a thief. There's no other way I can feed us both.*

"I liked those ladies." Shell's eyelids drooped.

"I know you did." Her fingers ached against the steering wheel, and her neck felt hard as concrete. She'd just walked away from a job.

If it really was a job. I didn't see a single customer the whole time I was in there. God, please help me. Please tell me what I'm doing wrong. What did I do to deserve this?

"I don't want to go, Anya. Want to stay here." Shell folded his arms.

"I'm going upstairs, Shell," she returned, in a thin, brittle voice like fine glass. "Please come with me. You can watch cartoons."

"Want to stay."

She could see a fit coming on. His eyes drooped closed, his lower lip pooched out again, and his hands began to pick at his shirt.

Anya uncurled her fingers from the wheel, reached down, and touched Shell's hand. "You're going to come upstairs with me," she said in her softest voice, sparks tingling under her fingers and her eyes suddenly burning with laserlike pain. "You're going to watch cartoons and be calm."

Shell's pupils dilated. She didn't use very much Persuasion. It was tricky, and if she gave Shell too much he might go into a screaming fit instead of calming down.

The familiar sense of euphoria swamped her, draining out through her fingertips and into his skin. "Be calm. All right, Shell? Be calm."

"Calm," he muttered, and Anya's heart twisted under her ribs with sick guilt. She shouldn't be doing this to him. Shell didn't deserve to be manipulated.

What if the Persuasion is what makes those things chase us? she wondered suddenly, and nausea hit below her breastbone like a club.

She managed to get Shell out of the car and up the stairs just as the rain broke, a hot white spear of cloud-to-cloud lightning stabbing the sky. Shell flinched and Anya let out a soft cry of surprise, almost breaking the key in the lock. She hustled him into the room just as another jagged spill of thunder shook the vaulted sky.

I hate this weather. "Go potty, Shell." She guided him into the bathroom and closed the door. Anya trudged back to the front door and opened it wide, looking past the covered passageway to the parking lot below, breathing in cold rainwashed air.

Rain poured down so heavily the world blurred gray and green. Anya sighed wearily, flinched as thunder boomed again. The motel crouched sleepily under the onslaught, like a big concrete creature dozing in the middle of the savanna.

A hungry creature. With big teeth.

I wish my imagination didn't work so well. Anya flinched again.

I think I just went crazy. It was actually a relief. There was no other way to explain what she'd seen at the Rowangrove— a swordhilt sticking up over the golden-eyed man's shoulder, guns in holsters at his hips, and knives strapped to his chest. Not just that, she'd *also* seen the funny necklace Elise wore shift and strain, the supple dragon carved into red stone twisting so convincingly Anya had almost heard scales rasp.

And she'd seen a beautiful green glow around Theo, reaching out and dyeing everything in different shades of deep emerald haze.

I'm crazy. I can start screaming or curl up in a little ball and cry. It doesn't matter. Nothing matters.

She watched the rain splat down as Shell lumbered out of the bathroom and dropped onto his bed. He played with the remote control and turned on the television. Cheery cartoon music warred with the sound of thunder. He said nothing. He wouldn't speak until tomorrow morning, since Anya had used the Persuasion on him.

I wish I hadn't done that. I wish none of this was necessary. She wiped at her tear-slick cheek, surprised after all to find herself crying. Rain made a sound like dry fingers rattling a tin cup.

The calm, flat, faintly-accented voice came from her right, from the part of the walkway leading to the stairs. "I would suggest you shut the door, at least."

Anya jumped, her heart hammering.

The gray-eyed man in the long, dark leather coat stepped in front of her. "My apologies," he said carefully, as Anya backed up, her throat filling with copper fear.

Shell was in a helpless trance. He would stay on the bed with glazed eyes and watch cartoons until he fell asleep, unable to move. Anya almost tripped on the carpet, recovered, and stood trembling, staring at the man. How had he found her?

"May I come in?" Each word carefully delivered, he halted just on the other side of the door.

All resistance drained away. If he wanted to kill her, she couldn't stop him. She was exhausted, hungry, and utterly spent. "What?" The word turned into a squeak halfway.

"May I come in? It's raining, and you're safer with the door closed." He paused. "I won't hurt you."

Anya swallowed, her throat clicking with the motion. "I can't stop you," she said miserably, and moved to her left, between Shell and the door.

"I won't hurt *either* of you." He stepped over the threshold. Water dripped from his coat, and his eyes blazed. He took up too much room—tall and wide-shouldered, with a fume of danger and darkness clinging to him.

Anya blinked. She saw it again—swordhilt, guns, knives. His long leather coat moved oddly, and he pushed stiff fingers through his dark hair, shoving it back out of his eyes.

I'm hallucinating. She tried to swallow again and failed miserably, making a small hurt sound in the back of her throat.

"I mean it." He swept the door closed and locked it in one efficient motion, without even looking. His eyes fixed on her so intently she almost expected to feel a warm draft against her skin. "I won't harm either of you."

"If you're going to kill me, get it over with," Anya flung at him, her hands fisted at her sides. "But leave Shell alone. He doesn't understand."

"I am not going to kill you," he said slowly, distinctly, as if she was an idiot. "I'm here to protect you."

"Protect me from what?" Her voice broke on a jagged, splintering laugh. *I'm crazy. I've finally gone off the deep end. I'm crazy.* Her breath came in short, sipping gasps.

"From whatever broke open your house and set it on fire." His tone dropped, became confidential. He leaned back against the door, seeming not to notice the sword strapped to his back. "I'd guess it smelled like smoke and copper, didn't it? Tall thing, but it hunched down, six legs, red eyes, mouth full of razor-sharp fangs."

"Stop," she whispered, tremors running from her scalp to her feet. One of her ankles buckled. She pulled herself back up, her head full of rushing noise. "Just stop."

He stopped, both hands shoved deep into his pockets, and watched her intently, his dark eyebrows drawn together. She suddenly realized he was attractive, in a strong-jawed stubbled kind of way.

He was blocking the only exit.

Her heart beat so fast she felt faint. "What *are* you?"

"Jack Gray. I'm a Watcher." He nodded, as if tipping his cap to her. "I'm here to protect you."

"Please don't hurt me." She didn't realize she was backing up until the back of her knees hit the bed Shell lay on. She dropped down to sit, the strength running out of her like water. The noise from the television blurred into the sound of the rain, thunder rattling again. Onscreen, a cartoon rabbit administered a thumping to a hapless cartoon hunter. Anya sat on the bed and stared at the gray-eyed man.

"Of course I won't hurt you." He pulled his right hand out of his pocket. He held a plain white envelope. "Here."

He approached cautiously, holding it out. Anya reached up with numb fingers, smelling rain, the anonymous scent of a hotel room, and the new smell of leather and danger that had suddenly invaded.

As soon as her hand closed on the envelope, he retreated back to the door and leaned against it again.

Gingerly, as if it might bite her, she slid the flap up.

Inside was a clutch of hundred-dollar bills. Anya stared at it—enough money to pay first and last months' rent and a security deposit. Enough money to pay for groceries for a few weeks as well. More money than she'd seen in a long time.

She raised her eyes to his face, blinking furiously. "I don't understand."

"I'm a Watcher," he repeated, each word weighted just slightly differently. "This qualifies as an emergency, so I've got some funding. That's about half of what I've got on me. Circle Lightfall will send more and we can get you out of here, but that will take a few phone calls."

"Circle...Lightfall?" *I sound like an idiot.*

"You're pale. You could go into shock. Have you had something to eat yet?"

"Why are you wearing *guns?*" she blurted, heat rising to her cheeks. This was not heading the way she'd imagined craziness would go.

"How else am I going to fight the Dark?" He shrugged, dismissing the question. "I think you should have something to eat, ma'am."

"Quit calling me ma'am." The envelope crumpled in her hand. *Isn't he going to kill me? He smells just like those other things.*

He nodded, dark hair falling into his eyes. "What should I call you?"

You could start with terrified and finish up with confused. "Anya. Just Anya."

"Just relax, Anya." He slid his hands into his pockets again. "You're safe now."

The monumental silliness of that statement hit her like a fist to the stomach. She began to giggle, then laugh. She laughed until tears ran down her face and her ribs hurt; laughed until her stomach twisted in on itself like a black hole. Through it all Jack Gray stood at the door and watched her as she finished the process of laughing like a lunatic. Then, for the second time that day, she burst into tears while thunder rattled the roof.

Twelve

The boy lay tucked into bed, sleeping heavily, his breath wheezing through his mouth. Anya was curled on the other twin bed, soundless, but Jack could tell from the radiating stillness of her aura that she was asleep.

He sighed and pulled the clunky, pink-upholstered chair away from the table. This hotel was clinging onto the margins of "flophouse," but it was clean and the linens were fresh. Jack had warded the walls as soon as she was asleep enough not to notice, and the resultant bell-jar feeling of still air had made both sleepers mutter and toss uneasily. Anya had murmured in her sleep, curled into a ball, and dived deeper into unconsciousness, her glossy dark hair winging against the pillow.

She'd refused to eat, just sobbed until she was limp and red-eyed. Then she'd stripped the sheet and blanket back on the bed the boy wasn't occupying and fell onto it without even bothering to take off her shoes. He had waited until her breathing evened out and gently pulled off the black heels, drawing the covers over her. He'd stared at her for a long moment and then retreated before he did something he shouldn't.

Like touch. Or even look too long.

Jack dropped down onto the chair. *Well, that went about as well as could be expected, I guess.*

He had dealt with plenty of hysterical witches, but never before had he wanted to grab and *shake* one, then slide his arms around her and hold her until the sick trembling under his ribs went away.

Pain kept a Watcher from wanting to touch a witch—every time he saw a Lightbringer, his bones would run with hot lead, and the older he got the worse it was. He couldn't even remember what touching another human being *felt* like. Jack had simply clinically, coldly, and calmly taken care of them, finished each rotation and moved on to the next, going from city to city, fighting off *kalak* and *s'lin* and numerous other predators, easing frightened Lightbringers into safehouses, shepherding them through crisis after crisis.

He had never before wanted to touch one of them.

I want to feel her skin even if it hurts. His hand found the gun kit in one pocket. He took out his right-hand gun and began maintenance. His fingers moved with the ease of long practice, cleaning and oiling, making sure everything was in perfect working order. He hadn't expected her immediate move to put herself between him and the boy.

Boy? He's not a boy, he's a full-grown problem. Why is she carrying him around?

Terrified and exhausted, she'd still moved to protect the kid. The thought made an unfamiliar smile tug up a corner of Jack's mouth, made his fingers itch even more.

Just one moment. Just one touch—maybe her soft cheek, maybe her hand—and the constant agony of the thing melded to his body would go away, soothed. The true relief of painlessness would be a reward he didn't deserve.

No touching, Watcher. Not for you.

Jack finished cleaning one gun, started on the other. Watchers rarely used guns. There were only a few things they would even affect, and having to dig your bullets out of walls after a fight to defy both police ballistics and anti-Watcher sympathetic magic got tiring. But you never knew when you might need them, and a Watcher's gear was how he protected a Lightbringer. He would have to be ready for anything.

Ready for anything. Of course. He restrained the urge to look across the room. His fingers paused in their habitual movements. *Ready for anything and everything except this.*

When he finished cleaning and re-consecrating every weapon, including his *flechettes*, he washed his hands in the small sink. Then he pulled the chair up so he was leaning against the door, stretched out his legs and let out a sigh.

It's happened. He couldn't stave off the realization any more. *She's my witch.*

An untrained air witch with an aura pulsing with distress, calling in every predator and piece of Dark in the city. It was a pure miracle she had survived this long without someone looking after her.

Maybe she has a guardian angel—if you believe in guardian angels. The thought was unexpectedly, grimly amusing, and Jack let out a short chuff of sound passing for a soft laugh. *If she didn't before, she certainly does now. That is, if there's anything angelic about a Watcher.*

He closed his eyes, sinking into the light trance that passed for sleep among Watchers. The Dark symbiote took care of the body, but every mind needed a rest, even minds as clear and cold as an arctic waste. He thought he had ruthlessly torn out every last shred of hope along with the echo of his native speech in his head.

He was wrong. Sometimes his semi-sleep deepened until he could...

...smell the smoke, hear the screams and crackle of flames eating wood, smell the unwashed crowd pressing close and the collective indrawn breath of wonder as the fire took one more soul to heaven—or somewhere else.

The memory faded as he brought himself back. Jack moved restlessly and resettled. He didn't want to think about the past. Not now.

His resting trance was full of nerve-tingling awareness. His witch. *His* witch, the only Lightbringer whose touch wouldn't hurt him. All the struggling, the striving, the fighting, the watching—and this was his reward.

I don't deserve it. He listened to the boy's snuffling wheeze and her almost soundless breathing. He could hear her pulse too, he listened so intently.

I don't deserve to be alive. I don't deserve to have another chance.

He especially didn't deserve an angel with flawless pale skin and large gray eyes fringed with charcoal, whose aura filled the air with sweetness. He most *definitely* didn't deserve to find the one thing every Watcher prayed for, hoped for, and endured for.

Not after what he'd done.

Jack touched a knife hilt for reassurance, checked the perimeter again, and waited for morning. He had all the time in the world, now.

Until she found out who he was, and what he'd done.

Thirteen

Shell screamed. It was the sound of a rabbit caught in a trap.

Anya scrambled up out of bed, barely feeling her feet hit the floor, and instinctively launched herself toward Shell's cry.

Jack half-turned and caught her shoulders, pushing her back. She stumbled backward and sat down on the bed, hard. She bounced up again, her bare feet rasping against cheap carpet, and Jack Gray's broad back was suddenly there, solid as a wall, between her and Shell.

"*Stop* it!" Anya yelled, raising her fists to pound at his back. At the sound of her voice, Shell's scream hitched to a halt, and something in the set of Jack's shoulders told her he'd frozen between one movement and the next.

Her heart thudded in her ears. She dropped her hands, shook them out, and took a deep breath.

"Shell?" She pitched her voice low and soothing, trying to peer around the man's bulk so she could make eye contact with Shell and calm him down. "It's all right, I promise it's all right. Calm, buddy. Be calm."

"Anya?" Shell's voice was a thin husk. Anya pushed at the large man's leather-clad shoulders. She could feel muscle standing out hard as tile even under the thick coat. *He could hurt both of us. He could have killed us both in our sleep. I shouldn't have slept.*

What was he doing next to Shell's bed?

"Anya?" Shell's voice broke on the word, like a five-year-old disoriented after a terrible dream.

"He's just upset." Her voice shook, it wasn't her usual clear tone. She pushed down the urge to make her hands into fists. "Please. Don't hurt him."

"Him?" Jack's voice rumbled and the walls shook. The window rattled in its frame. Anya flinched. "I don't want him to hurt *you*. He was thrashing around."

"Don't be ridiculous," she snapped. "Shell would never hurt me. Get out of my *way.*"

Amazingly, though his expression was reluctant, he swung aside, stripping his hair back from his face. The gesture looked habitual.

He didn't meet her eyes. "I'll watch." The words were loaded with such menace Shell whimpered.

Anya skirted the man, brushing against the hem of his coat. Shell sat straight up on the bed, his blond hair sticking up in soft spikes. His mouth was wet and loose, and he stared at Jack as if all his personal nightmares had come to roost in a cheap motel room.

He always had trouble with new people, and the tall leather-clad man was hardly the most reassuring thing she'd ever seen.

Anya climbed up on the bed, her knees dimpling the creaking mattress. "Shell. Shell, look at me. *Look* at me."

His eyes jittered over to her and flicked back toward the tall, glowering gray-eyed man. Jack didn't move, but his entire frame exhaled danger. It filled the room like his smell of leather and violence. She could *feel* his eyes on her, and she shook the sensation away, suddenly acutely aware that she'd slept in her sweater and slacks.

I must have been tired. Nobody in their right mind sleeps in her bra.

"Look at *me,* Shell." She didn't want to risk the Persuasion, not in front of Jack.

Shell's sleepy blue eyes found hers. "That's right, buddy," she crooned, reaching out tentatively, two fingers stroking his chapped knuckles where they clutched the sheet to his chest. "It's okay, Shell. Didn't I promise you I'd take care of you? You're my Shell, my buddy. I told you I'd take care of you. It's okay."

"Don't like him, don't like him," Shell chanted breathlessly. "*Bad*, he's *bad.*"

"He's here to help us," Anya insisted with a certainty she didn't feel. *He could have killed us both last night. Why am I not more frightened?* "Really, Shell. You trust me, don't you? I'm your Anya, and I say he's okay."

"He smells bad. Like those things."

Anya's nose wrinkled. He *did* smell strange, leather and male and the smell of steel, and a nose-stinging smell like peppery adrenaline. Now that she wasn't trembling on the fine edge of exhaustion, she could tell that the smell was...different. Not quite as threatening as the scent of the things that had chased them.

It might even have been comforting, if his face hadn't been so set and still with disapproval. She cleared her throat, wanting all Shell's attention on her. "I think he's all right. And he's helping us, for right now at least. So let's just pretend, all right?"

Shell blinked. "I don't *like* him. Make him go away."

He's going to be stubborn. Anya sighed. The sense of Jack's attention focused on her was an almost physical weight. *Why is he staring at me?* "Please, Shell."

Jack spoke up, quiet but with undeniable force. "I'm not going away. But I won't hurt you. Either of you."

"There, you see? He won't hurt you, Shell." Anya wished she believed it even as she said it.

Inspiration struck as Shell eyed her doubtfully.

"Come here," she said over her shoulder. After a single heartbeat of hesitation, Jack did. "Give me your hand, Mr. Gray."

His hand was callused, scarred, and much bigger than hers. The tendons stood out on the back, and his hand felt very, very warm. In fact, his skin felt feverish.

Anya folded his thumb and fingers down, except for his pinkie. He went completely still, his hand pliable in hers but strangely resistant.

"It's a pinkie promise." She hoped he'd hear the seriousness in her voice. "Shell, Jack Gray pinkie-promises not to hurt you, but you've got to give him your pinkie."

It took a good ten minutes, but finally Shell was convinced, and Anya guided Jack's hand through the motions.

"There," she said. Jack stayed eerily motionless through the entire process. Anya was acutely aware of him looming next to her, his heat radiating against her skin. "We're all friends now. You'd better go get washed up, Shell. Hurry, I want to take a shower."

"Okay." He slid out of the bed on the far side, shivering, and padded toward the bathroom, giving Jack a wide berth. She waited until she heard the shower start up, glad that she'd put a fresh set of clothes for both her and Shell in the bathroom yesterday morning.

Anya looked up at the gray-eyed man. "Thank you. That will make it easier, I hope."

"I'll keep it in mind," he replied, gravely. "You slept."

Well, what did you expect me to do? Her sudden venomous irritation both shocked and braced her. "I did." She wished she didn't sound so stunned, adjusted her tone with an effort. "Look, um, I don't mean to be rude, but who the hell *are* you? Why are you carrying around guns? And what...*who* are the people at the Rowangrove? Why have you decided to do this to *me?*"

Though she couldn't exactly put into words what he'd done to her, beyond frightening her to death and giving her money. Which seemed to put him, for the moment, into the category of "helpful" even if it didn't remove the scariness of guns in her bedroom.

"It's not important who I am." He stepped back from the bed, his hands plunging back into his pockets. "What's important is what you are. You're a Lightbringer. A witch."

"A *what*?" *Nice. If Shell didn't wake everyone up by screaming, I probably just did.*

Jack shrugged. "*Witch* isn't a bad word, to us. You're a Lightbringer. Psychic."

Now *that* made a weird kind of sense. She studied him for a few moments, trying to figure out if he was crazy.

He didn't look crazy. He looked serious. Dead serious.

Does he know about the Persuasion? Air caught in her throat. She swallowed heavily, took a deep breath. "When you say *witch*, what do you mean?"

"I think you should have some coffee before I start explaining." Now he looked slightly amused, one eyebrow arching up and his mouth softening a tiny bit. He removed one hand from his pocket long enough to scratch at his stubbled chin. "It could take a little while."

I wonder if he ever shaves. She studied his gray eyes and the thatch of dark hair falling over them. *Just my luck to meet a guy who's crazy and carries around enough metal to get his deposit back at the recycling center.*

Anya sighed, her shoulders slumping. She might as well listen to him. It would make just as much sense as anything else had lately. She had to admit he hadn't done anything harmful yet.

She struggled with caution and ran up against her own utter helplessness. Figuring this out without caffeine didn't sound like a good time. "I'll warn you, I don't have any cream or sugar." *And not much coffee, either.*

He shrugged, a lazy economical movement, and said nothing. But his eyes, gray like hers but cold and flinty, were fastened on her face. He had barely looked away from her. She had rarely been studied so intently, and, of course, it had to happen while she had a weed-whacker haircut and a serious case of paranoia.

"All right," she said. "Coffee. Good. I'll make coffee. *You* start talking."

Fourteen

"What do you know about witches?" Jack's wrist still tingled with the touch of Anya's soft fingers. The feeling—not even painlessness, but pure narcotic pleasure—was as jolting as the day-to-day agony of the symbiote. It had taken all of his control to stay still while she touched him. Hell, it had taken all of his willpower to remember to *breathe*. Because when he inhaled, he smelled jasmine, and her hair had been temptingly close. He had imagined bending down just a little further, filling his lungs with the scent of her, and that scraped his control down to a hair-thin thread. It was a good thing she'd put some distance between them. Or so he tried to tell himself.

Anya settled herself gingerly in the pink chair by the table, holding a cup of coffee. The shower was still running, but she didn't seem concerned. Apparently the boy could take care of himself.

"Witches?" She took a sip of coffee, obviously thinking over the question. Even rumpled from sleep and obviously uncomfortable, she still examined him sharply, quick intelligence moving in her soft rain-colored eyes.

He stood by the door, his back to the wall and his hands shoved deep in his pockets. Waiting.

Finally, Anya spoke again. "Pointy hats. Broomsticks. They don't like girls from Kansas or little dogs."

Jack sighed. *This is going to be a little more difficult than I thought.*

"In the 1500s," he began again, regretting the fading feeling of her skin against his, "there was a power struggle going on. The Pope, Innocent VII, had been convinced of the existence of witches by two Dominican monks. The clergy seized this opportunity to start slaughtering everyone in their way, including poor village wisewomen and midwives. The idea of a Crusade had spread and it didn't just include the infidel, but the unruly population the church ruled over as well. A certain Cardinal Givelli—called the Gray Demon—brought an idea to the Pope."

Jack took a deep breath, fixed his eyes on the floor. *A good idea, he told me, an idea that could give the Church something it sorely needed—a spiritual enemy to unite Christendom against. Unite the faithful and the Church is secure.* "They started a military order to hunt down women like you.

Lightbringers. There were several branches of this Order. The Watchers call it the Crusade, but the true name is Lupus Dei—loosely translated, the Wolves of God." *Not a grammatically proper translation, but it gets the point across.*

"Why did they want to kill those women?" Her eyes were as wide as a child's at bedtime, gray ice lit with spring sunlight.

Jack tore his gaze away. If he kept looking at her, he would have to tell her everything. Drop down on his knees and beg for mercy, perhaps.

There's no mercy for you. Just do your job, Jack.

"Two reasons. First of all, they're called Lightbringers; they have a light inside them that makes them able to do what they do. They generally ended up being healers, midwives, that sort of thing. They were people you came to when you couldn't go to your priest or doctor. That made the priests—and the doctors, who were also the priests—very angry. It challenged their grip on the commoners. And, more importantly, on the nobility."

Anya nodded. "All right. I think I saw a PBS special about something like this."

Great. She gets her ideas about what she is from television. This is definitely going to be harder than I thought. "The Lightbringers call that period the Dark Years. They were *this* close to being hunted to extinction. We don't really know what makes a Lightbringer; it seems to skip around. It does tend to run in families, but not predictably." *Except for when a Watcher and a Lightbringer bond.* He winced inwardly. He didn't want to tell her about that. "Anyway, there was another reason. The Seekers—the things Lupus Dei used to find 'enemies of the Church'—could see this type of psychic power. They ended up hunting Lightbringers almost by default. Before anyone knew it, the Wolves descended, and woe to the woman caught in their jaws."

"What about men?" She shifted uncomfortably and pulled the hem of sweater down a little more. He deliberately didn't look at her legs under her slacks, stared at the cheap pink and beige curtains pulled closed over the windows. Tried not to let his eyes wander to the V-neck of her sweater, showing a fascinating triangle of pale flawless skin. "Psychic men?"

"There are a few guys, Lightbringer men, but they're...well..."

"What?"

"Not as powerful. And mostly gay, though we don't know

why." He stared at the floor, the door, the curtains. Silence stretched between them.

Finally, he dared to look directly at her.

She sat in the chair, her head cocked and her sleek black hair mussed. Her eyes were fixed on him, an attention he would have enjoyed if it hadn't made his breath shorten and his hands tingle with the urge to touch.

He began to talk again, almost unaware of what he was saying, he'd said it so many times. "There was a knight, Gideon de Hauteville. He married a woman—Jeanne Tourenay, who had saved his life after a battle. She was a healer, like Theo. She was also a part of Circle Lightfall."

"Circle Lightfall?" She took another sip, and her eyebrows drew together. The shower stopped.

He had almost forgotten about the boy. Jack brought his attention back to the present. "The Lightbringers banded together to survive. They found that when a certain number of them gathered in a city, the rates of sickness and crime went down. So they came together, and some of them even tried to bring back the pagan ways. Teachers came to teach them, and they tried to protect themselves from the Dark and the Crusade. Anyway, when Lupus Dei tried to murder Jeanne, de Hauteville fought to the death to defend her. The stories are garbled, but basically he made a deal with something Dark and was given the power to protect Jeanne. He fought off the Crusade and decided to make more...Watchers. He was the first."

"Watchers." She took a gulp of coffee, made a face. "So what are...I mean, you just expect me to believe all this?"

It was a common reaction, one he'd seen too many times. She thought she wanted proof, but what she really wanted was validation.

His tone dropped. He hated this part of the process. "The thing that chased you, did it stalk you for a few days? Your head hurt, nothing seemed to go quite right, you knew something was waiting for you. Then you woke up, probably in the middle of the night, and knew you didn't have much time. You threw what you could into your car and escaped just as it burst into your house. It smelled like copper and smoke, and it was so hot the paint caught on fire when it brushed up against the walls."

Her hand shook and she set the cheap ceramic mug down. It chattered against the table's plywood top.

Bingo. A karak'ai. *She escaped a red burner.*

The satisfaction of narrowing down exactly what had almost caught her warred with gut-clenching relief. Did she know how close she'd come to dying? Probably not.

"How do I know you're not one of them?"

It was a good question, but just like a Lightbringer, delivered too late. "If I was one of them you'd be dead by now." His hands turned to fists inside his pockets. *I would never hurt you. Never.* "If you hang around a little bit more, you'll probably see me fight off something nasty. It's what I do. There are other predators that feed on Lightbringers. The world's a little dangerous for you, in case you haven't noticed."

"Excuse me." She was so polite she sounded almost prim, her perfect mouth pursing. *Gods above, she looks*—He shut that thought off in a hurry. He was not going to think about how her mouth would feel or how soft her skin was. "I have a question. Am I going to have to move out of town?"

Huh? "What?"

"I mean, the next time one of those things comes for me. They weren't too bad when I was younger, but now every six months or so, something tries to eat me or tear up my house or k-kill me." Her voice trembled slightly, but she sat up very straight, blinking at him.

There's more to that story than she's telling me. He noted the tension in her shoulders, the way her aura pulsed. She wasn't emitting like she had yesterday, but the waves of distress were still there, muted but still sharp. The wards he'd placed in the walls—Watcher wards, as careful and powerful as he could make them—vibrated uneasily, trying to contain her distress.

"The next time one of those things comes for you, I'll kill it," he told her. "You don't have to worry. You're with a Watcher now. You're safe." *As safe as inhumanly possible. Get it, Jack? Inhumanly possible. Ha ha.*

She absorbed this. "What if I don't want a...Watcher...with me?"

As if you have a choice, piccola. "Then I'll retreat and do my best to make sure you don't see me."

"But you're not going to stop watching me?"

"Would you want me to?" Bright nails of pain drove into his palms. He made his fingers relax.

The bathroom door creaked open. Shell wandered out, scrubbing at his wet hair with a towel. He wore a red T-shirt and a pair of very blue new jeans. He saw Jack and visibly flinched, his bare feet moving uneasily against cheap carpet.

Anya hopped to her feet. The sudden motion made her breasts bounce slightly under her sweater. Jack leaned back against the wall and forced himself to scan the perimeters once again.

"So you're saying I'm...one of these Lightbringers?" she said. "And those things are going to keep chasing me, no matter what I do?"

He nodded, unable to trust his voice. His throat was dry, his hands tense. *I want to touch her; I need to touch her.*

No. Just take a deep breath, Jack.

"And you're supposed to protect me?"

He nodded again. *Not supposed to. I will protect you.* His neck was full of iron rods. For the first time, the light pouring out from a Lightbringer didn't twist his bones into acid-drenched powder. Instead, being in the same room with her was like being dipped in something warm and thick, coating his skin and easing the constant agony. It unsettled him more than the pain ever had.

"I don't like this." Anya's chin lifted. Her eyes flashed once, and Jack's heart almost stopped.

"I'm sorry," he offered inadequately.

"How do I know you're telling the truth?" Anya waved her hand then, dismissing the question. "Never mind. It makes sense, and you're not lying." Tears glittered in her eyes, she fiercely blinked them away.

I'm not lying now. You should have seen me when I was younger. He struggled desperately to stay in one place, fighting the urge to touch her, to comfort her. What comfort could he give? He was just a Watcher. Just a single, stupid, solitary Watcher. Cannon fodder.

The only protection she had, now.

She sighed. "Shell, I'll get you breakfast in a little while. I need to take a shower and brush my teeth."

"Anya?" The boy sidled nervously, like a horse.

He's like a child. Jack took a closer look. In the long ago, dim time of Jack's youth, a man like this would be called 'simple,' forced to begging or work as a laborer or a rich man's capering fool, adrift in a hard world. No wonder he clung to her.

"It's all right," she soothed, and the boy instinctively leaned toward her. Jack found himself leaning slightly forward too, impelled by the throaty sweetness of her voice. *She could tell a man to walk off a cliff and he'd be in the air before he even thought to say 'okay.'*

She disappeared into the bathroom. After a few moments, the shower started again, and Jack took a deep breath. The boy eyed him suspiciously, the wet towel hanging limp from one hand.

"I don't like you," the boy announced.

I don't like you, either. You're a drain on her resources. But for her sake, I'm going to try diplomacy. "That's a shame. How am I going to look after Anya if you don't help me?"

The boy mulled this over, dropping the sopping towel. His wide, flat face transformed into the picture of realization. He paced forward on bare feet. Jack's instinct to draw himself up threateningly tall warred with Anya's obvious care for this too-big child. Finally Shell stood within five feet, his sleepy blue eyes fixed on Jack's face.

"Bad things chase Anya. She cries."

"I don't want her to cry." *I'm talking to an idiot, but a perceptive idiot.* "And I won't let the bad things hurt her." *We can do this the easy way or the hard way, bambino. You can decide not to make a fuss, or we can shake everything out now and set the tone for our entire relationship.*

Shell studied him intently for several seconds. Jack heard a clatter from the bathroom, and his attention momentarily split between Anya and the boy. *Dropped shampoo; nothing to worry about.* A tingle of pain ran through him. He had spent so long with the grinding constant low-level pain of a *tanak*'s presence in his flesh, the brief relief of his witch's presence made the ache seem more intense when it reappeared.

The boy was a puzzle. He was borderline-psychic, but his aura was oddly 'hard,' pulsing and weakly pulling at the ambient energy in the room. He was a low-level Feeder, addicted to psychic energy. No wonder he stayed so close to Anya. She wouldn't notice it; the drain on her would be minimal. Still...

"I don't like you," Shell repeated. "Anya will make you go away. She always does. Boyfriends don't stay."

I wonder how often you've interrupted her relationships with other people. "I'm not a boyfriend." Jack's fists ached and the *tanak* woke fully. His neck hurt, his entire skeleton dipped in hot lead. The brief relief from Anya's fingers on his made the return of the pain worse. "I'm her Watcher, and you'd better not get in the way."

Shell backed up, his loose mouth turning down. He gave Jack a darting, venomous glance and retreated to his bed, where he sat down and started rocking back and forth, the mattress squeaking under him.

Jack's mouth thinned. *He's going to make trouble. I don't have time for this.*

What, precisely, do *I have time for? She's my witch. I'm not going anywhere. Which reminds me, I'd better start working.*

Jack settled himself back against the wall, his attention sweeping the perimeter of the defenses he'd set up. Shell rocked back and forth, humming to himself. When Jack was sure all the defenses were as they should be, he pulled the cell phone from his pocket and dialed.

Three rings later, it picked up. "Report." The voice was clipped, mature, a woman's voice spiced with slight Power but without the usual kindness of a Lightbringer.

"Jack Gray," Jack said, and gave his access number. "Stationed in Zone Forty-Seven, Santiago City. I've got a flyer here, and I need some help. We're going to have to start from scratch."

Fifteen

Anya felt bedraggled and moth-eaten, worn thin. By the time she'd finished her shower, her skin tingling from hot water and scrubbing, Jack had a sleek black cell phone out, obviously finishing the last of several calls, A few minutes later, he'd ushered them into the car—Anya had only a moment's worth of unease at handing him her keys—and smoothly drove them to Willow Street as if he'd lived in the city all his life. The house was a small, white pseudo-Victorian two-story set back in a straggling garden. There was a red *For Rent* sign in the front window.

The cheerful, round-faced real estate agent who met them in her SUV took one look at Jack and positively beamed. She wore the obligatory suit jacket and a floppy, blowsy red necktie. "You'd like to rent?"

She didn't give Anya or the Taurus a second look. Anya rolled the window back up, not wanting to hear any more.

The cloud of red-black darkness around Jack pulsed once. Anya shivered. She held Shell's hand in the backseat of her car, both of them wedged uncomfortably between suitcases. The woman handed Jack a sheaf of papers and he signed two of them, then handed her something that looked like a check and another sheaf of paper. His aura pulsed again, that darkness shoving at the woman.

What's he doing? For a moment she could almost *see* the cloak of energy rippling, but it was gone too quickly for her to make any sense of it. She'd fought her strange gifts and hallucinations for so long that now, when she needed to understand what he was doing, the curse failed her.

Of course. Isn't that the way it always is?

Shell's fingers tightened on hers. "I don't like him," he whispered. "Make him go away, Anya. He's mean."

I don't think he's quite that bad. But you could say I'm not the best judge of such things. Bile rose in Anya's throat. "I know you don't like him, but we have nowhere else to go, Shell. If he can keep the bad things away like he says he can, we *need* him."

Not to mention the fact that we don't have another option. This is the end of the line. She shifted uncomfortably. The faint persistent odor of smoke in the car was drowned out by the smell of leather and musky, peppery male.

Shell made a small dissatisfied noise. "We don't need him. I don't like him. He's mean."

Anya took a deep breath. "I hope he's meaner than those things chasing us," she muttered.

Shell flinched. "Anya. I don't *like* him."

"Shell, *please*." She didn't raise her voice, but he stopped, staring at her with his sleepy blue eyes. "I'm out of ideas, buddy, and this guy seems to have a good handle on what he's doing. Let's just wait and see, okay?"

Shell said nothing else, but he mumbled softly, rocking back and forth. That was a sure sign of trouble. If he kept rocking, he would work himself into a fit and Anya might have to use the Persuasion. Using it in front of Jack would cause questions and problems. She'd hidden her talent for so long that the thought of someone else knowing filled her with a sinking, unsteady feeling.

The day was turning out cloudy and cool, brief spots of sunlight pouring down to outline the house. It looked like a nice place, even if its garden had been neglected for a while. The front door was painted a cheerful red, and the roof looked new.

Jack opened her car door, waving good-bye to the round-faced woman, whose SUV roused and shook itself as she drove away. Anya blinked.

"It's safe." He bent down so she could hear him. "Want to bring your purse in and take a look around? I'm sorry there's not more of a choice, but we're working on limited time."

"What do you mean limited time?" Her breath caught in her throat as she slid her legs out of the car, trying to pull her fingers from Shell's. He refused to move.

Jack shrugged, an elegant movement. He really was just like a cat, a big gray-eyed cat. Oddly graceful, with a shuttered handsome face and a peculiar intense gaze. The real estate woman had not seemed to notice his guns, or the sword hilt. "Dusk is coming. Night's the most dangerous time for you."

Anya closed her mouth with something resembling a snap. The things chasing her had always attacked at night. "How did you find this place?"

"Made a few calls. Circle Lightfall technically can't operate inside the city limits, but they can fund me through the infrastructure and give me a list of contacts. There's a list of things we do in a situation like this. We'll have a couple of deliveries today. Furniture, groceries, things like that."

He glanced at the street, his attention seemingly everywhere at once—and fixed on her at the same time. It seemed nothing escaped his notice, not the faintest expression on her face or the slightest breath of air. It was exhausting just *watching* him pay that much attention to everything around him.

"Why can't they operate inside the city limits?" She tried not to sound too curious.

"Because the Guardians won't let them."

"Guardians?" *I'm beginning to sound like an idiot.* She tugged on Shell's hand. He didn't let go, but he didn't move either. Anya twisted awkwardly in the seat, her arm stretched behind her. The small bones in her wrist ground together briefly, and she stopped, flinching.

"The Rowangrove. Theo, Mari, Elise. They're Guardians, responsible for protecting the city. They decided they didn't want Circle Lightfall here. They don't trust them."

"What about you? And the—the other Watchers?" This was interesting, she had to admit, even if she had to struggle to believe it.

You can't afford to disbelieve, even if this is a fairy tale. Hey presto, he waves a magic wand and all of a sudden everything's taken care of. She pulled even harder on Shell's hand. His fingers bit into hers, and he pulled back, probably surprised by her sudden movement. Anya's shoulder gave a hot flare of pain, and she bit back a short gasp at Shell's stubbornness.

"The other Watchers have bonded." He glanced up at the street again. "Look, we'd better get you inside so I can ward the place. Being out in the open makes me nervous."

Despite the fact that she couldn't imagine *him* nervous, she tugged on Shell's hand again.

"Shell, come on," she said, a little louder than she'd meant to. She twisted to look back over her shoulder. "We have to go inside the house."

Shell's face was white and his lower lip pooched out. He shook his head, trembling.

Anya sighed. She didn't want to use the Persuasion again. "Please, Shell. I have to get out of the car."

The Watcher—*Jack,* she reminded herself—tensed very slightly. "Is he hurting your hand?"

"Of course not. He would never hurt me." Anya's tone was sharp. "Let go of my hand, Shell."

She finally managed to extricate her fingers, but Shell's lower lip pushed out even further. He began to rock back and forth slightly, the car moving on its springs as his bulk shifted.

"Oh, no." This was the very *last* thing she needed.

"Here." Jack pressed a small piece of jagged metal into her hand, somehow avoiding touching her bare palm. "Go on up and unlock the door. That works for both the deadlock and the knob." He managed to close his hand around her wrist without brushing skin by wrapping his fingers around her sagging sweater-sleeve. "I'll bring him, and I'll be gentle. I promise."

"I don't—" Anya began, but he had already pulled her out of the car, his grip firm and gentle but irresistible.

"It's all right. I'll bring him. Go on in and see which bedroom you like. It's got two."

Her mouth went dry. "But—"

"Please, Anya." Now his tone was less flat and more...what? Pleading. He was pleading with her.

Anya cast one more worried look at the car, rubbing at her shoulder, but she couldn't see Shell. It was useless; she was out of ideas. She had a grand total of fifty dollars and her car, some clothes, her grandmother's jewelry, her coffeemaker, and a box of Triscuits. And Shell.

Plus the envelope of cash Jack had given her. She had to admit the grim-faced man carrying guns was looking like the best option for her and Shell's continued survival. Unless he was one of *them*, the dark things that chased her. But they had never spoken to her before, just tore down her house and tried to eat her.

Why am I so sure they want to eat me? She dismissed the question with a flare of annoyance at her own stupidity. What else did a monster do when it caught you?

The garden walk was granite flagstones, fitted closely together. A huge rosemary bush crouched by the dilapidated gate. Anya touched it and took a deep breath of its crisp scent. The sun broke from behind clouds and poured down, edging every ragged leaf in gold. She saw a hydrangea bush, a mass of chamomile, peony bushes, the distinctive leaves of foxglove, and more plants she couldn't identify.

I've always wanted a garden. Maybe we could stay here. It looks nice.

She shook her head, chiding herself, and strode up the walk through last year's fallen leaves, probably from the oak tree in the lower left corner of the yard. A few lone leaves still clung to the oak's branches. It would shade the house in summer. The fence leaned crazily.

"Well, it doesn't look like much," she murmured, examining the house. At least the windows weren't broken.

It feels nice, she decided, looking at the porch. It seemed solid; the steps didn't squeak when she climbed them.

Anya reached the front door. The red paint was oddly pristine, and sunlight turned it a glowing, rich crimson. It was an old house, and she'd always loved old houses. This one looked like it had been built in the twenties, an imitation Victorian, graceful and trim. It felt welcoming, and she felt her shoulders start to drop, weight slipping away. There was a certain relaxation in being utterly helpless. *I'll keep the money. Hide it somewhere safe. Just in case. After all, he gave it to me, didn't he?*

I wonder what he gets from all this?

The sunlight drained away, clouds moving across the sky. A chill wet breeze full of the smell of rain whistled between the porch supports.

I could plant jasmine, or honeysuckle. It would be nice to sit out here on a summer evening and watch the garden get ready for night.

The thought of nightfall wasn't comforting. Anya shivered, and put her key into the lock. The door opened easily, and she stepped inside.

It felt, again, like coming home. Except Anya knew how fragile that feeling could be.

Let's just hope this place doesn't burn down around me.

Sixteen

Dusk slid through the sky. Jack closed the front door and spread his hand against the chill wooden surface. The property wards were woven as tightly as he could make them in so short a time. He'd brought in all the suitcases from the car. The grocery delivery had startled Anya, but she'd covered it well. Better than she'd dealt with the furniture delivery. In the end, she'd just retreated to the kitchen and prowled around the breakfast bar until the deliverymen left. He didn't blame her— ordinary people were probably a reminder of her essential difference, and their messy, blaring minds would scrape her sensitive edges to no end.

Two box springs, two mattresses, a couch, and a kitchen table with chairs was the best he could do on short notice. There was no way to get bed frames. He hoped she wasn't affronted by so little comfort.

A moment's worth of concentration triggered the wards he'd laid on the house walls, springing up and folding over the physical structure, overlapping seamlessly. Red-black Watcher power spread like a bruise, a wall to keep the Dark out. It wouldn't completely hide her glow; she was a wildly random distress signal. It would, however, make most predators think twice before attempting to attack. He'd also laid the street with traps and defenses, which would warn him of anything approaching.

I'm going to have to clean out the city, too. Keep her undercover until I can make it a bit safer out there.

He took his hand away from the door, feeling the sense of dead air that meant the wards were tight and impassable. As usual, there was a slight stickiness, the energy wanting to cling to his palm. He shook it away and felt the familiar bite of acid in his bones. The Dark symbiote melded to his body was restless, searching for Anya, only slightly mollified by the fact that she was in the house and safe.

He heard light footsteps on the stairs behind him. Bare feet. A woman's feet. He knew almost nothing about Anya. He still didn't know what her calling was. Of course, Circle Lightfall would fund her indefinitely, but most Lightbringers had a specific vocation. He would bet hers was in social services; her firm handling of the boy seemed to say so.

"What did you say to Shell?" she asked from the stairs, and

his body tightened involuntarily. Even her voice plucked at his control, made him want to touch her.

He turned on his heel. The foyer was high and narrow, the living room off to the left, and the kitchen and dining room toward the back, stairs and a study to the right. The balustrade, carved oak in a fluid sinuous curve, seemed to almost vibrate with happiness under her hand. She was no longer emitting a high-pitched flood of distress; her aura was calmer.

Thank the gods, I can't answer for my temper if she gets that upset again.

"I didn't really say anything." It was his first lie since becoming a Watcher. "What's wrong?"

"Nothing's *wrong.*" Warm electric light from the foyer's fixture glimmered blue-black in her hair. Her gray eyes were soft and ringed with dark circles. She'd kicked off her shoes, and he made a mental note to make sure the heat was on. He wouldn't feel chill temperatures, but she would. "He's been remarkably obedient. It's not often he changes his mind about someone."

If you hurt her again, I'll take her away, he'd snarled, driven past patience. The fool of a boy had hurt her. She'd been favoring her shoulder when she got out, rubbing at it absently. *You don't want me to do that, do you, Shell? You do what Anya says. Now.*

He hadn't *pushed* the boy—the developmentally disabled were more resistant to the peculiar sort of mental pressure Watchers could use—but he had let a little Power leak out, knowing it would make his eyes glow and his voice turn harsh. The boy had let out an undignified squeak and scrambled out of the car. Making the kid hate him wasn't a good move, but Jack didn't have time to be gentle.

Not with him, anyway. Anya would need all the gentleness Jack was capable of scraping together. After so many years of being a Watcher, he wondered just how much he had left.

"I told him to do what you said," he clarified. "It'll be easier if he stays out of trouble while we're getting you settled."

She nodded, crossing her arms and cupping her elbows in her hands. The sweater—dove gray, just like her other one—made her skin glow even more. "He's playing with his marbles upstairs. We'll take the smaller bedroom, you can have the other—"

"I thought you could have the bigger bedroom, and he could have the smaller one." He dared to interrupt only because she looked so uncertain. "I'll probably be standing guard most nights."

"What about sleeping?" She sighed, pulling even further into herself. "I need to find a job, too. Unless they were serious about hiring me at the Rowangrove."

"I don't need much sleep." If he put off the trance for more than three or four days, he would need something more like human sleep. It didn't happen often—after fighting off two *belrakan* and bringing a witch into a Lightfall safehouse, he'd slept for twenty-four hours straight, his psyche reeling from brushing so close to death. He stuffed his hands in his pockets. The temptation to take a single step forward, then another, was overwhelming. "There's no hurry. Circle Lightfall will help you."

She held up a slim, pale hand. "I don't want to hear it. Not right now. Tomorrow."

He nodded. "All right. Are you tired? Hungry?"

"A little of both." She shivered. "What did you do? To the walls, I mean."

So she can see. I'd wondered. "It's basic warding. Shields."

"Shields." Her lips thinned and her shoulders came up. It was a habitual movement, taking on a weight. "I suppose I'd better start learning how to do that, right?"

Jack shrugged, easing his sword harness over his shoulders. The coat settled against him, a familiar heavy comfort. "The other Lightbringers will be able to teach you."

"What about you?"

He dropped his eyes, her voice stroking him. *She could make a man beg with that voice.* He felt a grim smile touch his face and banished it with an effort. "I can't work Lightbringer magicks. No Watcher can."

"But could I learn to do…shields?" Her eyebrows drew together, a look of puzzlement and inquiry mixed. "That seems like it would be pretty useful."

He nodded. "They can teach you. I'm just a Watcher."

"The things that keep chasing me." She shifted on the stairs, and he felt the movement in his own body. He was becoming acutely attuned to her. "I thought you were one of them."

No wonder she'd bolted, if she was so sensitive to the Dark. "I feel like it, don't I? It's called a *tanak*, it's a symbiote. It gives me greater strength and endurance, makes me able to beat the Dark at its own game." He dared to look up—she wasn't fleeing in terror, just standing on the stairs, staring at him. "I won't hurt you," he repeated, wishing he knew what to say to take that look off her face.

"All right." She sighed. The air turned golden, her aura spreading out. She was relaxing. That was better, because her fear would trigger his rage. It was also worse, because her steady glow would show no matter how well he warded the house. "Look, Shell needs dinner and you probably do too. What do you want to eat?"

He shrugged. "I'll be fine. I'm more worried about you."

"I think I'm beginning to recover from the shock," she replied dryly. "Will you at least eat something, so I'm sure you're human?"

I haven't been human for a long time, piccola. And with the tanak *in me, I don't need to eat if I get into enough fights to feed off the bloodshed.* He wondered why he wasn't planning on how to ease her into a safehouse, maybe in another city. Wondered when she would figure out he wasn't strictly human at all. "I'll eat if you like."

"Don't do me any favors." She stamped down the stairs and brushed past him, heading for the kitchen, sparks almost popping from her wake. A quick mood change, from vulnerability to irritation. Normal for a woman who had just been put through the wringer. He had to banish another smile.

Then she stopped, looking over her shoulder. He had to tear his eyes away from the curve of her hips under her gray slacks.

Her tone softened. "I'm sorry. That wasn't very nice of me. You don't have to eat. I just thought you'd be hungry. Or something."

A Lightbringer apologizing to *him?* Jack's jaw threatened to drop. "Don't apologize," he said through the sudden, surprising lump in his throat. "I'll help you fix dinner. Just tell me what to do."

That earned him a slight smile that did something strange to his normally calm, orderly head. *Wait 'til you bond, old man,* Hanson's voice echoed in his memory.

"Well, since it looks like you had enough food for twenty people delivered, I'm sure I can figure something out." Her wry smile softened the already-gentle sarcasm.

"Standard operating procedure." He followed her down the hall into the kitchen. "We bring a lot of Lightbringers in from the cold. First shelter, then food, then comfort."

"In from the cold?" She opened the fridge, bending slightly. Her spine had a beautiful supple curve.

"It happens more often than you think." *Down, boy. Be calm.*

She was still smiling, a good sign. "You thought of everything. Even paper plates."

"There's a list. Circle Lightfall's barred from physically being present inside the city limits, but the support infrastructure's here. Computers were a godsend." He realized he was talking too goddamn much and shut his mouth. Taking in a deep breath, he told himself to calm down.

"Toast." Her head was still in the fridge. "And some apples. Shell likes apples. Did you get any bacon?"

"Most Lightbringers are vegetarian," he mumbled, looking down at the counter. Someone had evidently loved this house. Everything was in good repair. The kitchen cabinets were pale wood, the appliances were new, and the countertops were a burnished pale blue that suited Anya. The floor was laminate, a lovely light wood, and electric light washed the kitchen in mellow gold. Outside, the last of the day was dying, and a flutter of rain brushed the windows.

"Well, it's going to be peanut butter toast and apple slices, then. And scrambled eggs. Maybe I can coax Shell into drinking some milk."

Her voice broke on the last syllable. She closed the blank white fridge, turned around, and suddenly slumped against it as if all the strength had vanished from her legs.

"Anya?" Alarmed, he checked the shields again. Intact. The house was clean and protected, he'd made sure of it. "What's wrong?"

"It's okay." She took a deep breath. Tears glimmered in her eyes. Her throat worked for a moment. "This reminds me of...let's see, two cities ago. I had this house with stripped pine cabinets and wooden floors. It was beautiful."

"What happened?" He used his softest tone, wishing his voice wasn't so harsh compared to the husky music of hers.

"Something tore the house apart in the middle of the night. We couldn't stay. Shell had a broken foot and I think one of my ribs cracked. It hurt for a long time."

He had to take a deep breath, rage sliding up his backbone and twisting in his veins. "I'm sorry," he offered inadequately. *Sorry I wasn't there to protect you.*

Anya shook her hair back, her chin lifting slightly. "It wasn't your fault." She wiped at her cheeks, pushing the tears away. "You're not surprised." She didn't sound surprised either. "You know what I'm talking about. You've seen those things."

I've seen far more than you can probably imagine, piccola. Jack's fists tightened in his pockets. He leaned against the breakfast bar and regarded her steadily, trying to breathe through the rage. The thought of her alone, without her Watcher, stranded in a city with the Dark tearing her house apart, wasn't good for his continued calm. "I've seen a lot. You aren't the first."

"It's just...I'm not crazy. Or if I am, I'm at least crazy in the same way you are, and those women at the Rowangrove. I suppose I just wasn't prepared to be sane. And I don't really have any choice but to trust you. I hope this isn't some sort of...some sort of game." She shivered. He could see the goose bumps rising on her arms since she'd pushed up her sleeves.

He shook his head, wishing he knew what to say. With any other Lightbringer, he would have known the right explanation, the right serving of truth to calm her and bring her into the Circle.

Why am I not locking her down and clearing the streets? Because she's fragile right now. If I left her in here, she might bolt again. I can't afford to let her out of my sight for a minute, she's completely unskilled. And if anything happens to her...

It was official. He was no longer Jack Gray, Watcher of Circle Lightfall. Now, he was strictly Anya's Watcher. He had a complete novice of a Lightbringer with enough Power to light up the city *and* a boy-in-a-man's-body to corral as well. The gods certainly had a sense of humor.

"Jack?" She watched him closely, the dark circles around her haunted eyes taunting him.

"Don't worry." The harsh rage in his voice made the kitchen window rattle slightly. One of the cabinets groaned. Anya's eyes widened. He pushed the fury down, his nails driving into his palms as he clenched his fists. "It's not a game. It's deadly serious. I'm here to look after you, Anya. Get used to it."

With that, he turned on his heel and stalked for the hall. If he stayed here any longer he would be tempted to touch her again, to see if the jolt of euphoria returned. He knew it would, knew she was the only witch who could ease his pain. Knew it with a sick certainty that twisted his gut and made his fists ache. She was *his* witch.

When she found out exactly who he was, he would lose everything.

Seventeen

Two weeks later, Anya stared critically at the bookshelf, her eyebrows drawing together. "A Technical Analysis of Tarot Archetypes," she muttered, shoving her hair back and tucking a few strands behind her ear. "You have *got* to be kidding me."

"Put it in General Tarot." Theo sounded amused. She lifted a wrought-iron candlestick free of crackling paper and arranged it on the shelf. "By author, remember."

"Oh." Anya found the Tarot section. She was slowly beginning to find her way around the store. Funny how it looked so small from the outside, but it was actually roomy enough for a lot of merchandise. "Ms. Morgan—"

"I told you," Theo replied with maddening patience, "call me Theo. No need to be formal. Now, can you repeat the four elements?"

"Earth, water, fire, air." Anya gritted her teeth. "Earth is patience, power, solidity; water is sexuality, emotion, and purification; fire is passion, drive and cleansing; air is communication, quickness, and insight."

"And the fifth element?" Theo arranged the candlestick, turning it so the star carved on its front could be clearly seen, swept up a white taper and stuck it in the top. It had been a busy day, a flood of customers wanting everything from cards to crystals to one woman who had bought seven hundred dollars' worth of hemp clothing. Anya was slowly learning how to coddle the recalcitrant, antique cash register and direct people to the right part of the store without having to fumble and look at Theo. She had doubted the store's ability to make a profit, but apparently there was a thriving New Age population in the city.

"The fifth element is spirit or soul," she answered. *Might as well ask a few questions of my own.* "Look, you keep making me repeat this. I want to know how to protect myself better."

She heard the demand in her own voice—*like a whiny little kid*—and took a deep breath, steadying herself as she shelved the book and turned to face Theo, her arms crossed defensively.

Theo nodded, brushing back her dark sandalwood-scented hair. "I expect you do. I wish Suzanne was here. She was the Teacher. I really don't even know where to start, Anya. I'm sorry. I'm doing the best I can."

It was impossible to be angry at Theo. She was so good, so impossibly calm and patient, that all anger just seemed to drain away around her. Anya sighed, guiltily. Theo hadn't said a word about Anya running away pell-mell. When she'd returned to the store, Theo had only hugged her and stroked her hair, saying she was glad Anya hadn't been hurt.

It was enough to make you hate her, if you could hate someone so kind and calm. "Who was Suzanne?" The question blurted out before Anya realized the rudeness.

"My friend. *Our* friend, our Teacher. She...died." Theo shook her head, sighing. "She would have known how to teach you, I think. Me, I'm just a healer."

Saying you're "just" a healer is like saying a Porsche is "just" a car. It was still surprising other people couldn't see the color and light around Theo—but they could certainly *feel* it. Every day, damaged and hurt people sought her out, and she would make them better, often at the cost of her own strength.

Guilt bit at Anya again. She'd heard Dante pleading with Theo to take care of herself. Oddly enough, he was the Watcher she felt most comfortable with, even though he was so big. Anyone could see how much he cared about the healer, and it made him seem much less threatening.

"I'm sorry." Anya shoved her hair back, impatiently. It was almost long enough for a ponytail, but until that blessed day she had to live with it falling in her eyes all the time. At least she'd managed to steal an hour at Supercuts in the mini-mall down the street from the Rowangrove. It no longer looked as if she'd been hacked by a two-year-old.

Theo shrugged, smiling. There was a suspicious glaze to her eyes. "Well, I know she's not really gone." She glanced up at the clock. "Shell and Elise should be along any minute."

It was a graceful subject change, and Anya appreciated it. "He's really proud of being able to work," she said, just as the air pressure inside the store plummeted. Anya's stomach plunged, and she shivered. It meant the Watchers were coming down from the roof or "patrol" or whatever they did while she was working. She supposed she might eventually get used to the sudden feeling of gravity shifting beneath her—but not yet.

"There's Dante." Theo's face lit up. She turned, her gray skirt swirling prettily, like a dancer's. She pushed up her sweater-sleeves. "And Jack, probably," she added belatedly, glancing at Anya.

"Go ahead." *I don't think Jack will be happy to see me. He seems to avoid looking at me unless he thinks I won't notice.* Anya spread her hands, shrugging. "I'll hang out up front."

Theo bit her lower lip, obviously torn, but then she heard Dante's voice and headed for the back door.

Anya sighed. Two weeks of working here hadn't helped anything. Well, *some* things—Jack swore she wouldn't have to move again unless she wanted to. He swore she was safe. And she'd begun to relax. Nothing had descended on her house to tear it apart, and nothing had chased her yet. That was an encouraging sign.

But Shell had retreated further and further into his own private world, not acknowledging Jack and sometimes not even acknowledging Anya. She hadn't had to use the Persuasion on him yet, but it was probably only a matter of time. *That* would open up a whole new jack-in-the-box of questions. Was hypnotizing people with a stare Anya's special talent? Theo could heal, Mari had visions of the future—Anya believed it— and Elise could light a candle with a fierce look.

The first time she'd seen Elise do so had been one of the more startling moments in Anya's life. The curious sense of not believing her own eyes had warred with a funny queer faintness. Anya had swayed on her feet, unsteady, and Shell had whistled tunelessly, unfazed.

The only thing more terrifying than being alone with her gifts was to find someone *else* with freakish abilities. The terror was only matched by a sneaking unfamiliar feeling of comfort.

Slowly, Anya had learned to build something called a "shield" around herself, but it was still thin and weak. Jack said she didn't radiate as much, and she supposed that was good, but learning to use whatever made her different was like trying to pedal a bicycle with a pair of flippers—hard, exhausting, and clumsy. Theo and Elise said it would get easier, but Anya wasn't so sure.

She stopped by the front door, looking out at the darkening street. It hadn't rained for a few days, but the clouds stayed thick. It was normal weather for this time of year, Theo said, but Anya wondered how people lived here without any sunlight.

A bike messenger whizzed by, heading for the foot of the Ave and the high buildings of downtown. A bus lumbered in the opposite direction, and a police car slid past. Dim evening light made the concrete even grayer. The trees had lost their leaves and the air had taken on a deep chill, a mild winter but winter nonetheless. She would have to get Shell new shoes, and maybe another warm jacket.

Voices murmured behind her. Anya didn't pay any attention—she probably wouldn't understand what they were saying anyway. Stuff about patrols and Darkness and talents and powers.

It was, she reflected, like being caught in a particularly bad sitcom. All it needed was a laugh track and commercial breaks.

Anya tilted her head. *What's that?*

"*Help! Help!*" The call was faint, coming from the street outside. It pricked at her ears, the world snapping into focus around her.

Anya jumped as if stung. She looked back over her shoulder, expecting to see Theo or Jack. Theo always seemed to know when someone was in trouble, and Jack's hearing was a lot more acute than he let on.

"*Help!*" The voice was faint under the seashell sound of traffic.

None of the people passing by seemed to hear. Anya shook her head slightly, trying to dislodge the sudden pressure between her temples. A black-haired woman dressed in a dark-blue business suit hurried by, her head down and her heels making faint sounds against the pavement.

"*Help me! Help me! No! NO!*" A woman's voice, frantic, raw with sobbing.

Why does it look like nobody else hears that?

The bell jingled as she pulled the door open. She stepped outside, shivering. Damp, chill air wrapped around her. She only wore jeans and a thin gray sweater, gooseflesh rising on her skin as she peered up the street.

"*Help! God, help me!*" The voice, screaming hoarsely, came from her left. Up the Avenue.

Anya didn't stop to think. She started up the street, walking quickly.

She passed two teenage boys walking with their heads together, whispering.

Don't they hear her? Maybe it was just big-city callousness. Or maybe Anya was the only one who could hear. That thought made her stomach flip uncomfortably.

Squares of light from the shop widows dappled the pavement. She passed the Glazed Fire Ceramic Shop and a Thai restaurant, her pace quickening as a long, indistinct scream came from up ahead. Nobody else seemed to notice or care. She ran now, her heart pounding in her chest and her lungs burning.

"*Help! Help!*"

The call echoed. A man walking in front of her shook his head, glancing around as if he heard, then hurried away across the street, his raincoat flapping.

There. A brick apartment building with blue-painted steps. Her breath came harsh and rasping. She was running flat-out, without any idea how she'd started.

"*Help! Help! Please help, someone help!*"

The alley; it's coming from the alley. Anya's sneakers slapped the pavement. She heard footsteps behind her, running quick and light. *Good, maybe someone else heard her. It sounds like she's really in trouble.*

Walls lifted up on either side. The light failed suddenly, as full dark dropped like a blanket over the concrete. There was a Dumpster set on one side, and the hot slippery smell of garbage rose, a thunderous stench under the rain and cold. Anya pounded down the alley, her feet moving of their own accord. It felt like a red-hot wire wrapped around her middle, pulling her on, inescapable as a hook in a fish's mouth.

There was a fire escape at the end of the alley, but Anya whirled and ran for a door showing a slim wedge of electric light around its edges; scarred metal that had once been painted blue. Anya jerked it free, the wooden wedge used to hold it slightly open skittering off into the alley. She realized as soon as she stumbled into the fluorescent-lit glare that it was a laundry room. It was brightly-lit, warm, and sweet-smelling, holding three washers, two dryers, a table—and a young woman lying on the yellow linoleum floor, staring up at Anya with wide, dark terrified eyes.

Anya blinked, almost overbalancing as the wire around her middle snapped and she was left breathless and disoriented, gasping because she'd just been running as fast as possible.

The man crouched over the woman's body blinked back. He was taller than Anya, whip-thin, with a greasy little moustache and a blue windbreaker. The woman's wrists were duct-taped together, and her shirt was cut down the front, revealing her blue lace bra. Something had been jammed into her mouth, which was duct-taped too.

Anya's gasp echoed against the metal of the washing

machines and fell lifelessly against the floor.

The man hopped to his feet and held up a long thin knife, fluorescent light running wetly over the blade's flat surface.

"On the floor!" he barked, his voice surprisingly high and unsteady. He pointed down with his free hand, grime under his nails in black half-moons. "*Now!*"

Anya, frozen, looked down at the girl. *Her mouth is taped shut. How could I hear her screaming? Oh, God.*

She felt more than heard the door swing shut behind her, locking automatically. Anya raised her shaking hands. "You don't want to do this."

All the air left her in a stuttering gasp when the man darted forward. *Use the Persuasion on him!* a dim voice screeched in the back of her mind. *Hurry up and use the Persuasion. Come on, Anya, do it!*

"Get on the *floor!*" the man yelled, making a short stabbing motion with the knife. The dark-eyed woman whimpered. Now Anya could see that her jeans were unzipped.

He'd been trying to take her jeans off.

Nausea rose in a swift, sickening wave. *Oh, my God.* "You don't want to hurt anyone—" she began, her voice bouncing high and squeaky off the walls.

The door behind her ripped itself open, metal screeching and snapping. Anya barely had time to take a startled, gasping breath before the air in the small room turned red-black and Jack moved past her, preternatural speed blurring him into a streak of black and silver. His leather coat flapped once, and he held the other man by the throat up against the far wall. The knife chimed as it hit the floor.

"Not on my watch." Jack's voice coated the room with ice. One of the dryers *pinged!* just like a car's hood after a hard race. "Not on *my* witch."

Anya swallowed dryly. She dropped to her knees with a jolt, her brain suddenly working again, and crawled to the woman lying on the floor. Tears slicked the woman's face and mucus ran down her upper lip, slicking down the tape. *How can she breathe? Got to get that off her mouth so she can breathe.*

"I'm sorry," Anya whispered, frantically picking at the duct tape. She finally managed to pull a corner of it up. The woman moaned deep in her throat, her eyes rolling.

Anya steeled herself and ripped it free.

There was a red ankle-sock jammed in the woman's mouth, Anya tweezed it loose.

"Anya." Jack's voice, harsh and low. "Are you hurt?"

It took two tries before her throat would work properly. Her heart hammered so hard she was afraid of passing out. *Don't you dare faint, Anya.* "N-no. We have to call the p-police—"

"No." He sounded *furious.* Anya had never heard such relentless rage contained in a single syllable. The darkness of Jack's aura smoked with twisting energy. "No police yet. The woman, is she hurt?"

The dark-eyed woman moaned. "Thank God. Oh, thank God, thank God, thank God." She struggled to hold her shirt together with her taped hands.

"I think she'll be all right." Anya started picking at the tape around the woman's wrists. Both of them were shaking so badly it seemed impossible, the strength had left her fingers. "I can't get this tape off."

There was a meaty thump. Jack turned away from the wall. "Here." He strode across the floor, knelt swiftly, and had a knife out before Anya could protest.

The knife was wickedly long and had a broad dull-black metal blade with thin traceries of red fire running over it in spidery, angular shapes.

Oh boy. We're not in Kansas anymore. The merry voice of lunacy whirled inside her head. Anya's stomach rose in rebellion. She swallowed hard, forcing the feeling away.

In one efficient stroke, Jack had the woman's wrists free, balling up the tape and sticking it in his pocket. Then the knife vanished, and Jack grabbed the woman's ripped shirt, hauling her to her feet. "What's your name?" His voice was flat and toneless as ever.

"M-M-mina. Oh, God. Thank you, thank you—"

Jack's red-black aura flared, shoving at her. Her dark eyes turned wide and blank. Her jaw slackened, and the thin moaning sound died in her throat.

"Go home and call the police. You were attacked down here, but you managed to fight the attacker off. You won't remember us, but you can give them a clear description of the man with the mustache. When the cops are gone, you'll go to bed and sleep. When you wake up, you'll feel much better. You'll know this particular man can't hurt you ever again. Do you hear me, Mina?"

Anya stared at his aura, her eyes blurring and watering. She could *see* what he was doing now, a type of Persuasion.

I thought I was the only one. She was unaware of her hand squeezing the duct tape from the woman's mouth into a ball, tighter and tighter.

Mina nodded. Her pupils dilated so far her eyes had turned black. The square of raw-looking flesh over her mouth hurt Anya to look at.

Jack's lips thinned. His aura flared again, but in a different way this time, less controlled and more general. Sweat stood out on his pale forehead, damping his dark hair down.

"There." Something in his flat tone told Anya whatever he'd done had been painful for him. "That should do it. Go on, Mina. Be more careful."

Anya gasped. The tape-mark on Mina's face was gone. *How did he do that?*

Mina moved like a sleepwalker, one slow step at a time, torn shirt flapping as her hands swung loosely at her sides. She vanished through the door, and Anya caught a glimpse of a staircase lit with the same glaring, buzzing fluorescent lights.

I really think I'm going to throw up. That would just cap off this whole damn evening.

Jack, meanwhile, grabbed the mustachioed man again and lifted him as if he was a sack of flour.

"Now the question is, what do we do with *you?*" he said, half to himself. The man's face was gray, and he hung limply from Jack's fist. Fist, singular, because Jack casually held him with one hand, as if he weighed nothing.

Anya made a thin, breathless sound. Jack glanced down at her, his eyes turned silvery and *cold.* "Do you want him dead?" he asked, as if it was the most natural thing in the world.

"*What?*" Her voice bounced off linoleum, brick walls, and metal appliances. *I sound like Minnie Mouse having a heart attack.*

"We don't have much time. Do you want him dead?"

"Of *course* not." *I sound horrified, too.* A black tide of unhealthy laughter rose below the surface of her mind. *Maybe because I am horrified. Imagine that.*

"As you like." Jack shook the man. "Wake up."

The man's eyes fluttered open. He began to make the same moaning, thready sound Mina had made moments earlier.

"Shut up." Jack's voice turned clear and flatly, terribly furious. His aura gathered itself and *shoved* at the man. He nodded his head toward Anya. "Forget her face and mine. You'll get the hell out of here. You won't ever come back. And if you ever want to force a woman again, you will beat your head as hard as you can against a concrete wall until the feeling goes away."

"Jack!" Anya gasped. Her heart still thumped and sang in her wrists and ankles, smacking so hard she had trouble hearing over its racket.

He carried the limp bundle to the door leading to the alley. "Now run as fast as you can," he snarled, and dumped the man outside.

Anya heard scrabbling feet and a thin moan before silence dropped over the laundry room.

Jack's eyes moved through the room in one smooth arc and settled on her. His hands curled into fists. "Are you all right?"

"I…" Anya searched for something to say. Out of all the words she knew, none fit. None even came *close* to applying.

"We've got to get you out of here. Did you touch anything? Anything at all?"

Anya found she was still holding the ball of duct tape. "I—"

He snatched the tape from her and stuffed it in his pocket. "Are you hurt? Did he touch you? I swear to the gods, if he hurt you, I will track him down and *finish* him."

"I-I'm fine." Anya forced herself to inhale. *Calming breath,* Theo called it. *Every witch's best friend.* "What did you *do* to them?"

Jack's eyes glowed silver. "It's called a *push*. I can only use it to protect you." He offered his hand. "Come on, Anya. If we're here when the police get here, I'll have to hide you completely and move at the same time, and that might be a little uncomfortable." He paused, still offering his hand. "For you," he added thoughtfully.

She closed her fingers around his, and he went utterly still, unbreathing.

What's wrong? Anya flinched and glanced at the door. "What is it?" she whispered. "Did he come back?"

"No." Jack pulled her carefully to her feet. She knew how strong he was—he'd picked up the other man one-handed, and he'd torn open the door. Had it been locked? "Never do that again, Anya. What were you *thinking?*"

"I heard someone screaming for help." The world wavered, like a static-laden television signal.

"It could have been a trap." His eyebrows drew together. He held her hand, staring down at her, his stubbled jaw set and harsh. His skin was callused hard and fever-hot. "It could have been the Dark. I would have come with you. You *cannot* run off like that. Do you understand me?"

The carefully controlled, iron vehemence in his voice was stunning enough. The fierce protective rage flooding out from him made her head spin, overwhelming the weak wall she'd managed to build around herself.

"I don't feel so good," she whispered, swaying. She'd never drowned in what someone else was feeling like this—the intensity of the emotion pouring out of him made her reel. Her stomach gurgled once more, decided maybe it wasn't quite worth the effort, and subsided.

"I don't doubt it. Can you walk?"

"I think so." Her own unsteady voice suddenly made Anya furious at herself. *What just happened to me? Am I losing my mind?* "I couldn't stop myself. It was like I was being pulled. Am I crazy?"

"Of course not," he replied, and the sudden relief flooding her was ridiculous in its intensity. "Mari has precognitive visions, and she's insensible to the world while she has them. This might be similar." He let go of her hand and slid his arm over her shoulders. "Come on. Let's get you out of here."

He half carried her to the door, pushed it open slightly to peer out into the dark alley. The door looked like a bomb had hit it, the frame wrenched and the innards of the doorknob lying in scattered shrapnel.

"Clear," he said. "It's not improbable that you heard this because you were meant to. You were moving too quickly. I've never seen a Lightbringer move that fast unless she was under a compulsion."

"Great." Her breath hitched in her throat. *I'm glad you know what the hell is going on. I don't have a clue.* "A compulsion?"

"I'll explain in a minute. Stay close to me. I'm going to hide you. The less people see us, the better."

Anya leaned against his shoulder. Prickles raced over her skin, and a wonderful feeling of warmth spread over her entire body. She sighed and saw the red-black bruising of his aura closing around her, weaving in little filaments. It seemed a spectacularly comforting, not to mention useful, thing. "I wish I could do what you do."

"Don't wish that, *piccola.*" He half dragged her down the alley. Her head wouldn't quite obey the command to stay on her neck, lolling drunkenly.

"I'm glad you showed up." Her voice sounded funny, high and breathless.

"Just breathe, Anya. I'm here." Warmth flushed her skin again. Dusk had turned into early night, the sky gone dark and cloudy, streetlights blooming into life. They reached the mouth of the alley. "I'm taking you back to the Rowangrove. The healer can help you."

"Shell." The thought roused her. He was coming back with Elise, but if Anya wasn't there, what would he do?

"He'll be fine. He's a lot stronger than you think." Jack's red-black aura flared slightly, and a group of giggling teenage girls walking down the sidewalk separated to let them pass. Anya noticed none of the girls even glanced at her and Jack.

She shuddered. *He had a knife. What was he going to do to her? Or to me?* Anya would have been helpless to stop him from hurting either her or the other woman. She hadn't even been able to summon the Persuasion. Instead, she'd frozen, like a stupid, silly rabbit.

Stupid and useless, not to mention weak, she scolded herself. Her pulse was acting strangely, speeding up into a weak, thready rapidity. *I have to start figuring this out.* "I want to learn. I *have* to learn how to protect myself."

"Just relax, Anya. I'm here. Just breathe." Jack sounded grim.

Anya opened her mouth to ask him something else, but blackness took her. For the first time in her life, she actually fainted.

Eighteen

"What happened?" Theo checked Anya's pulse. The healer's clear glow made Jack's bones twist and writhe, especially after he'd felt the brief relief of his witch's skin. "She's flaring all over. Gods above, what *happened?*"

"She looked like she was under a compulsion." He wished he could stroke Anya's hair back from her pale forehead. He stilled himself, his arms steady under his witch's slight weight. She lay cradled in his arms as if she belonged there, her gray sweater rucked up to show a slice of pale midriff. Tendrils of black hair clung to her cheeks, and she was flushed and breathing shallowly. He'd given her as much Power as he dared, the little heat-tingle that all Watchers learned to use in order to bring Lightbringers out of shock. He'd never had a witch faint on him like this before, and he had never in his life as a Watcher felt this sick, unsteady fear.

If she gets much worse I'll have to treat her shock the old way, skin on skin. I wonder what she'd think of that? Jack steeled himself and answered the healer's question. "She ducked into a laundry room and came across a crime in progress. I cleared it up, but she was pretty shocked."

Theo's wide soft eyes met his. "A crime in progress?" She didn't quite sound sarcastic, but there was a definite edge to the words.

"Use small words so I can understand," Dante said, calmly enough, from the door. The black-eyed Watcher scanned the street outside, sweeping the perimeters every now and again. "I'm a little confused."

"She went straight to where a serial rapist was tying up his next victim." Jack wished he didn't have to explain with a Lightbringer here. No Lightbringer should have to hear or see such things. They weren't made for it.

"How do you know it was a serial rapist?" Dante sounded only mildly curious, but his shoulders had stiffened.

"He was too prepared to be a first-timer. Had all his supplies ready." Jack's voice made the air turn close and hot, and he closed his eyes briefly, willing himself to control. He looked down at Anya's high cheekbones, her mouth with the bottom lip fuller than the top, and the shadows under her eyes.

Theo's fingertips settled on his witch's cheek. "Anya," she breathed.

Power folded around Anya. Jack had rarely seen this kind of skill before. The healing was focused, intense, not a whisper of it bled through to rub against Jack's aura. Which was a blessing, because he felt the beginnings of a headache coming on from being so close to Theo. His neck felt like iron rods had been jammed into it and twisted mercilessly by a demented little imp.

But Anya was safe.

Thank you, gods. I don't deserve this, but thank you. I got there in time. Thank you. She's safe. The thought calmed him just barely enough so he could open his eyes and look down at his witch.

Anya blinked, stirring. He waited until he was sure she could stand, and slowly, carefully bent to put her on her feet. Her left sneaker was untied; she probably hadn't even noticed. Her sweater was still disarranged, but that fascinating glimpse of white skin was gone. It was a good thing, too, because his control was frayed. He wanted to shake her until her head wobbled and demand she never, *ever,* do anything like that again, or he would—

"Oh, wow," she said in a high breathless voice. "That wasn't fun."

"I'll bet not." Theo put her hands on her hips. "What were you thinking, Anya? You could have been seriously hurt."

"I heard screaming, so I had to help. Nobody else seemed to hear. Or care."

Theo stopped, a curious look spreading over her face. "Really. That's odd."

Anya unconsciously leaned against Jack and he made himself a rock to steady her. He had to move slightly to make sure a knife hilt wouldn't jab her.

A deep shuddering breath worked its way out. Her gray eyes cleared, and she lost the staring look of shock. "Jack said something about a compulsion. Like Mari."

"Here comes Elise and the boy." Dante said from the door.

Anya flinched, then straightened. "I'm all right. Just...maybe a cup of coffee, or something. I feel a little sleepy."

"You can't work tonight," Theo said firmly. "Dante, will you make coffee? Elise will probably want some too."

Dante must have nodded, because he slipped past them and

through the curtain into the back room. Jack wondered briefly if the other Watchers ever felt this killing fear. He had understood intellectually that if a Watcher bonded with a Lightbringer, the constant grinding pain of the Dark would ease with the witch's touch. What he hadn't realized was the gut-wrenching fear of losing that peace, the only chance for redemption a Watcher had.

He hadn't counted on a witch so beautiful it made his eyes hurt to look at her, either.

"I have to work," Anya said colorlessly. It did something strange to chest to hear that wounded little voice. "I *have* to...I mean, I can't depend on Jack forever."

Yes, you can. That's what Circle Lightfall is for. That's what I'm for.

"Don't worry about that," he said.

Theo's eyebrows drew together. She knew enough about Watchers by now to look up at him, folding her arms. "You've been giving her money?"

As well as anything else I can. "My duty as a Watcher is to care for her well-being. You've barred Circle Lightfall from the city, so it's been a little tricky. But we've managed. They've funded her as they would any Lightbringer."

"We're going to have a talk about this later." Theo's tone was mild, but something flashed in the depths of her eyes. She looked back at Anya. "Sweetie, don't worry about the money right now. I suspect Jack knows what he's doing. I think you should go home and rest."

That seemed to galvanize his witch. "I'm fine." She stood a little straighter, Jack slowly unloosing his hands from her shoulders. "I'll stay. I'm okay. It was just...it was just a shock, seeing that. I'm glad Jack was there."

The bell over the door gave a strangled jingle. Elise breezed in, her long red hair braided into a thick rope. Her nose-stud winked merrily. "Hey everyone! What's happenin'?"

Jack braced himself instinctively for the wave of pain that didn't come. Anya's aura was tangled with his, and the Dark in his bones grumbled and went back to sleep. It wasn't the thorny pleasure of her bare skin on his, but it was an unexpected solace.

One I don't deserve.

The memory of screams and crackling flame rose, and he pushed it down. He hadn't thought of that in years. Had *trained* himself not to think of it, to keep his sanity.

"Oh, another crisis averted," Theo replied, just as merrily. "How was it?"

"It was good." Elise halted, folding her arms. Her camel coat and jeans made her look like a young, leggy college student. "You okay, Anya?"

"I'm fine," Anya repeated. "I just had a bit of a...disturbing experience."

"Yeah, they're coming fast and thick these days." Elise moved gracefully aside as Shell burst into the shop, his hair sticking up in blond spikes.

"Anya! Anya! I did tables!"

Jack felt the tremor that went through her. "You did?" Her voice was clear. Her aura suddenly firmed, and her shoulders came up, taking back the weight of responsibility.

Remy slid last through the door, his golden eyes dark and the smell of Watcher magick sliding off him. He caught Jack's eye and tipped his head slightly. The message was clear. *We need to talk.*

Jack left Anya exclaiming over Shell, noting Theo's move to take Elise's arm. Had the healer seen Remy's signal?

"What's up?" Jack halted right by the door.

"The boy's a jealous one." Remy's accent made the words a slow murmur. "If I didn't know better, I'd say he was flirting with my witch and deliberately trying to make her think I hate him."

"You too?" Jack was grimly amused. "What do you suggest?"

"He's two steps away from being a Feeder." Remy pushed stiff fingers back through his dark golden hair. It was a relief to talk to a Watcher, Jack realized. He didn't have to be gentle or try to explain, or hold himself carefully controlled. "I'd get him out of here before he starts trouble, but your witch is attached to him. This could go very badly."

"Tell me about it. What's Hanson doing tonight?"

"Standing guard over Mari at some staff party or another. Why?"

"I think my witch has a compulsion." Jack laid it out in a few clipped, brief sentences and saw the other Watcher shake his head.

"Sounds like it to me. I don't envy you, *homme*. Need help?"

On any other day, Jack might have bristled at the implication that he couldn't handle himself or his duty. "We need a Teacher.

The healer told me she's been having no luck with Anya." Jack glanced up, his attention sweeping the perimeter and his eyes finding Anya. She accepted a cup of coffee from Dante, who had moved between the Lightbringers and the front door, effectively shielding Jack and Remy, leaving them free to continue their conversation.

"You've bonded." Remy's tone was flat and unsurprised. "Fire, water, earth, air, and four Watchers. I'd say the gods have something planned. I'll mention a Teacher to Elise."

"I gather she's the one that hates Circle Lightfall."

"If Elise hated them, she wouldn't have agreed to have *you* come in. She's just naturally suspicious, that's all. I'll talk to her about allowing a Teacher in, but don't expect much." Remy's eyes flicked past him, checking, then returned. "Wish we had a safehouse. Elise is my first witch."

Jack shrugged. *You lucky bastard, bonding on your first.* "I suppose we just do what we can. Like usual."

"Like usual. Watch out for the boy."

"Thanks for the warning."

They separated, Jack keeping watch at the door while Remy went to stand behind Elise. The redhead leaned close to Theo, talking in a low fierce voice, the Talisman around her neck shifting and straining.

Jack let out a shaking, almost painful exhale.

That was the worst moment of my life. Seeing the laundry room door in his mind's eye, knowing Anya was on the other side of it. Then, bursting through and finding her faced with a knife—

His heart gave another sick twist. *I can't take my eyes off her for a single second. If she's developing a compulsion, it's latent and it's only going to get worse. No safehouse to put her in. And she's still so fragile.*

Anya listened to Shell's excited babble patiently, smiling and making the appropriate noises. She was probably still near to shock—pale as milk, her hands shaking slightly as she pushed up her sweater sleeves. He might have missed those shaking hands if he hadn't been watching her so intently, in little sipping glances between keeping an eye on the street.

Jack scanned outside again. Night had officially fallen. The shields on the shop stirred slightly, sensing his attention.

The realization came out of nowhere, thunder after lightning. *She touched me.*

His mouth wanted to curl up in a smile, but there was nothing to smile about. His witch was mostly untrained and beginning to develop a latent power that could only mean trouble, the Dark was still crawling over this city, and he hadn't had time to start clearing the streets yet. But still...she wasn't frightened of him anymore. She had been glad to see him, even if it was only because she'd been facing a knife-wielding maniac.

His skin went cold at the thought of how goddamn *close* it had been. Even a stupid human sicko could rob a Watcher of his witch and condemn him to a failure-stricken death.

Jack scanned the street again. *Something's going to happen. I'll bet Remy's right. This is just a prelude.*

A deeper, instinctive voice rose. *I can't afford to lose her. What am I going to do when she finds out what I was?*

He told himself to worry about that another time and glanced back at Anya. No matter how dutiful, how obedient, how useful he was, the memory of his crimes hung over him like a dark cloud.

"*Lupo Grigio.*" His lips barely moved, his eyes scanning the street. "The Gray Wolf."

Then he shut his mouth. He had no time for the past; there was Dark out hunting tonight. The sooner he could work out how to protect Anya and clear the city at the same time, the better.

Nineteen

Anya drew up the blankets, tucking Shell in.

"Tell me a story, Anya." Shell's sleepy eyes drifted closed, opened again. "I did real good today. I cleaned tables."

"What story should I tell you?" *Please, Shell. I'm so tired I could fall down right here and sleep for days. Maybe I should get a teaching job again. It'll be easier than lifting boxes.*

She smoothed the quilt—Theo's, a patchwork of deep green and cheerful yellow—carefully. Blue ripcord curtains were drawn tight over the window.

Jack was downstairs. Anya could feel him, a steady dark glow of attention. Even separated by half a house, she could feel his awareness sweeping the halls and rooms, checking the defenses, coming briefly to rest on her and sliding slowly away.

"Tell me about Gran," Shell said.

Despite her exhaustion, a smile pulled at her mouth. *I should have known. That's his favorite story.*

As in every house, Anya had made a mobile out of wire hangers and string, dangling Goodwill-bought forks and spoons over Shell's bed. He liked to watch it moving before he fell asleep.

"My Gran lived in a small apartment in the city," Anya began, and felt Jack coming up the stairs. She suspected he deliberately made a noise, letting the stairs squeak underneath his feet. How did someone so big move so quietly?

Shell moved restlessly. "I don't like him," he whispered, as if reading Anya's mind. "Make him go away."

I don't think I want to. Anya smoothed the covers mechanically. "I'm telling you a story, Shell. Hush. Now, Gran always baked cookies when I came to visit, and she would always have them ready with a pitcher of lemonade, especially in summer. In winter it was hot chocolate. I still remember how it smelled."

He eyed her, visibly trying to decide if he could push the issue. Anya glanced away, toward the closet—firmly closed and checked every night—and his battered high-top sneakers obediently crouched in front of the wooden closet door. His Green Bay Packers sweatshirt was reverently draped over a straight-backed wooden chair Anya had brought home from the Rowangrove.

Go on, take it with you, Theo had said, laughing. *You need furniture, and I need the damn thing out of here.*

"Gran knitted, too. One Christmas she knitted me a sweater striped blue and purple, with sleeves that were way too long."

She continued the story, feeling Jack's silent and now-familiar presence in the hall outside. Was he listening? Why? Was something wrong?

Shell fell asleep halfway to the end of the sweater story. Anya stopped speaking, smoothing the quilt over his broad chest. She eased up from the bed, crossed the room quietly, and turned the light off, checking the Donald Duck nightlight. Leaving the door open the standard two inches, she stepped out into the shadowed hall and found Jack leaning against the wall, his hands stuffed in his pockets as usual. His eyes glimmered.

"Do you ever take that coat off?" she asked.

He seemed to give the question his full attention, considering it from every angle before opening his mouth, the ghost of an accent lingering behind his words. "Not often." He peeled himself away from the wall. "Are you all right?"

No, I'm not all right. Anya opened her mouth to lie anyway, and failed miserably. "No, I'm not."

"Want some tea?"

It was such a prosaic suggestion her shoulders relaxed slightly. "I think that would be a good idea. I have a couple questions."

"I don't doubt it." His eyes flicked down her body, returned to her face. "Is the boy asleep?"

"Of course. Look, I'm sorry. I know he's not easy to deal with."

Jack shrugged. "I don't take it personally."

"Is there anything you *do* take personally?" *I can't believe I just said that.*

The way the other women treated the Watchers was starting to rub off on her. The women were all three so confident, so self-assured—and they all sometimes dealt with the big weapons-laden men like not-too-bright little boys. There was a complete absence of fear in the women, even though the guys carried around guns, and swords. Oddly enough, it was difficult to be afraid of them, once you got used to how silent and diffident they were. She'd never heard one of the men raise their voices, even during Elise's rampages.

It was the Watchers that convinced Anya she wasn't crazy.

She could have denied the full extent of her own talents forever, but the Watchers wandering around almost invisible with that kind of weaponry—*that* made the shadowy predators and psychic powers much more believable.

He shrugged again, a lazy fluid movement. "Some things." He waited for her to go past him and fell into soundless step behind her.

"Jack?" It was easier to say when she wasn't looking at him. The hall opened up into the staircase, and she ran her fingers along the balustrade. *I could get used to this house, it's beautiful. Real potential here. I could make it stunning. And it has a garden.*

"Hm?" A noncommittal sound.

Halfway down the steps, she stopped, bracing herself. "Thank you. I just...thank you."

"It's my honor." He sounded like he meant it. "I'm sorry if I was harsh with you, Anya. I was concerned for your safety."

That wrung a short laugh out of her, and she started down the steps again. "So was I."

The kitchen now boasted dishes, the much-traveled coffeemaker, and a white enamel kettle Anya now filled and set on the stove, flicking on the flame. Jack leaned against the wall by the door, the black-wrapped swordhilt sticking up over his right shoulder.

I suppose it's true, a person can get used to anything. Even big, tall guys with swords and psychic women. "So you think I might start checking out and chasing down crimes?"

"It's too soon to tell. Hanson said Mari's visions started sporadically, once every couple of months, then started to come regularly. Now they come in waves, depending on what's about to happen."

Anya sighed. "I hope not, I can't afford to go wandering away from my jobs. What am I going to do? I can't work at the Rowangrove forever. I've got a *degree,* for God's sake."

"What do you do?"

"I'm a high school teacher. English." *Not very romantic, is it? Not like Theo or Elise.*

"Ah." As if the information confirmed a private hypothesis. Why did he always sound so damnably calm? "We can work something out, Anya."

The kettle began to creak, heating up. "I hope so." She stared at the counter and the dishes piled next to the sink. Shell had refused dinner, a sure sign of trouble ahead. Night pressed hard against the windows. She rubbed her bare feet against the floor. *I'm already thinking of this place as home.* "Look, Jack, I need to know exactly who you are."

He dropped his eyes. Even his shoulders dropped a few millimeters, a movement very much like a flinch. "I already told you. I'm your Watcher."

Anya got the tea bowl down. Elise had given her the fluid lovely bowl, painted creamy white and sunny yellow. *Welcome to the circle,* Elise had said. Theo had given her a Ziploc full of different kinds of tea bags. Mari had brought boxes of plates and bowls and silverware. Every day someone brought something that a woman who had lost all her belongings might need. Anya had never been welcomed so instantly into a group before—her talents had always kept her alone, isolated, afraid.

The big nasty things chasing her, ripping her houses apart, hadn't helped either.

"Elise tells me Circle Lightfall sends out their Watchers, and every Watcher eventually finds a..." She couldn't bring herself to say the word *witch.*

"A Lightbringer." He shook his hair back. It was starting to hang in his eyes. Added to his almost perpetually-stubbled cheeks, the effect was haggard and dangerous. His eyes glowed, a piercing silvery intensity.

Who am I kidding? She caught herself sneaking glances at him as she got down two cups. *He'd look dangerous even clean-shaven and dressed in a tuxedo.* "Like Theo and Dante. Elise told me that being around them—Lightbringers—hurts you."

He moved slightly, restlessly. "What else did Elise tell you?"

"She said that you know when you've found...the one Lightbringer, because it doesn't hurt you to touch her."

He nodded. "That's correct." His voice was flat, as usual. Were his eyes glittering? She couldn't tell.

"She said they...Circle Lightfall put something in you. Something like the things that chased me."

"No." His voice made the window rattle slightly. "Not anything remotely like that. It's a *tanak,* a symbiote. It's Dark, but not like the predators. It makes us stronger, faster—but not evil. We don't want to *eat* the Lightbringers."

"I didn't mean that." She sorted through the teabags and picked out Evening Delight, deciding that the last thing she needed was caffeine. "What kind of tea would you like?"

"Anything." He stuffed his hands in his pockets. His habitual pose, shoulder-slumped and seeming lethargic. She didn't believe it for a moment. She knew how fast he could move.

Inhumanly fast.

"Evening Delight for you too, then." She brushed her own hair back. "You know, the last house we lived in...I'd gotten some things into the car, I knew it was coming. I went back in to get Shell's teddy bear. I told him to stay in the car."

Jack leaned his head back against the wall, watching her. She had his complete attention, even with the waves of awareness he sent out, checking the borders of the house—concentric rings of alertness she could *see* so much more clearly now.

The teddy bear. God, I was so stupid. Anya's hands began to shake. She cleared her throat. "I went in to get his bear. I was in the hall when it broke open the front of the house. It was like...like...I don't know. Now I can imagine what it's like to get bombed. I hit the wall pretty hard." The lump on her head wasn't tender any more, but she rubbed at it anyway. "It stunned me. And the burning, everything just started to burn. It just exploded, it was so hot. I woke up, and Shell dragged me away. He'd come in, and he was screaming. So was I."

Jack's eyes glowed. He said nothing.

"We managed to get to the car. It demolished the house. I was bleeding. It was a miracle I was able to drive, I thought I might have a concussion and my nose bled. I drove away while it tore my house apart and burned it down. It tried to chase us, but something happened. It didn't go very far."

"Red burners never do." His voice was deeper, and the anger boiling off him made the air hot and still even if it wasn't directed at her. She couldn't work up the energy to be frightened of him just now.

Just concentrate on the tea. It didn't get you, you're in your own kitchen, and Jack's here. The kettle whistled and Anya clicked the stove off, her mouth dry. She poured the water, her hand shaking so badly boiling water slopped out of the cups and onto the pale blue counter. *Isn't that strange. I'm actually comforted by a man wearing guns in my kitchen.*

"The flame is a short-term attack mechanism," Jack said quietly, as if he wasn't vibrating with leashed anger. "They can't keep it up for very long, especially if their prey escapes."

"I wonder why nobody ever thinks to tell people about these things." She set the kettle down on an unused burner.

"Most people don't see, and don't want to know anyway." The air grew even warmer, heat sliding off him. Anya wondered how he did that. "Careful. You'll burn yourself."

"As long as it doesn't kill me." She hated the clipped, harsh tone in her own voice. "Right?"

"You're angry." He said it so goddamn *calmly.*

Her temper snapped. Anya whirled, her hair ruffling out. "I didn't *ask* for this!" she shouted. "I didn't *ask* to hear what other people are feeling or to be hunted down like an animal! I didn't *ask* to be driven out of all my homes. I didn't *ask* to—" She stopped short, swallowing her words.

Your anger can kill, Anya. Swallow it. Push it down.

For a moment she didn't want to. She wanted to lash out, wanted to hurt someone, and she had an easy target.

The temptation passed. It wasn't fair to be angry with him. He'd only tried to help her, after all. He wasn't responsible for her cursed talents.

His eyelids dropped slightly. He didn't look upset or even ruffled. Even his stubbled cheeks looked planned, a deliberate choice instead of scruffiness.

Nothing ever surprises him. It was comforting and infuriating at the same time.

"I want to show you something," she said, finally.

Jack didn't answer, but she could feel his attention sharpen, enfolding her. Nobody had ever listened to her so intently, as if every word she said mattered.

Anya's shoulders came up again, taking back the old weight. Her eyes began to burn. She took a deep breath, centering herself the way Theo had taught her—it was easier to use her strange abilities once she was centered completely in her skin. Anya stretched out with the Persuasion, the familiar euphoria flooding her. He was hard to affect, like pushing a boulder uphill—but she did it, the Persuasion finding the weak point and sliding home, making *contact*. He stiffened.

"Come here." Her voice crackled, her kitchen flushed momentarily with golden light.

He glided across the laminate flooring, his boots soundless, and stopped three feet from Anya, the light finding reddish highlights in his black hair. His eyes burned, molten silver coins.

"Give me your gun." Her eyes poured out hot streams of

energy she could taste as well as *see*, wrapping him like a cocoon.

Jack's hand blurred. He presented her with a silvery gun, spinning it habitually as he gave her the handle. It was strangely heavy, the metal cold. Anya knew nothing about guns, but it didn't look like it had a safety. Her fingers curled around it. The Persuasion clamped down over him; she sensed him resisting, struggling against her mental hold.

God, I hate doing this. Anya's stomach jolted under her breastbone. She tasted bile. It was difficult to keep him under her control, resistance dragging at her mental hold. "Now back up. Back *up.*"

He backed up, still eerily soundless.

Anya took a deep breath, pointed the gun at him, and gave another command. "Stand on one leg." Her head started to hurt. He was *hard* to Persuade. Even with the centering Theo had taught her, she had to concentrate more fiercely than she ever had. Something about him fought her much harder than a normal person. It was like trying to hold a slippery armored eel.

He lifted one foot.

"Flap your arms."

He did. Energetically, even. His coat snapped, his arms moving with weird mechanical grace.

Anya let the Persuasion go with a subliminal snap. She sagged against the counter, holding the gun steady even though her hands wanted to shake.

Jack's hands dropped to his sides. He regained his balance on both feet and studied her, his face expressionless again. Anya braced herself for his anger.

"I call it the Persuasion." Her voice trembled. The gun wavered in her hands. "I can make people do things. When it started getting...easier...the things started chasing me. I *brought* them, maybe. But I only used it to help people stop smoking or lose weight, things like that, until we were in Kansas, two cities ago, no food, nothing. I used it to...I made a bank teller bring me money. Since then, once or twice."

Jack studied her. Then he moved forward, with that spooky, blurring speed she'd seen him use not more than five hours ago, in the laundry room. He slid the gun free of her hand with one swift movement, holstered it without even looking. "You didn't need to do that." He didn't sound angry. Instead, he sounded oddly conciliatory, as if she was the one who had just been hypnotized into flapping her arms and looking like an idiot.

Anya set her jaw. "Theo, Mari, Elise—I'm not like them. They're..." *They're innocent, and I'm not.*

"I'm not worried about them." Was he smiling?

He *was* smiling. It was just a quarter-inch short of a grin. The corners of his eyes crinkled. Whatever reaction Anya had expected, it certainly wasn't this.

I just made him flap his arms like a chicken and took his gun away. Why does he look so stinking happy?

"Weren't you listening to me?" She folded her arms, glaring at him. A bead of sweat trickled down the shallow channel of her spine. Her head cleared, the ache behind her forehead from the Persuasion swirling away.

"I'll listen to you all night," he answered, and she believed him. "You're not alone. Several Lightbringers can use a type of *push*. The Watchers learned it from them. It doesn't draw the Dark, Anya. The Dark hunts what it can, where it can. You're a bigger target only because you glow. You're a Lightbringer— and they *eat* light."

I just held a gun on him. I just used the Persuasion on him, and he's not angry. "Jack—"

"You said you had questions." The smile didn't fade. Instead, he looked happy for the first time. His entire face had relaxed. "I'll answer them."

"Who the hell *are* you? What am I *doing* here? Why can't I have some kind of normal life?" Her voice broke on the last syllable. "Am I going to start running around stumbling over c-c-crimes and—"

"I don't know about that last bit just yet. But the next time you go running off as if someone's lit a fire under you, I'll be with you. And the next, and the next, *ad infinitum*. I'm your Watcher."

Anya opened her mouth, but whatever reply she would have made was lost. The shields on the house reverberated, reacting, and she felt all the heat drain from the air. The hair on her nape rose up, prickling, a familiar feeling.

Jack gripped her shoulders. "Stay here." He sounded calm enough, the words weighted with that faint trace of an accent. "There's something outside."

Of course there's something outside. Shivers spilled up her spine. *I used the Persuasion, and a lot of it. I've brought it here, whatever it is.* "I'm sorry," she whispered. "I just wanted to make someone understand."

"It's not your fault. Stay here. Do you hear me, Anya? Stay in the house. Please."

She nodded numbly.

There was a breathless prickle along her skin as Jack vanished down the hall. She grabbed for the counter, blindly, her hand hitting a mug. Boiling water splashed out, and she snatched her fingers back.

Get moving, her conscience shrilled. *You've got to get Shell out of here.*

"He said to stay." Her whisper fell into the still, doom-laden air. If something was going to attack, she couldn't stop it. There was nowhere to run to, either.

Anya's legs shook. She dragged herself over to the breakfast bar and felt for a stool, lowering herself onto it. Whatever happened now, she was helpless.

It was beginning to be almost familiar.

Twenty

Blood dripped wet and warm in Jack's eyes. His left side burned—the claws had stuck in his ribs. Blisters bubbled up his leg—a *gimmer* with a whip. Where had that come from? Whips were usually a Thain trick. Had the Thains started taking in *gimmerin*?

Can't let her see me like this. But when he made it to the corner, he saw the door to the white house was open, warm electric light spilling out onto the porch. Anya, clearly visible, stood in the doorway, her arms crossed over her stomach, her black hair shining with blue highlights. Her hair was starting to grow out, brushing her shoulders, but still looking a little haphazard.

She had to trim off all the burnt parts. Rage tightened his fists. Hearing how close she'd come to death made his skin go cold and tight. Every time he thought about it, he had to take a deep breath and invoke iron control. How had she survived without a Watcher?

Doesn't matter. I'm here now. One burned, beat-up guardian angel, at your service.

The thought startled him into a half-voiced laugh. He felt her reaching out, clumsily, her attention sweeping the front yard and wrapping around him. He saw her shoulders sag briefly. Was it relief, or was he just another burden to her?

Jack made it up the flagstone walk, through the ragged yard. She had already started gardening, tying some of the plants to stakes, weeding in small increments. His boots made the porch steps squeak slightly.

"Move back from the door," he told her, too tired to phrase it as a respectful request. "Something might see you. And the Crusade sometimes uses non-magickal weapons." *Like high-powered rifles. I'd hate to take a shot tonight. I already feel half-past Hell.*

"The crusade?" She shivered, but stepped back into the shelter of the house.

Jack's breath came harsh, but he didn't stop to rest until he reached her. He drew himself up, ignoring the grating pain in his side, his body shielding the open door—and her—instinctively.

Always with the goddamn explanations. "The Crusade. And

the Brotherhood. The Thains might be in town too. You can't be too careful. Why are you standing in the door?" He made it inside, wincing slightly as the symbiote fused the crack in his ribs together.

"I was waiting for you to come back. Good God, you're *bleeding*."

"I am." *I deserve to. Don't worry about me.* He swept the door shut, locking it. The Watcher shields reverberated—she wasn't leaking distress, but her aura pulsed slightly. "Be calm, Anya. Breathe."

She put her hands on her hips and glared at him. "You're bleeding all over and you tell *me* to breathe?"

I'm more concerned about you breathing than me bleeding. If you get upset I'm likely to go right over the edge. Jack swiped his hand over his face. The wound on his scalp closed. He drew in a long, deep breath, the symbiote converting pain and anger into Power. When he opened his eyes, Anya was staring at him, pale, her lower lip trembling.

"It's kind of odd to see the healing for the first time." He expended a little Power. It tingled, trickling down his skin, burning off the blood and grime, repairing his skin until no trace of the attack remained except the scars. "I'd better change out of these clothes." She still stared at him. Jack sighed. "Look, I know it's disturbing, but—"

Her entire body pitched forward. Just like a Lightbringer, trying to soothe the pain. "Does it hurt? When it heals like that, I mean."

He considered the question, shifting his weight slightly as the symbiote attended to the torn muscle in his calf. "A little. Not as much as other things." *Not as much as my conscience.*

She took a step forward, bare feet soundless. "I'm sorry."

The ludicrousness of it—a Lightbringer, especially this Lightbringer, apologizing to *him*—threatened to make his jaw drop. She didn't know; she had no *idea*.

"Don't be sorry," he managed, when he could speak again. "It's what I'm here for."

"Whatever it was would have tried to break into my house and eat me," she pointed out, practically enough. "And I used the Persuasion. So it's my fault."

Anger boiled behind his sternum. He forced it down. "It is *not* your fault. The Dark isn't your fault." He looked down at the shredded mess of his T-shirt and the blood soaking into his

jeans. It would take time and attention to repair his clothes with
Power. It would be more efficient to just wash them and use a
needle and thread. Here, though, he'd have to use Power on his
jeans. They were the only pair he had. He was down to his last
spare T-shirt, too. "I need to clean up. With your permission,
Lightbringer?"

Now she looked mystified, her charcoal eyebrows drawing
together, the corners of her mouth pulling down. *Isn't that
strange.* He studied her in the wash of golden light from the
overhead fixture. The smell of amber musk and jasmine ghosted
through the entire house. She made everything smell like
summer. *Watching her mouth do that makes me want to kiss
her.*

Jack shook himself free of the daydream. *Duty, Watcher.
Shut up and do your job.*

"My permission? You don't need my permission. Use the
upstairs bathroom. I just cleaned it. Do you...do you need
bandages?"

"No need, thank you." The words bit themselves off,
damming up everything else he couldn't say.

"Do you—um, I mean, have you got..."

He realized what she was trying to ask. "I have an extra
shirt or two, Anya. I don't need much. Why don't you go to
bed?"

"Go to *bed?* Like I'll be able to sleep after *this.*"

The rage rose, right under the surface. He was dangerously
close to the edge. He wanted to touch her, needed the feel of
her skin. *Gods above and below forgive me. I'm acting as if I
deserve to get within ten feet of her.* "Why don't you make
some coffee, then, and we'll stay up."

She nodded, slowly. "You swear the Persuasion doesn't
bring those things?"

"It doesn't draw the Dark, Anya. I swear." He waited,
watching the curve of her cheek, the faint blush that rose when
her eyes met his. A long, tense, breathless silence folded around
them both. Jack realized she was now blushing fiercely, staring
at his face. *I must look hellish.* He spared himself a grim internal
smile for the joke. "I'll go get cleaned up," he finished lamely.

Anya nodded. Her cheeks were crimson, and the flush only
made her prettier. "Go ahead. I've got to wash the dishes."

It hurt to push himself away, to brush past her and go up
the stairs. Each step was a kind of exquisite agony. But he did

it, reminding himself of his duty every time his boots hit the floor and his calf twinged, the burning twinges in his ribs settling as the *tanak* settled in to smooth out and repair the messy quick fixes to each shattering break the bones had suffered tonight.

It had been a vicious fight, for all its shortness. He was still close to the edge of combat, ramped up with nowhere for the adrenaline to go.

When he came back down ten minutes later, clean and presentable, he was in marginally better control of himself. He found her in the kitchen, scraping the dinner dishes while the coffeemaker burbled. Jack stopped in the doorway, leaning against the frame, watching the quick grace of her movements.

She didn't look over her shoulder, but she spoke to him. "The coffee should be done soon. Shell didn't eat his dinner. He gets more and more upset, each new place we land." Her voice shook only slightly, a light tremor making the huskiness even more charming.

He couldn't say what he wanted to, settled for something else. "You don't have to move again. Unless you want to."

Her shoulders came up, slightly. Taking back the weight of responsibility, of worry. "I want to believe that."

I've never met such a pessimistic witch. Jack took a deep breath. "Your shields are getting better." Then he took the plunge. "The healer told me she has some difficulty teaching you. Perhaps..."

She turned, her hands dripping with soapy water. "Perhaps what?"

"Perhaps I could try to teach you a little. I've seen enough Lightbringer magick, after all. If you wouldn't mind taking instruction from a Watcher, that is."

"You would?" The smile lighting her face was a thorny pleasure, her eyes suddenly shining. "Really?"

"I don't promise much," he cautioned. "I'm only a Watcher. But maybe I can teach you a few things." *Since the healer's having no luck, and you need all the training you can get. It's too dangerous.*

She took two steps, then a few more—then she ran lightly across the intervening space and threw her arms around him. Jack, shocked, caught her automatically, tearing his hands out of his pockets. Her slim weight against him, the smell of her hair and the jasmine-scent of her Power closed around him, teasing at his frayed control.

After a brief, squeezing hug, she stepped back. He had to force his arms to loosen.

"Thank you." Her eyes shimmered with tears. "Really. Thank you. For *everything*."

She's thanking me for that? Disbelief warred with the evidence of his senses. She was beaming now, all that sunny attention focused on him. It felt good—but it also ground home the fact that he wasn't worth it.

Not with the stain on his soul.

She forged blithely ahead, lighting up like a Christmas tree. "When can we start? What first? Do I need to read more of those boring books on theory or can you just show me? Can you teach me to keep them—those things—away?"

His heart plummeted. *Look what you've done now. What do you think she's expecting?* "I can teach you more about shielding, and how to make yourself practically invisible to normals. I can maybe teach you some of the defensive magicks, and I can teach you about runes. You know about runes, right?"

She nodded, her eyes shining, holding her hands awkwardly because of the soapy dishwater. "Theo explained some of it. How they concentrate power, and the more you work with them, the easier it is." She whirled back toward the sink. "Just let me get this finished. Pour some coffee, will you?"

Jack moved to obey, watching her as she hurried back to the sink and started clanking the dishes again. "Don't you like using the dishwasher?"

"It seems wasteful to use it for just a few dishes." She glanced over her shoulder, smiling at him and tossing back a fall of glossy dark hair. "What else can you teach me?"

Jack's chest squeezed in on itself. "That's enough for a start, isn't it?" He forced himself not to mumble. The circles under her eyes were appallingly dark; she looked tired and worn.

And absolutely beautiful.

He was suddenly, utterly, glad that she knew nothing about the Crusade—and nothing about the Watchers. Nothing about *him*. He had a little time before she found out. He could use that time to teach her—and maybe, just maybe, she might understand or forgive.

Stop that right there, he told himself sternly, getting down two mismatched coffee mugs—one a deep golden color from Elise, and a fluid blue and white painted one from Mari. He poured black coffee for himself, added two and a half sugars to hers, and put the coffeepot back in its spot. *You don't deserve forgiveness, Watcher. Remember your place. Duty, obedience, honor. That's all.*

"I suppose you're right." She pulled the plug, rinsed the sink, and dried her hands off on a sunny yellow towel, yawning. "As usual. Are you hungry?"

He shook his head, carefully holding her coffee cup so she could take the handle. *It's useless. The more I teach her, the better off she is—but the more I teach her, the closer she is to finding out who I was. Lupo Grigio.*

He forced away the shudder touching his shoulders. "Let's go into the living room, *piccola*. We can start by strengthening your shields."

Twenty-One

The envelope came in the shop's daily mail, addressed to Anya Harris, care of the Rowangrove. The postman, broad, fat, brown-eyed Frank, handed the sheaf of paper to Anya with a cheerful nod and went on his way, whistling in the intermittently-sunny afternoon. He wore shorts, though it was barely sixty degrees outside.

Anya set the rest of the mail—bills addressed to Theo, an advertising circular, a glossy ad from a carpet-cleaning company, and a New Age magazine—aside on the counter. She glanced around the store's regimented order, comforted by the neatness. Everything in its place.

Shell was with Elise, bussing tables. Theo had gone to the hospital with Dante to see one of her patients. Mari was supposed to come in to help with the usual evening rush. Jack had disappeared—she felt his presence above her, deliberately shuttered. He was on the roof. Perched up there like some black-leather gargoyle, watching the street.

The envelope was heavy cream-colored paper, obviously expensive. Anya looked at the typewritten address. Her mouth went dry. There was no return address, and no postmark.

And who on earth knows I'm here? Nobody, that's who.
Her heart began to pound against her ribs, a familiar sickening wash of fear turning her mouth sour.

Stop it. It's something about taxes, or something. Heaven knows I'm not hiding, even if I've moved all the way across the country. Quit being such a little coward, Anya.

She slid her finger under the flap and tore the heavy paper. There was one folded sheet of the same cream-colored stationary, she drew it out and opened it with a crackle.

It was a picture printed from a computer, of a slim black-haired woman seen from above, standing at what was obviously a bank counter. The teller across from the woman had a large floppy neck scarf and was holding out an envelope. The black-haired woman's hand was extended to take it.

Anya's heart leapt into her throat, turning into a stone.

Scrawled in thick red marker across the bottom of the sheet was her nightmare.

We know.

Anya let out a thin, hurt sound. Her hand shook. The small

sound of the paper brushing the air as her fingers vibrated scraped her ears. She looked up at the window, wildly, as if whoever had sent the letter would be standing right outside.

The air pressure changed. Anya crumpled the letter into a messy ball, scooping up the envelope and thrusting her hands behind her back just as Jack pushed the *Employees Only* door open. The door led down to the basement storage and a small space they called the "temple," with wood flooring, four beautiful altars, and a wooden statue of a pregnant woman. The statue was charred, but none of them would talk about *why*. And the Watchers somehow used the stairs to get down from the roof, but Anya wasn't quite sure how.

Jack's flat silvery eyes scanned the store. He seemed too big, too menacing, to fit inside the space. Now that she was used to seeing it, the swordhilt poking up over his shoulder was clearly visible unless she concentrated on seeing the shimmer of glamour hiding his weapons from other eyes.

"Are you all right?" His tone was calm and noncommittal, as usual.

"F-fine." *I'm not fine, I'm nowhere near fine.* "We know." *Who is it, who knows—and why are they sending me this? Oh, God, please—*

"You're pale." His eyes moved over her. The layers of Power shielding the shop resonated uneasily as he checked them, a nonphysical movement that stroked along the edges of her awareness. "Did you see something, hear something?"

Anya shook her head, unable to speak. *I told him about the Persuasion. I told him about the banks, so he already knows. What if...*

Jack examined her for a long thirty seconds and turned away, reaching for the doorknob. "I'll go back up, then."

"Wait!" The cry burst out, surprising her. He turned back, his coat rustling, and took two steps toward her.

Anya took a deep breath. "You have to promise not to say anything." She sounded queerly breathless, even to herself. "To the others—Theo, and them."

He nodded and irritably pushed his fingers back through his dark hair, forcing it back from his face. "Done."

Just like that? He doesn't even know what I'm going to tell him. Am I going to tell him? I can't tell him. For a moment, self-preservation warred with the need to tell someone, to relieve the awful pressure. *I can't possibly trust him that much.*

But he had followed her, and ripped open the door, and saved not only Anya but also the other woman from the terrible man with the knife. He had gone out and chased the Dark things away more than once in the past few weeks, coming back all bloody and exhausted. He had sworn to her that the Persuasion didn't bring the Dark. He had even started teaching her, quietly and with infinite patience, more than Theo could. How to shield herself, how to make Power obey, how to shape a bolt of the Power and fling it at the Dark—now *that* was something useful, even if Anya couldn't do it more than once without getting a blinding headache.

He stepped up behind the counter and glanced at the papers she'd laid aside. "The mail's early today," he noted quietly. Then he simply stood and waited, without any discernible sign of haste or discomfort, looking at the advertising circular as if it were the most interesting thing in the world.

Silence stretched between them, a thin cord of humming tension.

Anya's fingers tightened. Tears blurred her vision. She brought her hands out from behind her back and offered him the crumpled paper.

He took it, smoothed it flat on the counter, and glanced over it. Then he examined the envelope, turning it over in his hands. More pregnant silence ticked through the store's bright interior. A cloud drifted over the sun, plunging the sidewalks and other buildings into shadow. Anya shivered.

Finally, he glanced up at her, a single keen pale-eyed look. "When did this come?"

"With the m-m-mail." *I will not cry. I will NOT cry.* Her breath hitched slightly. "I had to, Jack. We were starving. I didn't take much—only enough to get to the next city. Only enough for food."

His eyes held hers. "I know." The windows in the front of the store rattled and the counter groaned slightly, responding to the leashed violence in his tone. "You wouldn't have done it unless you were desperate, Anya. I know."

Relief and fresh guilt swept through her. "If I hadn't had Shell..." She bit her lip. She couldn't blame Shell for this. It was purely and simply her fault alone.

"I know," he repeated. His tone changed to thoughtfulness. "There's no postmark on this. That means they're in the city."

"Who?" Her voice shook. *I will NOT cry.*

"Any number of groups. This isn't a Crusade trick; they just want to kill Lightbringers, not blackmail them. This is more like the Brotherhood. Remy told me they're in town; they tried to collect the fire witch not too long ago. "

How can he sound so calm? "Collect?"

"That's what the Brotherhood does. They collect Lightbringers and other psychics, other Talents. Then they brainwash them and sell them to the highest bidder, if they don't keep them for jobs ranging from corporate espionage to assassination."

Anya swayed. Jack dropped the envelope and caught her arm, his fingers sinking in. "Steady, Anya. Breathe."

"If they tell the p-police I'll go to jail."

"No you won't. If they were going to call the cops, they would have already. And I know how to keep a Lightbringer out of the way of the authorities."

"But—but—" Anya's lower lip trembled. She'd done it, even though she knew it was wrong. She'd *had* to do it. If they—whoever *they* were—told the police, she would go to jail. There would be nobody to take care of Shell. If she ever got out of jail, she would never be able to work as a teacher again. Her whole life, ruined because she'd had to do something she'd known was wrong.

"Anya." His voice was firm, losing its usual impersonal edge and gaining that faint rhythmic song of an accent. He held her arm, his fingers gentle though she could feel the iron strength in them. "Listen to me. I'm trained to keep a Lightbringer out of trouble. That means legal trouble as well as trouble with the Dark. You didn't do anything wrong. If by some miracle they manage to arrest you, I'll come get you—and Circle Lightfall will take care of the rest. Do you think this hasn't happened before? Now *listen* to me."

He didn't quite shake her, but his hand twitched, and she suspected he wanted to. "This is meant to throw you off-balance. It's meant to make you afraid. Fearful witches are easier to catch, because fear makes them silly and predictable. Take a deep breath."

She filled her lungs, the red-black bruising of his aura closing around hers. It was comforting, if a bit prickly. He was angry, fury he was careful to shove down so the only evidence of it was the set of his jaw and the glow of his eyes. Her own shields quivered nervously before they firmed the way he'd taught her.

"You're angry," she managed around the lump in her throat.

"Of course I'm angry. They're threatening my witch." He said this as if informing her the sky was blue. His eyes burned silver, a muscle flicking once in his cheek. "This is just an opening gambit. If you get any more of these, *don't* open them. Let me open it instead. All right?"

She took another deep breath. *Isn't that strange, I almost feel better about this.* "Why shouldn't I open them?"

"You don't know what they might *put* in the next one," he answered grimly. "Anya."

Startled, she looked up. His face was set, eyes glittering. His other hand came up and rested on her shoulder. Heat flushed down her skin—the warming-tingle all the Watchers used to bring a witch out of shock.

"I'm sorry," she whispered. "I had to. I'm so sorry."

"I know you had to." He tensed and slowly, deliberately, pulled her forward. Anya didn't resist. She laid her head against his chest, hearing his even, regular heartbeat thudding beneath her cheek. His arms closed around her. He smelled like leather and pepper and musk. Oddly enough, the scent that would have terrified her a month ago was now comforting.

Safe. When had that happened?

"Don't worry." His voice rumbled in his chest. He was scorching-hot through the thin cotton T-shirt. "Whoever it is, they won't get near you. I promise."

"Don't tell anyone," she whispered. "Please."

He paused slightly before answering. "Of course not. I swore, didn't I?"

She sighed. The heat was comforting, soothing as a hot bath. "I'm sorry."

"Don't be. You did what you had to. I'm sorry I—" He stopped suddenly.

Anya breathed deeply, centering herself. "Mari will be here soon."

He nodded. She could feel the motion even with her eyes closed. "She will. I'll take the paper, if you don't mind. If another one comes, don't touch it. Don't open it. Do you understand?" His voice was harsh, even though he bent down and said this into her hair. Then he inhaled, shuddering slightly.

"I understand." Even though she didn't. Who was sending these? Why did they want to frighten her?

Why was Jack shaking, a fine thin tremor like the humming from a power transformer? His aura almost crackled, folding tightly around hers. She could see more than she ever had before, and that should frighten her. It seemed the more Jack taught her, the more Theo tried to teach her, the more her senses sharpened. The more acute her senses became, the more Power leaked out and made her glow. Like right now—even Jack's red-black aura couldn't hide hers completely.

He let go of her reluctantly, as if unsure of her ability to stand. Anya braced herself, lifted her chin, and gave him a tremulous smile. "I'll be all right." She didn't sound very sure even to herself. *Stop being such a coward. You've done harder things than this.* "You're right. If they—whoever they are— wanted to go to the police, they would have by now. If they want to blackmail me, they're going to be very disappointed, I don't have any money."

"No. But they might think you could *get* a large amount for them. If it's the Brotherhood, your talent could be very useful. Worth a lot of cash."

She flinched. He scooped the paper and the envelope up, folded the paper neatly, and pushed it back inside the envelope. Then he safely stowed everything in a pocket of his big leather coat.

"Will they leave me alone if I ignore them?" She hated the childish quiver in her voice. *You'd think I could learn a little bravery, dammit.*

"Probably not. Don't *worry,* Anya. I'm here. They won't leave you alone if you ignore them—but they *will* leave you alone when I finish with them." His jaw set and his eyes glittered. Tightly-controlled rage made his aura swirl counterclockwise.

I should feel afraid of him. Why don't I?

She didn't want to think about that. It was a relief when the bell over the door tinkled. The after-lunch shoppers were just starting to trickle in.

Anya dredged up a smile and turned to the two teenage girls, obviously skipping school, giggling and whispering to each other. Elise called them 'witch-trippers' with a disdainful snort, but Theo would always chide her gently. *The more of them interested in the Craft, the more chance we have of being accepted,* Theo would point out. *And they're sincere, Elise. Even if they're not very serious.*

Anya thought privately that if the teenagers knew what a curse it was to see things, they might stop coming in altogether. That would certainly put a dent in the store's profit.

Come on, Anya. Pull yourself together, and quit being such a whiner. "Welcome to the Rowangrove," she said, as brightly as she could manage. "Anything I can help you find?"

Twenty-Two

"Good." Jack reached around Anya and traced another rune on the countertop, a backward-leaning X. It glowed briefly with red light, vanished into the glass. His skin tingled with her nearness. He took care not to crowd her. "And this one?"

"Naithuz." Her eyes danced as she glanced up at him, the smile hovering around her mouth. "The Closer of Doors. It can be used to lock or dispel."

"Very good." Theo grinned from the other side of the counter. "I don't know what we'd have done without you, Jack. I'm no good as a teacher, it seems."

It's all Anya, he wanted to tell them. *All I did was offer what I know. I'm not a Teacher.*

"Wow." Mari's blue eyes sparkled. She leaned against the glass on the other side, right next to Theo. "That's fantastic, Anya. I struggled for months with the runes. It's like a whole different language."

"It *is* a whole different language." Elise gave Anya a wide, dazzling smile. Her elegant fingers, nails lacquered with red polish, drummed the countertop. "I knew you'd be the brains of the operation."

"Hey," Mari objected good-naturedly, giving Elise a slight push.

"Oh, relax. You're the cute one." The redhead gave Jack a piercing look. "So I guess you've been doing some good, Mr. Gray."

Jack, standing behind his witch, met the redhead's look squarely enough. "I hope so," he answered, the balm of Anya's presence between him and the hurtful glow of the other Lightbringers. Anya had lost the dark circles under her eyes, and largely lost the sheen of nervousness and fear. She was no longer so thin and desperate-looking. But she still flinched at certain noises—and she checked the mail every day at the store with pale cheeks and trembling hands.

He leaned a little closer to her, meaning to comfort, and didn't miss her slight shifting back toward him. *Don't get greedy,* he warned himself. *And don't think it's anything more than it is. You're only useful, that's all. You're just her Watcher. Nothing more.*

Dante, his hands on Theo's shoulders, raised his eyebrows. "That's the first time I've heard you say something complimentary to a Watcher, firehair."

"Don't get used to it." Elise turned away and surveyed the inside of the store. Dusk was coming, and the golden electric light inside spilled out through the windows. The wind had risen as dark fell, whistling through the streets. The sign was turned to "Closed," and a full moon was rising in the sky outside. It was the first Full Moon of the new year. Anya hadn't wanted to celebrate the Winter Solstice, but the other three had dragged her to a party at Mari's house, and she had given in with good grace. The three Guardians, with perfect tact toward Anya's financial situation, hadn't exchanged presents this year, but Theo had given her a few days off with pay.

Remembering the party at Mari's made Jack think of driving home with Shell asleep in the back seat, Anya humming along with carols on the radio and yawning. He had never felt so at peace in his entire life as a Watcher.

There hadn't been another letter—or another one of those compulsions—for three and a half weeks, and Anya had relaxed somewhat. Jack, however, had not. He'd promised he wouldn't tell any of the other Lightbringers; and he hadn't told any of the other Watchers either. A few seemingly casual questions had elicited some troubling information, though. The Brotherhood was indeed a presence in this city, and the women—despite being Guardians—hadn't been able to bar them from entering. Since the Brotherhood wanted to *capture*, not *kill*, the regular Guardian binding didn't work. Mari was researching another binding at some library, but until she finished they were stuck with increased vigilance.

The Brotherhood was Jack's first guess at the identity of the letter's writer. Anya would be worth a lot of hard cash, either as one of the Brotherhood's brainwashed pet psychics or sold to another organization.

Jack's skin roughened at the thought. *Not while I'm here.* His hands ached slightly. He wanted to touch Anya and didn't dare. It was a pleasant torture, to be this close to the glow of his witch, unable to touch.

The other Watchers were also uneasy. There had been random incursions—a *kalak*, two or three *s'lin*, and a whole tribe of *gimmerin*—Grays—had attacked at different times. On New Year's Eve, the drunken normals and firecrackers had put everybody on edge. Now the city was curiously hushed, as if waiting for something. The wind rose almost every day at dusk, howling through Santiago City's concrete canyons. And once or twice, Jack had felt something—a brush against the borders of his consciousness, quickly gone. As if someone watching him had stepped into his sensing range and hurriedly backpedaled.

Shell came out of the back room, holding a green plastic cup. He didn't meet Jack's eyes, but he stopped, staring at the women, his sleepy blue gaze coming to rest on Anya's face. She smiled, pushing her hair back and tucking the crow-black strands behind her ear. A general murmur of laughter rose, and Anya blushed happily.

Jack watched a number of different emotions work their way across Shell's wide clumsy face, before he turned his attention back to his witch. The boy was no threat.

"I think I was trying too hard," Anya was saying. "After a while, something just clicked. I felt less like I was learning and more like I was *remembering,* if that makes any sense."

"It certainly does." Mari nodded. "I felt the same thing. Suzanne said it was a sign I'd finally started thinking like a witch." She grinned at Anya, her blue eyes snapping with mischief. "So, are you ready?"

"I think so." Anya glanced up at Jack, then, just as quickly, looked down at the glass counter. A power-crystal, slightly bigger than a human head, hummed quietly to itself on one shelf, the card in front of it reading, *Not For Sale.* Jack wasn't surprised—there was an elegant, powerful spell laid on the crystal and spreading through the store to discourage shoplifting. It had all the earmarks of Mari's light touch and sophisticated work. "Ready as I'll ever be. I had no idea people could...I mean, that there were other people who could do these sorts of things."

"Believe it, baby." Elise clicked her tongue, a sharp sound that made the shields on the painted walls shiver quietly.

As if by a prearranged signal, Remy appeared, opening the *Employees Only* door. "Everything's secure. Hanson's taking the perimeter this time."

"Good." Dante stroked Theo's shoulders. "Whenever you're ready, lady witch."

"I wanna watch," Shell said, for the fifth time, sloshing his water.

"Of course you can watch," Anya answered patiently. "Theo said you could."

Jack strangled a flare of dislike for the boy. *Dislike? No. I don't trust him. He's jealous of Anya, too possessive. And what did Remy say? Two steps away from being a Feeder.*

Although I don't blame him for being possessive. Jack allowed himself a few more moments of soaking up Anya's clear glow.

Dante followed Theo like a shadow, as she turned and headed for the door, her skirt fluttering around her ankles. The green witch's shields throbbed with anticipation. "Well, let's get started."

Anya looked up at Jack again, her hair falling back and a momentary shadow passing through her clear eyes. She seemed about to say something, then shook her head and moved to the side, stepping down to follow Theo and Mari.

Elise offered her arm. "You'll do just fine. I was nervous my first time too, but I swear it turns out okay." The redhead's tone was kind, for once.

"Performance anxiety," Mari tossed lightly over her shoulder. "Best thing for it is to go straight through."

Downstairs, the temple was lit by one lone white taper set on the main altar in front of the Goddess-statue. The air hummed with Power. Shadows slid and twisted, and Jack heard Anya take in a shallow, tense breath. He halted with the other two Watchers, at the temple's periphery, clearly marked by the edge of the wooden flooring. The rest of the basement was floored in concrete, boxes of stock neatly arranged. Shell perched on a stool they had carried down for him, leaning away from the Watchers.

Elise took her place in the south corner; Mari in the west. Theo was already standing with her back to the north altar. When Anya stepped in front of the eastern corner, with its simple altar hung with yellow cloth and decorated with an unlit white novena, two peacock feathers, and an incense holder, the subliminal *click* of a circuit completing itself made Jack's skin roughen. *She was brought here for some reason, and so was I.*

"Did you feel that?" Mari whispered.

"Did I do something wrong?" Anya asked, her voice pitched a little too high, breathless. Her nervousness teased at Jack's control; he pushed down his response.

She'll be fine. She's a Lightbringer, she was made for this.

"No, you didn't," Theo shifted slightly. "Elise?"

The fire witch exhaled. Power shifted, swirling like the Talisman the redhead wore. Then, with a crackle, light bloomed, the candles on the altars guttering into life, and the candles in front of the main altar and the statue of the Goddess blooming with flame.

Anya gasped.

"Ladies and gentlemen, I'll be here until Beltane." Elise sounded smug. "No applause, please. Just throw cash."

Theo laughed. The sound gathered Power, scattered it in bright silvery motes through the suddenly-charged air. "I'll start." Her voice dropped, took on new weight. "Northward stand I, mother and earth, I call on the powers of the Northern Ones. Be here now."

"Be here now," the women chorused, Anya's voice nervous, Elise's and Mari's harmonizing, and Theo's full of calm power.

You can do it, Anya. Jack shut his eyes, feeling the Power in the small space thicken.

He worried for nothing. "Eastward stand I, air and intention." She sounded as if she had cast circles all her life. "I call on the powers of the Eastern Ones. Be here now."

"Be here now."

Elise, now. Her voice had taken on a new calmness. "Southward stand I, fire and passion. I call on the powers of the Southern Ones. Be here now."

The Power was visible to the naked eye now, a tide of golden sparks floating around the women, the light in each clearly visible. Anya's aura was clear gold, Theo's a green flame, Elise a gold-red fountain of sparks. *"Be here now."*

"Westward stand I, water and calm." Mari raised her hands slightly, Power cupped in her palms, her blue glow swirling. "I call upon the powers of the Western Ones. Be here now."

"Be here now."

"The circle is cast," Theo said, and the click of Power closing in a completed circuit was no longer subliminal. It was clearly audible.

Dante let out a soft breath. Jack's eyes fixed on Anya—her head tipped back, her eyes closed, her hair brushed by a slight personal breeze. The Power was contained by the boundaries of the circle, four incredibly powerful Lightbringers—and something else. It was like seeing a whole safehouse of Lightbringers in Circle, the face of the sky opening to show the light of Creation itself at a solstice or equinox.

They've been chosen. Jack found himself unable to look away. He had never, in all his years of being a Watcher, seen this much power. Four elements, four Lightbringers—and he found himself blinking as a telltale silver glimmer spread from Theo, Mari, and Elise to wrap itself around Anya. *Guardian?*

But she hasn't agreed to that!

The disbelieving smile spreading over Anya's face stopped the words in his throat. Shell shifted on his barstool, humming tunelessly.

"Are we all right?" Theo asked softly. "Anya?"

"It's warm." Anya sounded dazed. "So warm."

"First time." Elise's voice sent a shiver of red through the sparkles floating in the air. "Nothing like it. Let's hope for no headache."

"Is a headache usual?" Anya whispered.

"With a lot of Power, sometimes it happens." Mari's Power was shifting tides, cinnamon and salt. She swayed as she spoke, moving slightly with the eddies of Power in the air. "Don't worry, kiddo. You're with us."

"What do we do with this?" Anya asked. "There's so...*much*."

Damn right, Jack thought. *Dear gods. I've never seen anything like this.*

"Well, this Full Moon we were thinking of reinforcing the protections on the city." Theo's voice calmed the restive Power, soothed the air itself into green sweetness. "Reach out...like *so*. Feel that?"

"Yesss..." At Anya's voice, the entire circle of fiery Power flushed gold, and a sunny smell of jasmine and amber incense filled the basement.

"Have you ever—" Remy whispered.

"No." Dante's whisper was just as shocked and disbelieving. He too had seen the great circles of Lightbringers in the safehouses, calling down the powers of Creation—but Jack would bet his sword and his knives he had never seen four lone women do *this* before.

"Reach out and help us," Elise said. "You can feel what needs to be done."

Theo started to hum. Mari joined her. Elise's contralto purred under their joined voices. The moment Anya's throaty, sweet voice joined in, the circling tide of energy snapped taut, overflowing. The Power crested. It was, like all great Lightbringer magicks, organic, growing in and of itself like a natural thing. The controlled burst of energy cascaded up through the layers of shielding laid on the Rowangrove and spread in concentric rings, expanding to the city's limits and even slightly beyond, forming a wall of Power. The statue at the central altar sang one long, sustained note, glowing silvery-white. Jack blinked, wondering if he'd seen the wooden arms move slightly, a gesture of blessing.

He stood slack-jawed, staring. The women, perhaps, had only a faint idea that they were the magickal equivalent of a hurricane. With Anya to complete their circle, they were unstoppable.

Unstoppable—but not invulnerable. Jack's hands tightened. A stray Dark predator or a Crusade Knight wouldn't think twice before erasing that light from the world. The Brotherhood wouldn't think twice before capturing one or all of these women, wiping their brains with drugs or worse, and selling them to the highest bidder.

Jack heard the crackle of flames again, heard the screams. *Lupo Grigio.* The Gray Wolf.

Memory rose from its kennel in the dark recesses of his guilt.

In the early years of Lupus Dei, there was no name more feared than that of Jacopo Givelli, Cardinel Givelli's bastard son. While the other Knights of the Crusade hunted with the Seekers, Givelli's son hunted only with the power that the Grace of God had bestowed upon him. Jacopo was psychic. Not as much as the women Lupus Dei hunted, but enough.

Lupo Grigio. The wolf of God himself.

Jack squared his shoulders, his eyes fixed on the curve of Anya's throat. Her head tilted back, black hair lifting slightly on an invisible breeze. Jack's bones twisted with fresh acid pain. Not even her presence could stop the bright tide of Lightbringer magick from etching agony into his body. The magick swirled, drifted, and drained, finishing with a single snap that crackled in the air.

Shell shifted on his stool, the wood creaking under him. Jack glanced at the boy and saw his eyes were open wide, his body leaning forward, straining. The pulsing of his aura drank in ambient Power.

Feeder. Jack's lip curled with disdain. *Much more of this, and we might have a full-fledged psychic vampire on our hands. I don't like that idea. It will be painful for Anya.*

"Wow." Elise stretched, sparks popping from her lacquered fingernails. "Did you feel that?"

"I did." Mari stared at Anya, peering over the statue's carved wooden hair. "The last time it was like that…"

"Was when Suzanne was here. Only not so powerful," Theo finished. "Yes. Anya's our fourth. Just like Mari guessed."

Elise laughed, a soft sound echoing with the hiss of a candle flame. "Seeing the future must be such a drag. Hey, Mari, what's the Lotto going to be this time?"

"Bite me." Mari's tone was uncharacteristically sharp. "It's official, then. Anya's our fourth."

"Did I do something wrong?" Anya blinked, swaying, straightened just in time. Jack tensed. He couldn't step over the barrier of the circle to catch her if she fell. His neck ached, tension in his shoulders twisting tighter and tighter.

"No, Mari just doesn't like anyone asking her about the lottery. Or horse races." Elise's grin glittered. She looked fey, her hair lifting as static teased at it. "Relax, Mare. Be chilly."

"You see? She's impossible." Mari rolled her eyes. "Don't pay any attention to her."

"Nobody pays attention to me," Elise answered, "so I've got to keep acting up."

"Now, now, ladies." Theo lifted her hands slightly. "Let's bring the circle down and get something to eat. I'm starving. It's all these pregnancy hormones."

"Eating for two." Mari grinned, brushing back her blond curls. "Any business before we close up the circle?"

Jack watched Anya's eyes open, their gray softly shining like the moon behind clouds. She tilted her head slightly, glanced out beyond the confines of the circle, looking at him.

Me? Why is she looking at me? But he knew. She was glancing at him for reassurance. She had trusted him with more than one secret and looked to him for guidance. His shoulders came up under the weight of that trust.

Every Watcher was taught that their witch would ease the pain, that if they could survive long enough to find the witch that could stop the relentless agony they would be *saved*. Jack had worked with enough of the others to know that salvation meant something different to each Watcher.

But none of the other Watchers were even remotely like Jack. None of them carried the same stain he did.

He watched as his salvation looked back at the other women in the circle, a disbelieving smile spreading over her weary, beautiful face. Her eyes glowed, the corners of her lips tilted up, and when she shook her glossy fall of hair back. Jack felt his heart pause for a moment.

They had not told the Watchers—had not told *him*—that he would feel his entire body go cold at the mere thought of her in pain. They hadn't told him that a threat to her would fill him with iron-tasting, clinical rage.

They hadn't told him, long ago when they trained him, that he would want to tell her about his crimes—and at the same time, fear the exposure of what he was and her inevitable disgust.

Or that it would be worth it, Watching her, even if she recoiled from him. He could accept that tearing pain if she was safe.

"Wow." Anya swayed again. Jack's body tensed, his fingernails sinking into his palms. "That was..." Her black hair clung damply to her forehead.

"Better than chocolate," Elise whispered. "You bet."

"Yeah." Theo's voice was soft, but firm. "Release the North, my thanks and blessings."

"Release the West, my thanks and blessings." Mari's eyes glittered and her mouth was a thin firm line, but she sounded satisfied.

"Release the South, my thanks and blessings." Elise grinned, shook her fingers. Sparks popped.

"Release the East," Anya whispered. "My thanks and blessings."

The circle folded down into the ground, power swirling to caress each of the women before it drained away. Anya took one unsteady step toward the center altar with its statue humming with foxfire power, tripped over her own feet, and her knees buckled.

Jack wasn't even aware of moving. He caught her, breaking the force of her fall as gently as possible, his knees thudding painfully against the wooden flooring, jarring all the way up to his teeth. Elise let out a short shout of surprise, and Mari gasped.

"Easy, *cherie*." Remy caught Elise's wrist. "Gentle. He's just making sure she's okay."

"He should *warn* someone before he comes running into Circle." Elise made a short, vicious sound of annoyance, matching the static crackling around her right hand. Remy murmured soothingly.

"Dante?" Theo's voice. "Is she hurt? Dante?"

"She's all right," Jack heard himself say. "Just a little bit of backlash. Anya?"

Her charcoal lashes, lying in perfect fans along her cheekbones, fluttered. Anya's eyes met his.

She blinked. The reverberation of Power in the air faded slowly, scraping against Jack's skin, taunting his nerves with rusty nails.

"Jack?" She grimaced, blinking, dazed.

"Headache?" *I'm not surprised, with that much Power. Gods above, she's incredible.*

"I...yes. Did I pass out?" She sounded stunned.

"It's normal. It goes away after the first few times." He tried to speak gently, wished his voice wasn't so harsh compared to hers. Moved his arm slightly so her head was cradled, and strangled the urge to lean down and press his lips to her damp pale forehead.

"Oh." She looked up at him then, a look that seemed to pierce through every careful defense he'd ever built. "I think I want to sleep."

"Then sleep, Anya. I'll be watching."

She sighed and closed her eyes again, moving slightly as if to cuddle into his arms. He looked up to find three witches, two Watchers, and Shell staring at him.

"I'll take her home," Jack said. He was glad Watchers didn't blush, but his face felt suspiciously warm.

Elise nudged Mari, who giggled. Theo, her hands glowing green, bit her lower lip. Dante held the healer's shoulders, keeping her still as she pitched forward, her entire body tense with the compulsion to help.

"She'll be all right?" the green witch asked. "The first time we...well, that didn't happen to us."

"You probably didn't cast a major spell with three Guardians," Jack reminded her, moving so he could slide his arm under Anya's knees and lift her, carefully. Leather creaked as he reached his feet. Her head rested against his shoulder. "Don't worry, she'll be all right."

"She's our fourth," Mari said. "Like Suzanne. Remember the awful headaches we all got after Circle the first few times?"

"Oh, gods. Worst hangover I *ever* had." Elise moaned, leaning back against Remy, who drew himself up, his golden eyes half-lidded. "Hope that doesn't happen to her."

Too late. But it'll fade, she's meant to do this. She's a Lightbringer. "She'll be fine," Jack repeated. "I'll take her home."

Twenty-Three

"Shell?" Anya stood at the bottom of the stairs, her hands on her hips. Her head hurt, her eyes were sandy, and her lower back felt as if someone had buried a bar of hot lead in the muscles. The half-circle window over the front door glowed pearly gray, the sun struggling through a foggy cottony morning outside. Anya tried again. "Shell, please. I'll be late for work if you keep this up. Shell?"

Jack closed the front door quietly. He'd been outside in the fog, and little droplets of water clung to his dark hair, dewing the shoulders of his coat.

"You should be in bed." His eyes flicked once over Anya, cut toward the stairs. "Problem?"

Heat flooded Anya's entire body. The silence of a heavy fog wrapped around the entire house, made even her heartbeat seem loud. Her cheeks were on fire. *How does he do that? How does he make me blush? He hasn't even touched me.*

Except to protect me. The blush was almost as bad as her headache.

No, nothing could be as bad as this headache. Her entire body twinged as she shifted her weight.

"Theo called." She wished her head wouldn't pound with each word. "Mari's at work and Elise is downtown getting an amp fixed. Theo wants to go visit someone in the hospital again. She told me not to come in, but I told her I would. Only Shell isn't..." She bit her lip, running her hand back through her hair. "Good morning," she said awkwardly, ashamed of her immediate complaints. "I suppose you brought me home last night, because I don't remember anything after the end of the...spell."

He nodded. Wonder of wonders, he'd shaved, even though his hair looked a little longer and more unruly this morning. The absence of dark shadows on his cheeks and chin made his face look even sharper—gaunt and set and handsome—his gray eyes fringed with black lashes under a shelf of dark hair. The effect was startling. She'd never noticed how good-looking he was, or how he seemed to go completely still when his eyes met hers, almost as if he was...afraid?

No, not afraid. Concentrating completely. Anya had never been the subject of such intense scrutiny.

If he didn't look so severe he'd actually be cute. Another flush scorched through her. It actually helped to clear her head a little, made the pain recede.

"I brought you home," he said, and Anya had to remind herself what she'd asked. "You were unconscious. I also put Shell to bed. He was upset, wanted you to tell him a story. I improvised a bit."

Wonders never cease. "You told him a story?"

He ducked his head slightly and raked his fingers back through his hair. He looked actually *sheepish.* "Of a sort. It's been a long time. I tried the Three Little Pigs and Rapunzel. That seemed to satisfy him."

"He likes to hear about my grandmother." Her cheeks were hot. Her eyes dropped to the silver butts of the guns at his hips. *I don't even know where he sleeps. On the couch maybe? I don't even have a spare blanket.*

"I'll go up and get him, if you want. Have you had breakfast?"

"What?" She stared at him. She hadn't even thought of breakfast—stumbling for the shower and crawling into clean jeans and a pale blue sweater had been the most she could manage.

"Have you had breakfast yet? Food will help the headache. Coffee, too. A little caffeine sometimes helps the backlash." One corner of his mouth tilted up, a slight sardonic smile. His eyes were soft, no longer flinty. His shoulders dropped, and his hands went in his pockets again. He seemed to want to make himself smaller, to fade into the woodwork.

How any broad-shouldered man armed to the teeth could fade into the woodwork, she couldn't guess. Nobody in their right mind would overlook him. "You know about the headache?"

Jack nodded. "It happens. You were the conduit for a lot of Power last night. It gave you...almost a hangover. Once you become accustomed to the amount of Power you can command and control, it won't be so bad. It'll feel almost normal."

"Oh." Anya rubbed the end of the balustrade absently and glanced up the stairs. No sign of Shell. Irritation rasped at her neck, drawing the muscles tight. She took a deep breath, trying to dispel it. *I'm the adult here. Shell's probably just oversleeping. We were up late last night. Any change in his routine throws him off.* "Jack, can I ask you something?"

"Of course." His voice was soft, none of the awful rage

she'd heard before. *How can he sound so different?* she wondered, noticing again just how *big* he was. It wasn't even physical size—it was the aura of awareness and danger he carried that made him seem to fill up a room.

"Where—um, where do you sleep?" The heat in her cheeks grew worse.

"I don't need much sleep. Mostly in front of the door." The smile grew slightly. Or was that her imagination?

Anya stepped into the hall, ignoring the instant scream of her lower back and the jolt in her temples. "You sleep on the floor?"

"Sometimes. It's all right, Anya."

She didn't realize she had approached him until he took a single step back, avoiding her gracefully.

"We should get you a sleeping bag or something. We don't even have an extra blanket for you to sleep on the couch." Her breath caught in her throat. *What am I doing?* She halted less than three feet from him, smelling leather and that strange peppery adrenaline that followed him, mixed with the smell of damp salt from the fog, an ocean scent coming up from the bay on little foggy cat feet.

"I don't need it," he answered, in a strange, quiet voice. As if something was caught in his throat too. His Adam's apple bobbed, and she saw his black T-shirt was torn. The left knee of his jeans was threadbare too. His boots were deeply scuffed.

He needs new clothes. And a haircut wouldn't be amiss either. Guilt rose inside her chest. He'd given her money, taken care of everything—and not taken a single penny for himself.

"No." She looked up at his face. "You do need it. You also need a haircut and a new shirt. And a few good meals. You're beginning to look a bit gaunt."

He blinked.

Anya reached up, wincing slightly as the movement made her lower back throb with pain. Jack didn't move. She laid her fingertips on his chin, feeling the odd vulnerability of freshly-shaven skin. His eyelids dropped and he went still, not even breathing.

"You haven't told anyone about the letter." Her voice trembled. "You've just done exactly what you said you'd do. I thought you were one of *them*—the things that hunted me." *Great, Anya. Why can't you say what you mean? You used to think that, but not now.*

His eyes opened slightly, and she felt a twitch go through

him. "I know you're not," she soothed immediately.

Just like Shell when he gets all tight-strung. She wondered why she hadn't seen it before. Jack's immobility wasn't inertness; it was hypervigilance.

She brushed her fingertips up to his cheek, slowly, going on tiptoe to reach his temple. "I just want to say thank you. I know I haven't been very nice to you. It's been so long since I could relax without worrying about when the next crisis was going to erupt. Thank you."

His eyes moved over her face. "No need to...to thank me." Husky, his lips barely moving. "Anya."

What am I doing? She dropped her hand to her side but didn't back up. *I don't even know him!* "I want to know about you. I want to know who you are. If I've been brought here—and Theo thinks I was *brought* here—and if you were brought here too, there must be a reason. I feel like I *know* you, but I can't say how or why. Like the runes, or the spells. So I want to know about you."

The color drained from his face. Anya, her head and neck suddenly tensing with new pain, closed her eyes and took a deep breath.

His hands curled around her shoulders. "I'm your Watcher, Anya. That's all that matters."

Anya opened her eyes to find his face inches from hers, his eyes burning, jaw clenched. His fingers tightened, but she felt no fear. The prickling heat surrounding him wrapped around her, eased the pain in her head and the burning in her neck. Oddly enough, it relaxed her. Just like an electric blanket.

"But who were you before you were a Watcher?" she persisted. "Jack Gray's not your real name, is it?"

His eyes turned dark, haunted. That was it, *haunted.* He looked like a man just awakened from a nightmare.

"It's close enough." His voice was low and harsh enough to heat the air in the foyer. "I'm your Watcher. Nothing else matters, Anya."

"But—"

He straightened his arms slowly, pushing Anya away. Then, gently, with exquisite care, he loosened his fingers until she stood barefoot on the hardwood floor, staring at him.

"It doesn't matter, Anya. I swear to you, the person I was before I became a Watcher is *dead.* And good riddance to him. He was nothing. He doesn't exist." He dropped his hands down to his sides, stuffed them in his pockets.

He's sweating, Anya realized, with dazed wonder. *And shaking.*

"I'll go get Shell up," he said. "Make some breakfast, Anya. It will help with your headache. I could do with a cup of coffee, myself."

He brushed past her. Anya's chest ached. "Jack."

He stopped, his booted foot on the first step.

"If I ordered you to, would you tell me?" *Why am I angry? God, please don't let me be angry.* The thought of her first and only brush with the power of her own anger rose to taunt her. She couldn't afford it; she knew what her anger could do. Her hands curled into fists.

His tone was as brittle as it was frigid. "If you *ordered* me to, I would do anything. Duty, obedience, honor. That's what it means to be a Watcher."

"So you're only here out of duty." *I'm an idiot. I am SUCH an idiot. Thank God I haven't done anything stupid.*

"I came here out of duty. I will stay here because you are my witch, Anya. You don't know what it's like—" He stopped short, as if choked.

"If you don't *tell* me, how will I know?" She turned away to face the hall, her fists lifting slightly. The anger rose to her head, made her pulse pound and her neck hurt.

"It's *not important*, Anya!" The stairs creaked under his voice. Anya flinched. "I'm sorry," he said immediately, softer. "If you want me to, I'll tell you. But it's not...pretty."

"Never mind." Anya fixed her eyes on the floor and stalked through the foyer toward the kitchen. "I don't care anyway."

He reached out as if he would catch her arm as she passed him. Anya stopped, still staring at the floor. The anger quivered, straining at her control and making her head pound even worse—just like Power.

His tone gentled even further. "I'm here to watch over you, *piccola.* Believe me when I tell you nothing will harm you if I can possibly stop it. No Watcher likes to talk about what he was. I'm sorry."

"Pickle *what*?" She couldn't help herself. He sounded genuinely sorry. The anger drained away, leaving only an unsteady sort of nausea in its wake.

"It's Italian. An...a nickname, of sorts."

"Oh." She looked up, pushing back her hair with one hand. He stood on the bottom step, making him seem even taller, but his shoulders were slumped as if he carried something hopelessly heavy. "What does it mean?"

He actually fidgeted, a small sharp restless movement. "It means *little one*."

Is he blushing? She took a closer look. He *was* blushing, a faint stain of red high up on his freshly-shaven cheeks. From pale to blushing in less than five minutes, because of her.

Maybe I'm not such an idiot after all. Anya studied him. "I like it," she said, finally. "All right. I'll stop asking you about your past if you promise to be extra-gentle with Shell."

"I would anyway. For your sake."

I actually believe him. I wonder why he doesn't want to talk about before he was a Watcher. The idea of getting one of the other women alone to pump her for even more information about this whole thing made her head hurt. "All right." Her throat felt coated with sand. "Do you want breakfast?"

He began to shake his head, then stopped, studied her for a moment, and nodded deliberately. "Yes. Please."

"Breakfast it is." She turned on her heel and stamped toward the kitchen. The phone began to shrill, and she surprised herself by cursing as she stubbed her toe, running to scoop it up in the kitchen. "Hello?"

"Hey, baby." It was Elise. "I'm at the Rowangrove. I'll stand in for you while Theo goes and ministers to the lepers and cripples."

"I'm sorry," Anya began immediately.

"Oh, don't." Elise's voice crackled, brisk but not impatient. "They won't be finished with my amp until tomorrow, and I've been meaning to do some research with the books Theo has here anyway. And if you're feeling anything like I felt the first time I cast a major spell, you should be in bed with that big hunk waiting on you hand and foot."

Anya felt heat stain her cheeks again. *I have to stop blushing like an idiot.* "Really, Elise, I can come in."

"No. Go to bed. That's an order, baby-cheeks. Your head's probably pounding and you feel like you've got the worst cramps since PMS was invented."

"I do feel a little—" Anya started.

"Good. Stay home, have that Watcher wait on you. He's big enough to carry a breakfast tray. And not bad-looking." Elise laughed. "Oh, stop it. Remy's making faces at me. Well, *ciao*. Call in tomorrow and let us know if you feel any better."

"But—"

"No ifs, ands, or buts. Rest. That's an order." Elise laughed again. "Bye, sweetie. Get some sleep."

There was a click, and the dial tone rang in her ear. Anya knew enough now not to be offended; it was just how Elise was. What most people mistook for brusque rudeness was just Elise's natural running-speed. *If the world is moving at fifty-five miles an hour,* Mari once remarked, *Elise is clipping along at seventy. With the radio up and all her windows rolled down.*

Anya laid the phone down in its cradle. *Well, that's a fine how-do-you-do. I've got to get another job. I can't depend on someone else's goodwill forever.*

The phone rang again.

Anya picked it up. "Elise?"

"Anya." The voice was male, pleasant, and crawling with evil. Anya's entire body turned to ice. "Anya Harris."

Anya swayed, her fingers curling around the edge of the counter. "Who is this?" Her voice trembled.

"We know, Anya. We know about the First Continental Bank and Detroit National." The voice crawled chill through the phone line, touched Anya's throat. Her hand started to tremble. Her head cracked with pain, her eyes suddenly dry and hot as if full of sand. "And the Gratston Credit Union. Have I left anything out?"

"Leave me alone," Anya whispered.

Shell stumbled into the kitchen, fisting at his eyes, then stopped, staring at her. He was barefoot, wearing his sweatpants and a yellow T-shirt. Jack loomed behind him, his gray eyes suddenly burning over Shell's shoulder.

He pushed Shell aside and stalked into the kitchen.

"We're watching, Anya. We know. We want you to help us, and we'll help you. Don't trust the Watchers. They know more than they're telling. Ask him, Anya. Ask him about the Gray Wolf and the Crusade. See what he says."

Her gaze stuttered up to Jack's face. He deftly extracted the phone from her nerveless hand and lifted it to his ear. Anya clasped her cold hands together as he listened, his face going still and hard as a granite cliff. His eyes flashed silver-hard.

He laid the phone down, cutting off the sound of the chill, evil voice. "Interesting." Then he caught Anya as she swayed. "Sit down. Shell, bring her a chair."

Shell shook his head, his blue eyes wide.

It didn't deter Jack in the slightest. "No? Fine. Here, *piccola,* sit." He dragged the lone wooden stool from the breakfast bar and guided her onto it, then held her shoulders. "Anya, are you all right? Look at me. *Look* at me."

She shivered, a galvanic thrill tightening her nerves. Her head ached. "I don't feel so good." Her stomach revolved, cramping. "Elise c-c-called, and then he—"

"Don't worry about it. I told you, they're only trying to frighten you."

"Doing a damn g-good job of it," she said wryly, and he smiled. He was trying to comfort her, she knew, but his smile was only painted over a dark simmering well of rage. Yet his hands were gentle. He stroked her shoulders, a soothing touch.

"Anya?" Shell sounded plaintive. "I'm *hungry*. What's for breakfast?"

"Leave her alone," Jack snapped over his shoulder. His voice made yesterday's dishes rattle in the rack and the cupboards groan. He checked her damp forehead with burning-hot fingers.

"No," Anya protested, weakly. "Leave Shell alone, he doesn't understand."

"He understands far more than you think. You're chilled. You should be in bed."

"Shell—"

"I can make toast as well as anyone can, *piccola*. And coffee. Don't worry. Come."

With that, he slid his arm under her knees, bending, and picked her up.

"No, wait—no—*Jack*—" she blurted. She had never in her life been literally *picked up* before, especially not by a broad-shouldered hunk who acted as if she weighed no more than a sack of flour.

"Hush. I can make toast, and he'll be fine."

"I want Anya to make me breakfast!" Shell pouted, stamping his foot.

Oh, no. Anya tried to wriggle free of Jack's arms. *He's going to throw a fit.*

"Too bad." Jack pushed past him, cradling Anya in his arms. "I'll make you coffee, Anya."

"This isn't necessary."

"It is. You'll make yourself sick."

She shivered, her teeth chattering. "I d-d-don't—"

"They want you sick and predictable and weak with fear. Don't worry about it. Shell will live without you to coddle him; he survived for long enough before he met you, I'd guess. How are you going to take care of him if you drive yourself into a nervous breakdown?"

He reached the head of the stairs and turned toward her room. Her head gave another terrific squeeze of pain, and her back burned. He kneed her door open and deposited her on the ransacked bed. Then he swept her legs up and pulled the covers over her. "Don't move. I'll feed Shell and bring you breakfast and coffee."

"But—" She began to protest.

He folded his arms and drew his eyebrows together, his gray eyes gone dark and cold. "I'm to look after your well-being, *piccola*. I can't do that if you insist on harming yourself. Rest."

Anya sagged back into the pillows as her head throbbed again. Lying down did seem to make the pain more bearable. "All right. I give up. You win. Shell likes his toast with peanut butter, cut diagonally with the crust trimmed off. And orange juice. And he has to have a spoon in his orange juice."

"I *know*. I've seen you do it." Jack turned to the door. "I'll bring you breakfast and the newspaper."

"Jack?"

He looked back, his hands in his pockets and his face pale and set. Gray morning light filled the room—she'd pushed the curtains back when she got up. The light helped, showed her bare white walls and the open closet, the pale-blue dresser Elise had painted and brought to the house in her newly-bought Volkswagen. Mari had started bringing sweaters and jackets and boots, and Theo had brought her a whole collection of silverware just this last week.

They've taken me in like I took Shell in. She felt abruptly thankful that she'd chosen Santiago City.

Still, she had to tell him. "He said to ask you about the Gray Wolf. And the Crusade."

A flush of red went through Jack's aura. His face set, his eyes turning light and hard as ice. His upper lip peeled back, and heat slammed through the room, fogging the window. Anya propped herself up on her elbows, her pulse pounding in her throat.

He looks dangerous. Her pulse ran slow and thick, heavy in her chest.

"The Gray Wolf," he said slowly, "was the name of Cardinal Givelli's bastard son. He hunted Lightbringers through Europe. He was the most feared of the Live Knights of the Crusade, when Lupus Dei was new and the terror fresh. He killed many

Watchers, and many Lightbringers."

Anya's mouth went dry.

Jack half-turned, looking at her closet. She saw his profile—
long nose, strong chin, his mouth turned into a thin line. "He
was a murderer, a killer of Lightbringers. He sent many of them
to the stake and killed many good Watchers. When he appeared
at the safehouse in Prague and begged to be taken into the
Watchers, there were those who wanted to kill him on sight."
Jack's voice dropped to a thread, barely audible. "The High
Council of the Lightbringers said differently. They said he was
to be given the training, and if the gods allowed him to live
through the binding to a *tanak*, he could start paying his penance
for the lives he had destroyed."

"Jack—"

He turned his back to her. "I'll get Shell his breakfast."
Without another word, he was gone.

Anya let out a sigh. Her head hurt too much to make sense
of everything. The soft, evil voice on the phone seemed to crawl
inside her head, twisting and sharp. *Don't trust the
Watchers...Ask him about the Gray Wolf.*

But he's so gentle. She turned over, closing her eyes,
burrowing into the comfort of the pillows. *And he's so nervous
when I get close to him.*

It felt good to lie still, with her eyes closed, in the warmth
of the bed. Inside the shields Jack had put on the house were
the layers of shielding he'd patiently taught her how to weave,
and she felt his attention slide along the layers of energy,
checking them. Felt him pause, checking the shields around
her room, testing them, and sliding away.

He's very attached to me. She wished her head didn't hurt
quite so much. Now that she wasn't focusing so hard on staying
upright and moving from one thing to the next, the pain was
overwhelming. Her back ached until she settled into a
comfortable position on her side, not even caring that she was
going to sleep in her clothes.

Attached? No. He seems more than attached.

But she fell into a light, uneasy sleep before she could finish
the thought.

Twenty-Four

Anya slept almost all day, tossing underneath her blankets. Jack brought her coffee and a breakfast tray, but she was so deeply asleep he didn't dare wake her. Gray light played against her pale skin, and her glossy hair was spread along the pillow. She lay on her side, her hand outflung, her eyelashes a perfect arc against her beautiful cheekbones. She looked so peaceful his heart almost stopped, and he retreated, closing the door quietly.

The boy pouted all through breakfast, watching Jack fiddle with the toaster and the coffeemaker. Then he ran up and down the stairs until Jack collared him and told him in no uncertain terms not to disturb Anya's sleep. Sulking, Shell returned to his room, playing marbles all through the afternoon and occasionally sneaking out to peer at Anya's door. Jack made him a grilled-cheese sandwich with a quartered apple and a glass of milk for lunch.

Jack leaned against the door as evening fell, arms folded, glowering at the hallway. The boy would wake Anya if he could, probably to complain about Jack. Nervous and fretful, denied the glow of the Lightbringer's presence, he crept closer and closer until he was crouched at Jack's feet.

"When will she wake up?" he whined, almost daring to touch Jack's boots.

"When she wakes up. She's sick." Jack took a firmer hold on his temper, restraining the temptation to push the boy away.

Boy? He's almost as tall as Dante. Strong, too, unless I miss my guess. And he has her wrapped around his little finger.

"She was never too sick to play before." The boy scratched at his shaggy blond hair. He blinked and stretched his legs out, tapping the opposite wall with his callused feet. "You made her sick."

"You probably worried at her until she gave in, even when she was sick," Jack snarled. "Stop that. *Don't* wake her up, or I'll be very angry."

The boy glanced up at him and stuck out his tongue, his broad face screwing up into a picture of childish disdain. Jack gathered the last few scraps of his patience and took a deep breath. He was on edge, and not because of Shell.

They had told her.

She knows I am a monster. How could she not? They told her, when I would not. Who knows what they told her on the phone before I took it? She knows now.

His thoughts turned to inventive curses in his native tongue, curses he muttered as he stared at the opposite wall. The rhythm soothed him—English was such an unlovely language, not like the song of his early years.

He had not spoken his childhood tongue in a very long time. It brought up too many memories. He had stripped every nuance of the past from his speech with each passing decade, listening for new words, mimicking the accent of the other Watchers around him. It was part of the reason why he'd requested an American assignment; every mile of Europe reminded him of something unpleasant nowadays.

It was a curious comfort to half-sing the filthiest words he could think of to himself as he cursed whoever had been on the other end of the phone line, wishing them ill-luck and God's fury down unto the seventh generation.

Now that he was a Watcher, it might even stick.

"She doesn't like you." Shell scooted over to the other side of the hall, bracing his broad back against the wall. "She thinks you're ugly and mean."

He was feeling so savage toward the soft evil voice on the phone the childish taunt didn't even sting. "Is that so." *Of course she wouldn't like me; I'm a monster. The best I can hope for is to be allowed to protect her.*

Jack closed his eyes. The stench of smoke and the sickly-sweet smell of roasting flesh rose, screaming and struggling in his memory. He pushed it down.

"You *are* ugly. And mean. I don't like you. Anya will make you go away. She does what I want."

Jack's gaze came down, met Shell's. The boy flinched back. "I am not going anywhere," Jack said, slowly and distinctly. "I am here to protect Anya, whether you like it or not. If you get in the way of Anya's protection, I will be very displeased." He let a little bit of a rumble creep into his voice. Shell quivered, but stared at him.

"She'll make you go away. She hates you."

Jack found that his lips had curled up into a mirthless grin. *A Watcher doesn't belong to Circle Lightfall after he has found his witch. Even if she orders me back in disgrace, I won't go. I'll stay and protect her, from afar if I have to. And if you get in*

*the way, man-child, I will wait for a time when she's not looking
and make sure you don't interfere. If I have to frighten you to
protect her, I will.*

It was a relief to think of frightening the boy into behaving.
Jack shook himself. It would make Anya mistrust him even
more. The fool wasn't responsible; he was unable to really
understand the consequences of his actions. It was unworthy of
a Watcher to think such things.

I am to kill the Dark, not menace the innocent, he reminded
himself. *Duty, obedience, honor. That is what you are made
for. You're not worthy of her touch.*

Shell rocked back and forth, tapping the wall with his
elbows.

"Stop that." Jack heard movement inside Anya's room. He
fixed the boy with a steely glare. "If you've broken her rest…"

Anya opened the door, yawning and scratching at her temple
under her mussed hair. She blinked drowsily up at Jack, her
room falling dark behind her. He saw that the top button of her
jeans was undone, and her sweater's neck slipped down,
showing one pale shoulder. His entire body tightened.

The only language that could do her justice was the soft
blurred rolling song of his youth, and he had to force himself to
think in the speech of the here-and-now.

She looked up at him, soft gray eyes meeting his. Time
seemed to stop. He held his breath. *She doesn't look angry.* He
examined her face, her lips slightly parted and her cheeks flushed
from sleep. *Maybe she won't order me away.*

He told himself sternly not to hope.

"How do you feel?" he asked softly, with the last breath he
had left. The syllables fit oddly in his mouth.

"Better." She yawned. "Hungry."

"I can—" he began, but she shook her head.

"I'll make something. Were you waiting for me to wake
up?" She looked past him, to Shell. "What's wrong?"

"Nothing. He's been waiting for you all day. I've been
keeping guard at your door so he didn't burst in and pester
you."

"He's mean!" Shell burst out. "He's mean and nasty and *I
don't like him!*"

Anya sighed. She buttoned her jeans and ran her hand back
through her hair, then looked up at Jack. He waited, his hand
curling into a fist.

If she tries to send me away, I will find whoever's stalking her and make them wish they had never been hatched. Then I will deal with the boy. I can frighten him into behaving, at least.

Amazingly, Anya smiled. "I don't think he's that bad, Shell. He's kept the dark things away, hasn't he? Let's go make dinner."

She reached up, her fingers spread, and rested her hand on Jack's chest. The touch burned him even through his T-shirt, the delicious heat of her skin not quite reaching through the thin cotton fabric and dipping him in electric honey.

"Jack," she continued, as if reminding herself who he was. "I think we should talk."

He nodded, not daring to hope even now. "Whatever you like," he said, harshly. "Anya."

Slowly, deliberately, she stepped closer and went on tiptoe, her soft hand sliding up to curl around a strap of his leather harness and pull slightly. He bent down, automatically obedient, and her lips met his stubbled cheek.

Fire raced through his veins. He inhaled sharply. *I don't deserve...* he thought, before the pleasure rose in a giddy spiral and drove every coherent thought out of his head.

She retreated, two soft steps on her bare feet. He'd turned the thermostat up early in the afternoon, and she looked flushed and sleepy.

"I'm not sending him away, Shell," she said quietly, but with a tone of finality. "So you'll have to get along with him." She offered the boy her hand. "Come on. I'll make fried chicken, if you want."

"Fried chicken!" Shell scrambled to his feet and grabbed her fingers. He squeezed too hard, Anya winced, and Shell gave a sneering glance back over his shoulder as he followed her.

Jack's fist clenched. *He knows he hurts her.* Rage prickled along his spine. He followed mechanically down the stairs, the feel of Anya's soft touch on his cheek enough to stave off that rage. *Careful, Watcher. As long as she lets me stay, I care not what he does.*

It wasn't true. He *did* care. There was simply nothing he could do about it at this point.

He knows he hurts her, the deep voice of his conscience rose to taunt him. *He knows. What's to stop him from hurting her even more?*

He heard the downstairs toilet flush, and Shell's voice. "Anya? Anya?"

Leave her alone, she's in the bathroom! He swallowed the words. His hand tightened on the balustrade until the wood groaned and he had to unlock his fingers one by one.

"If he hurts her," he murmured, stopping at the last step while Anya continued down the hall, Shell babbling, the softer music of her replies, "if he hurts her I'll..."

What can I do? If I frighten him into behaving, she'll hate me, even if I could prove to her that he understands more of what he does. Her innocence blinds her. He is only a Feeder, not something Dark.

He spared himself a grim smile for the position he was in. Still, he would enjoy scaring the boy into treating Anya better.

I am not a very nice person.

It took a touch of the Dark to understand what the Dark was capable of. Lightbringers didn't understand hatred, or violence, or greed. Their very natures couldn't comprehend Darkness. It was another thing that made them vulnerable.

Jack continued down the hall and into the kitchen, now brightly lit against the gathering dusk. Even though the days were getting fractionally longer, it was still dark early. Imbolc, the witch's Festival of Light, was right around the corner.

Anya moved around the kitchen, occasionally yawning. The coffeemaker gurgled. Shell perched on the stool. He saw Jack and stuck out his tongue.

"Now stop that," Anya said sharply, though her head was in the fridge. "Don't be rude, Shell."

The boy bridled. Jack halted, leaning against the doorway, his arms folded. "He understands more than you give him credit for, *piccola.*"

"Mh." She surfaced and gave him an arch glance. "I suppose you think I should send him to an institution, or a home?"

"No. You're fond of him, I wouldn't tell you to do that." *Even though you should.* "I just think you should be aware that he knows when he's hurting you."

She opted for a graceful subject change. "Mashed potatoes with garlic. We're almost out of milk. And what about steamed broccoli? I want to use this before it goes bad, though I'm not a big fan of broccoli. It's good for you."

Jack shrugged. "I suppose." He wanted to ask what the soft evil voice on the phone had told her, held his tongue. "You like to cook?" The instant it was out of his mouth, he cursed himself for saying something stupid.

"I do, actually." She smiled at him, pushing a strand of raven hair behind her ear. "It's a type of magic I understand. Putting raw ingredients together, adding a little something extra, and making something edible. Pour me some coffee, and get the flour down, will you?"

He moved to obey almost before he thought of it. "Are you going to send me away?" The question took him unawares, and he had to translate it inside his head before he discovered what he'd said.

She paused, holding a blue frying pan. "What?"

He jerked his chin at Shell, who hummed to himself, tapping on the countertop. "He says you'll send me away. Now you know what I was. What I...did. Will you try to send me away? Do you—" He ran out of words, staring at her.

She looked almost shocked.

A long, taut pause stretched between them. "Pour me some coffee, okay? And of course I'm not *sending* you anywhere. You're an adult. You can go if you want, of course—but I'd like to know a little more about how to protect myself before you do."

Over my dead body, witch. "I will not leave you. Not unless you order me to—and even then I'll do my best to protect you, Anya. I'm your Watcher."

Her face changed slightly. "Get down the flour, too. I can't reach it."

"Anya—"

"Not now, Jack. Later." She turned back to the stove. "Some cream in my coffee, please."

Obedience, Watcher.

He did as she asked, silently. When she had the potatoes boiling and the smell of frying chicken began to fill the air, she started to hum, only pausing to give soft orders.

"Shell, would you set the table? Forks on the right, remember. No—take the glasses one at a time. Jack, that bottle of wine Elise gave us—yes, a red, it needs to breathe." More humming. "One at a time, Shell, we don't have enough glasses to break."

By the time it was all done, she turned to Jack, pushing her hair back. He had to force himself to look away from the slight sheen of sweat on her neck. "Do you suppose you could take your coat off? Just to sit at the table?"

"Of course," he managed around the lump in his throat.

"Anya?"

"Hm? Oh, damn. The salt and pepper shakers. Can you?"

"I'll take them." He deftly snagged the wine bottle at the same time. "I only wanted to thank you."

"For what?" She waved a pair of tongs absently before she turned back to the stove. "Shell! Come on, I need you to carry the potatoes!"

Jack retreated. He brushed past Shell into the dining room and chose the seat with its back to the wall. He set down the salt and pepper shakers and the wine, then took a deep breath and shrugged out of his coat, hanging it carefully on the wooden chair. He thought for a moment, and decided to leave his rig on. It was bad manners, but he felt almost naked without his weapons.

He glanced up and saw his reflection against the darkness pressing against the dining room windows. The swordhilt poked up over his right shoulder, the knives rode easy in their sheaths, the guns at his hips. He saw the holes in his shirt—one under his left armpit, the other two low on his right side. His jeans were worn and old, and his hair looked more like a bird's nest than anything human.

It brought him back to the present with a jolt. Memory wasn't his friend, it would only distract him. No distractions were allowed.

His eyes glowed against the screen of dark glass, half-lidded silver coins, flat and deadly. He *was* ugly—and he was mean too.

I just hope I'm mean enough to keep her safe.

Twenty-Five

Shell poked and prodded at his food, but Anya was still too tired to scold him into eating. She was hungry, so hungry she finished everything on her plate and took seconds of fried chicken. "I'm still starving," she said finally, "but I can't eat another bite."

"It's the backlash." Jack ate slowly, often pausing and sending out those invisible waves of awareness. "Magick uses physical energy, and you need to replace that energy." He spoke slowly too, as if he had to pause and remember the words.

She wiped her lips with her napkin. "What about you? I hardly ever see you eat."

"The *tanak*. It lives on anger and pain. And the released Power, when I kill something Dark."

Maybe I shouldn't ask these questions. "Oh." She took a long drink of milk and put her glass down. "So you need to...kill?"

"No. It just feeds me. Without the Dark, I need more human food." His eyes flicked past her, checking the dining room. "I can live for a long time on very little. Any Watcher can."

She thought about this, stifling a yawn with the back of her hand. "Shell, are you done?"

His sleepy blue eyes met hers. "Want dessert."

She examined his plate. "But you didn't eat your potatoes. Or your broccoli."

"Don't feel good." Shell's mouth turned down. "Want dessert."

She pushed herself up. "I don't know, Shell." Her chair legs scraped the floor. "You'll have to help me clean the table."

He brightened. This was an old game; pleading for dessert and cleaning the dishes.

Anya paused, looking down at Jack, who was slowly unfolding himself from his chair. "You want some more coffee?"

"Sure." He gathered up his own plate, stacking silverware efficiently. "Let me take that."

"I can handle my own dishes. But you can bring the salt and the butter. And your glass."

Anya turned her back on him, ignoring the way Shell was sticking his tongue out. Her hands still trembled slightly and the headache threatened right behind her eyes. *It's a good thing*

I didn't drink any wine. I opened that bottle for nothing. "If magick makes you feel like this, what's the use?"

"Only the first few times. You have to learn to accommodate that much Power." He followed her into the kitchen. "It gets better. You're a Lightbringer, you're meant to carry it, cast those spells."

Shell dropped his dishes in the sink with a clatter. "Dessert!" he crowed.

Anya stopped, silverware chattering against the plate as her hands shook. *I just think you should be aware that he knows when he's hurting you.* She examined Shell, who moved his weight from foot to foot, his blond hair sticking up in every direction. He was big—and he hadn't really hurt her before Jack showed up. Not even in the middle of his fits. But in the car, and just before dinner, he had deliberately squeezed her hand too hard.

Is it true? Does he know that he hurts me?

It was a horrible thing to think.

"Dessert! Anya? Dessert?"

She approached him and put her dishes in the sink. "I don't know, Shell. You didn't eat your dinner."

He pouted. "Anya..." His eyes filled with tears. Big, shining crocodile tears. She'd dealt with enough juveniles to tell the difference. She shook the thought away. She didn't want to think that perhaps Shell could deliberately mislead her.

"Sit down. Over there." She pointed at the stool. He pouted, but he did it. Anya scraped the plates and loaded the dishwasher. Jack put everything else away and took care of the leftovers, stacking two bowls' worth efficiently in the fridge. He poured her another cup of coffee and gently pushed her aside when she had the sink full of soapy water. He put the coffee cup in her hands and started scrubbing the pans.

Anya stared, her jaw dropping. A big, tall, broad-shouldered, shaggy-haired man up to his elbows in soapsuds, his threadbare black T-shirt straining at his muscled back and the oiled leather straps holding his knives and guns and other little metal things resting against the cloth. *I don't think I would believe it if I wasn't seeing it right in front of me.* "You do dishes? My God, you're like the *perfect* man."

The smile he gave her was openly shocked and pleased at the same time. "Hardly."

Anya leaned against the cupboards, folding her hands

around the hot mug. "You brought me home last night, you took care of Shell this morning, and you do *dishes,* for God's sake." Anya was hard-pressed to stop a grin. *Is he blushing?* "Are you blushing?"

He shrugged. "I don't think so." The halting pauses eased out of his voice. He rinsed the pot she'd boiled the potatoes in and put it in the rack. She set her coffee aside, picked up a towel.

"I'll dry." She glanced over at Shell, who had wiped away the tears and was now watching her, his face slack and lifeless. Guilt pricked at her. "Don't worry, Shell. There's ice cream in the fridge. When we finish the dishes you can have some."

His face lit up. "Gee, Anya! Thanks. I been a good boy. I really been!"

"I know you have," she soothed, drying the pot and putting it away.

Jack, as if reading her mind, handed her the wrung-out dishcloth. She wiped the pale-blue counter near the stove, suddenly stopping to take a breath. *I haven't thought about running away, or felt something chasing us for weeks, now.*

A queer light happiness began under her breastbone—a happiness that was just as quickly doused by the memory of the soft voice on the phone.

Who was threatening her? And why?

I suppose the Persuasion would be worth a lot of money. If I wanted to rob banks, or do other nasty things. The thought caused a little shiver, her entire skin shrinking like a sweater in the dryer. Her head didn't hurt as much as it had, but suddenly each sound seemed painful. *But I wouldn't...I wouldn't do anything like that, ever.*

But if someone had no compunction about sending her blackmail notes and trying to frighten her, they would perhaps hurt her, try to make her use the Persuasion for bad ends. Her idea of just what "they" might do was hazy, but when she turned back to hand the rag to Jack, her eyes snagged on the black-wrapped swordhilt, the guns, and the knives.

"Jack?" She picked up the towel again and lifted the frying-pan he had just rinsed off.

"Hm?" He rinsed the vegetable steamer and set it in the rack with solicitous care.

"The people threatening me. What would they do to me, to make me do what they want?" She dried the frying-pan and hurriedly bent to put it away in the drawer underneath the new oven. She looked back up at Jack, sweeping her hair back from her face.

"Nothing," Jack said. "They won't get near you. I promise."

"But if they did. Just...what if?"

"They won't." His eyebrows drew together. "I'm here."

"Jack. Please."

He rinsed the rag, wrung it out, and started wiping down the other counters. Shell squirmed on the stool, eager for ice cream, but one warning look from Anya made him go still.

"If it's the Brotherhood, drugs and alchemical magick. If that doesn't work, more standard brainwashing techniques, starting with sleep deprivation and going through rape and torture as well as other more heavy-duty drugs. Freelance groups don't have the alchemical facilities, so they just go to the standard brainwashing techniques first." He rinsed the rag out again, wrung it out, and pulled the plug.

"Ice cream?" Shell asked tentatively. He squirmed on the stool again, making it creak.

Anya straightened. "Ice cream." Her voice was steady enough. *Brainwashing. Rape. Torture. Drugs.*

"They won't take you, Anya." Jack's hand curled around the edge of the counter. "I told you, I'm your Watcher."

"I know." She opened the freezer and took out the carton of mint chocolate chip ice cream, setting it on the freshly-wiped counter to soften. "I just wanted to know." *And now I do.* "Do you want some ice cream?"

"No, I'm going to check the street outside. It feels too quiet."

"Quiet's good." She shivered, hung the towel up, and regarded him. "Right?"

"It is. But not *too* quiet. Too quiet means someone's planning mischief."

Anya opened her mouth to ask what he thought *they* were planning and who exactly he thought *they* were, but the sound of the phone's shrill ring cut through the kitchen.

She jumped, letting out a thin cry.

Jack touched her shoulder. "Don't worry." He picked up the phone. He didn't say hello, just held the phone to his ear. A long pause. Then, "Sorry about that. She's right here." He handed it to her, mouthing *Theo*, and she held it to her ear with a trembling hand.

"H-hello?" Anya's voice trembled.

"Hi, sweetie." Theo's voice was deep and calm. "I know you're not feeling well, so I'll keep it short. I think I may have found a job for you. One of my patients knows the headmaster of a private school. The pay's good, and they need an English teacher. She'll recommend you."

Anya's heart actually leapt. "Really? That's...but how can I—"

"Did I mention the headmaster also owes Mari a favor? She took care of some not quite mundane problems he was having not too long ago, so he owes her. And I'm sure your Watcher can help. Just thought I'd give you the good news, sweets. Now, you rest up. I'll come by tomorrow to see how you're feeling." Theo sounded amused. "I think Elise and Mari will come too. We need to have a meeting and we can't do it without you."

"Why not?" Anya saw Jack getting the bowls down for ice cream. A brief flash of unreality unloosed her knees, and she leaned against the counter. "I mean, is it about the store?"

"No. We can't have it because you're our fourth, and a Guardian besides. And we have a few things we need to discuss."

Anya's stomach flipped. "Do you take in everyone like this?" *I didn't ask to be a guardian, whatever that is.* She remembered the silver flash last night, the feeling of something snapping around her, an extra layer of shielding. Her head hurt to think about it.

"Not everyone. But you're our fourth, Anya, and you're meant to be here. Last night proved that. Besides, Mari had one of her visions again. The four of us, in the park, working a collective magick. She says it was beautiful. Not only that, but Elise likes you very much—and that doesn't happen every day, let me assure you. She's an excellent and very tough judge of character, our firehair." Theo paused. "I think it speaks well of you that you wouldn't consider a job unless you could take care of Shell. You seem to have fit into our little group very well—almost as if you were *meant* to. And...well, it appears you have Suzanne's approval too."

A chill touched the back of Anya's neck. "I thought she was—"

"She's only dead. Not gone." Theo's smile was audible. "Go to bed, you shouldn't even be up. That's healer's orders."

"Yes, ma'am." Anya heard herself, sounding confident and light. *Is that me?* "I'll be going back to bed right after dessert."

"Mh. Can't miss dessert. See you tomorrow." Theo hung up.

"I suppose so." Anya hung up. She looked at Jack, who had pried the lid off the ice cream and was looking for a spoon to scoop it with. Then she stared at the phone as if it might bite her, hugging herself.

"What is it?" Jack asked, frowning slightly as he hunted for a spoon.

"Try the drawer next to the stove." She looked up at him. "Jack?"

"Hm?"

"Theo says I'm one of their group now. A Guardian."

He shrugged, the swordhilt moving. "It seems you are."

"I was *brought* here."

"Maybe."

"By...the gods. Their gods." *They believe in gods, don't they? They don't say much about it, but they believe.*

"Or yours. You want some?" He indicated the ice cream, his eyes not quite meeting hers.

"I never believed much in God." She looked at the window over the sink, night pressing against the glass. "But I suppose if I can believe in big, burning, razor-toothed things that want to eat me, God isn't so much of a stretch."

"*I* want some ice cream," Shell announced. "Are we gonna go see Theo? I miss Elise. Wanta go to work."

"Tomorrow Elise will come to visit us." Anya rubbed at her forehead gently, the headache threatening to come back. "Theo says she might have found a job for me at a private school."

"That's good news." Jack had filled a bowl for Shell and gave him a spoon. "Here you are, Shell."

Shell took it, gave Jack a glare—only slightly mollified by the prospect of dessert—and dug in. Anya cupped her elbows in her hands, hugging herself even harder. She watched Jack's ghostly reflection put the ice cream away in the fridge, a brief slice of cold light illuminating him. Then he dried the rest of the pans and put them away, moving quietly and efficiently, no motion wasted. Finally, he leaned against the counter, surveying the kitchen with a satisfied air.

She saw him turn to look at her, his gray eyes reflecting bright in the glass. "I should go check everything. With your permission, Anya?"

Her heart gave a sudden leap and fell crashing back into her chest. "Um," she said. "I don't think anything's out there, Jack. I really don't."

He shrugged again. "I should go anyway, just to be sure."

She turned to face him, her hair swinging out as she almost banged her hip on a drawer pull. "I want you to please stay in tonight." Her throat threatened to close on the words. "If you don't mind."

Elise or Theo would have made that sound better. Even Mari would have known how to say that. He's going to think I'm a nincompoop.

After a long, measured pause, he nodded. "Of course. If you like."

What? She hadn't expected simple compliance. "Oh. Um—okay."

"I'm going to go get my coat. Did Theo say anything else?"

She glanced at Shell, who was taking huge mouthfuls of mint chocolate chip ice cream. "Just that I should go back to bed. She thinks I need more sleep. I've slept all day, though."

He looked suddenly thoughtful. "Do you feel sleepy?"

She did. She still felt exhausted and still hungry, though her stomach felt full and slightly uncomfortable. "Not too much," she lied. "I want to talk to you, after I put Shell to bed."

"Whatever you want." His eyes moved over her face, and she had the odd idea he was agreeing to more than staying inside. He watched her so closely she could almost feel a physical pressure from his gaze against her skin, and his red-black aura touched the very edges of hers. Heat rose to her cheeks again.

"You really mean that, don't you."

"I'm done." Shell rattled his spoon against his bowl. "I want a story. Story, Anya!"

She glanced at him. "Go and brush your teeth and wash your face. You need to start saying please, Shell. You're not being very nice."

He pouted, knocking over the stool as he slid down, landing heavily on his feet. He stamped out of the kitchen and blundered up the stairs. Anya sighed, her shoulders rising under the familiar weight.

Jack said nothing, but the silence was suddenly hard and tense.

"It's hard on him when his routine changes," she said, wishing she didn't feel as if she was defending Shell to a hostile audience. "He doesn't understand."

"He's jealous. Wants you all to himself." Jack's eyes hadn't moved from her face. "I can't blame him."

"Weren't you going to go get your coat?" She sounded breathless even to herself.

He nodded, his eyes not leaving hers. "I was, wasn't I."

"You were." *I sound like an idiot. But he's staring at me. Why is he staring at me?* "Jack, I'm not like Theo. I'm...I've done things—used the Persuasion. I'm not innocent. Those people, whoever they are—they might even hurt the others, and it will be all my fault."

"They have Watchers too, Anya. I wouldn't worry too much about them." Jack took a couple of steps back, gracefully avoiding the breakfast bar. Then he turned and stalked into the dining room.

Anya let out a soft breath, looking at the kitchen window. Darkness stroked the glass. She could see part of the back yard lit by a fluorescent light with a motion detector. The wooden back fence was six feet tall, strong and new, and the gates were locked with padlocks.

Anya leaned against the counter, staring out the window. She was so absorbed in her own thoughts she almost missed the movement.

Almost.

Anya gasped. Something low and black, red eyes flashing for a moment, streaked for the back fence. It leapt and caught the top of the fence with clawed hands made of black paper.

She backed up a step. *I didn't feel a thing. Why didn't I feel that? Whatever it is, it's quick.* Her breath came short and harsh. *If it comes back I have to get Shell out of here.*

She heard Jack's soundless step. He barely paused to open the back door, moving so quickly he blurred. The door shut itself with a bang and locked behind him, the house shields quivering.

"Jack!" For a moment Anya considered going to the door and throwing it open. Then she realized that the thing—whatever it was—had been running through the back yard at a slight angle. It had probably muscled itself over the gate at the side of the house, and Jack was chasing it.

As soon as she thought it, the phone began to shrill again.

Anya, her hands cold, picked it up mechanically. She copied Jack, though—she simply lifted it to her ear, not saying "hello."

A burst of static gave birth to a feedback squeal. Then the soft, evil voice teased at her again. "Anya." A pause. "Come to us, and we'll leave your friends alone. They don't ever have to know. We just want to talk to you, Anya, make you an offer. That's all. Come to the Wescorp building downtown, the corner of First and Aventine. Go inside and tell—"

"What if I don't?" Anya whispered.

"Then we'll tell your new friends, and the police, what kind of a thief you are." The voice laughed. "I'll see you tomorrow."

"You can't—" she began, but the line went dead.

Anya laid the phone gingerly back down. "Great," she whispered. "Just great."

Twenty-Six

She was waiting when Jack came back, the entire house quiet and serene. Anya sat on the stairs, her arms wrapped around her knees, the ringing silence telling him she'd put the boy to bed.

"Anya? It was only a stray *thuryik*, nothing big. I drove it—Anya?" He took one look at the tension in her shoulders and the way her hands shook slightly. A curse rose in his throat and was savagely repressed. "A diversion. What was it, *piccola*? Another phone call?"

Her face was pale, her gray eyes huge. She nodded. "They want me to come to a building tomorrow. Just to talk."

"If you were a frightened witch without a Watcher you might, and they could pick you up neatly." Fury settled under his breastbone. "This looks like the Brotherhood. Other groups aren't this finicky. They think they can simply—" His jaw worked for a moment, then clenched shut. He was going to say something truly filthy if he kept talking, and not in English, either.

"I think I should go," she said quietly. "He said they just want to make me an offer. Maybe if I listen to them they'll go away."

What? For a moment he thought his ears were playing tricks on him. "Anya." He couldn't even begin to tell her how foolish that was. "These people are *not* going to just go away. They will keep trying to acquire you until it's too expensive for them to continue. They will not go away because you ask politely. They will only leave you in peace when a cost-benefit analysis tells them you're too dear to be bought."

She held up a hand.

Jack's mouth snapped shut. *She's a Lightbringer,* he reminded himself. *Duty, honor, obedience. You're misbehaving. Cool and quiet, Jack. Be still.*

His entire body went cold at the thought of Anya walking unprotected into a Brotherhood trap.

"If I go and explain to them that I'm with you and don't want to work for them, they might leave me alone. It would be a better way to solve the problem than all this fighting."

He wasn't sure whether he should feel like celebrating because she had implied her acceptance of him or cursing because she was evidently determined to risk her life negotiating

with the Brotherhood instead of listening to him. He settled for
a deep breath, his hands in his pockets, and a short nod.

"And," she continued, "I want you to watch Shell while I
go tomorrow."

"No." One short, clipped word. All the sworn obedience in
the world couldn't make him agree to that.

"Jack, I wish you'd listen."

"No."

"But I need you to—"

"*No*, Anya. I'm your Watcher, not his. I cannot and *will* not
let you go alone into what is almost certainly a trap." His neck
began to feel as if iron rods were being rammed down his spine,
and his bones started to twist with pain, reacting to the thought
of her in danger. He took a deep breath, seeking to calm himself,
a soft voice in his head that sounded suspiciously like hers trying
to tell him to be quiet.

"I could use the Persuasion on you." Her eyes were
luminous and terribly sad.

"That would be foolish," he told her through gritted teeth.
The air began to warm up, the Dark symbiote bleeding heat
through his aura, and his voice made the stairs groan slightly.
"And you are not a fool."

Oddly enough, that made her smile, as if pleased. That small
smile eased his neck. He took two steps forward and sank to
one knee, daring to reach forward and take one of her hands in
both of his. Her skin was cool and smooth, full of light that
eased his pounding pulse and aching muscles.

"Don't do this, Anya. Please. They're liars. Whoever they
are, they've already blackmailed you, and they probably think
I don't know about it. They're counting on you being scared
and silly, not prepared."

"If you're with me, I don't have anything to worry about,
do I?"

His heart thudded against his ribs even harder. *She'll let
me stay. I'm almost sure she'll let me stay with her. But I told
her—and they told her, too, told her what I did. Who I was.*

To be absolutely fair, though, he hadn't told her everything.
He'd only told her as much as seemed necessary. She obviously
didn't understand the full implications. It would give him a
little time, at least, until she found out the rest.

"I won't let anything harm you," he promised. "But if you
go straight into their trap—who knows what they have planned?
They might not be able to kill me, but they could hurt me and

try to take you. Please, Anya. Don't do this."

"But..." She sucked her cheeks in thoughtfully, her mouth puckering, obviously rethinking the whole thing.

Good. Don't do it, Anya. It's not safe. It is not safe at all. His thumb slid over her knuckles, the feel of her skin blurring up his arm and spilling through his bones. He searched for calm, for a soft tone to convince her. "Besides, if they only wanted to make you an offer, they could have come to the Rowangrove. Or sent you a letter instead of a threat. Yes?"

She nodded, her hair falling forward, a glossy sheaf of clean darkness.

"If they only wanted to make you an offer, they wouldn't threaten to go to the police and leave Shell without anyone to look after him."

That was her vulnerable spot, and he felt a sharp pinch of guilt for using it. Her free hand clasped around his. The wash of spiked pleasure through his veins made his eyes half close and his lungs cry out for air. He'd stopped breathing.

She nodded, once, very slowly. "And if they wanted my help, they wouldn't tell me bad things about you, would they? Unless they wanted to make me afraid of you."

He looked down at her hand covering his. Fine-boned, pale, long, tapering graceful fingers, her nails bitten down almost to the quick, a smudge of grease just under her thumb from cooking. His hands were larger, scarred and callused, his skin a different tone, darker and rougher, his fingers blunt and indelicate.

"I hunted witches for years." *I'm about to tell her the truth,* he realized dully, hopelessness already starting to twist at his chest. He had to fight for the breath to continue. "My father, the Gray Cardinal, used me as an example to Lupus Dei. I was the first true Knight of the Order because I was his creature entirely. I would have done anything to please him. He gave me the undead Knights and later the Seekers to control, and sent me out to kill." His voice dropped. "I knew no better, Anya. You have to understand, I did not know. I was so young. And all I heard from the Church—the *Church*, the sole arbiter of right and wrong—was that these women were evil, were witches, *maleficia.* I grew skilled, and I grew cold, then I stopped caring. I killed without mercy or remorse."

"You don't have to." Her voice sounded oddly strained. *Is she disgusted? Of course she is. Who wouldn't be?*

Jack pressed on. "I fought a Watcher. The last one I ever

murdered. He gave his life to protect a woman, and with his last breath he cursed me. But she—the Lightbringer—she knelt down by the body of the Watcher and looked up at me. She told me she forgave me, and the Seekers came and..." A dry, hoarse sound barked out of his throat, too harsh to be a sob. *The blood smelled of iron, and I was secure in my love of God. I felt nothing but contempt until it was too late, until I saw what I had done and I begged God to kill me. He did not listen, He never listened.* "I could not comprehend how a *maleficia* of Satan could exhibit such forgiveness, forgiveness the Church would say was Christian. And for the first time, I saw the Light inside her. I destroyed the Seekers and returned the undead Knights to their rest. Then I went in search of answers."

His head dropped even further, and he stared at her bare toes. Anya was utterly still, listening. He would have liked the feeling of her complete attention, if he hadn't been telling her his shame.

It was too late now. The words spilled out, tripping over each other, his accent wearing through. How long had he been wanting to tell someone, miserably impelled to scratch the itch of confession?

"The Watchers wished to kill me, and I could not blame them. But the Grand Council is made of Lightbringers, and they told the Watchers I was to be given a chance to earn redemption. The Watchers did not believe it, but they obeyed." A bitter half-laugh tore at his throat. "I saw true obedience among them. And true forgiveness—the Lightbringers never uttered a word of reproach, though I'd killed so many of them. The Watchers—gods alone know how many of them I condemned to despair, killing the Lightbringers as I did. Every time I see a Watcher without a witch, I think perhaps I am the one responsible, and the pain..." His voice broke.

Anya's free hand left his. He waited for her to pull away, waited for her shock and disgust.

She stroked his hair, her fingers light. Silence stretched down the hall. The furnace clicked on, and warm air soughed through the house.

"When they tell you to be frightened of me, it is for good reason," he admitted painfully. "I do not deserve to be near you. I do not even deserve to know you *exist.*"

I have never deserved it. I fight the Circle's battles and I atone, but it is never enough.

When she spoke, it was almost too softly to be heard. "You

didn't know. You didn't know any better. Just like Shell."

The thought that she might pity him made a fierce flush of rage rise up his backbone, but he set his jaw and shoved it down. Pity was better than anger, and if she felt sorry for him she might let him stay.

"Anya..." *There is nothing I would not give to take it back. I wished I'd never heard of Lupus Dei. I wish I had not been born to be such a blight on the world.*

But if I had not, I wouldn't be here now, able to protect you. Dear gods. Is it worth it?

"What did you think I'd do when you told me?" She stroked his hair, her fingers infinitely gentle. "Did you think I'd tell you to go away? You didn't know, Jack. You *didn't know.*"

"I enjoyed it," he whispered, watching her feet. "I murdered them with joy. I consigned them to the flames with a heart full of happiness, I thought I served God and made my father happy." *Even though I was only a bastard son,* he finished silently, seeing again his father's tomb. He had gone back once as a Watcher, and hadn't had the heart to destroy the marble edifice.

But oh, he had been tempted. And each year folding into the next did not make the memories any easier to bear.

"Well." Her soft fingers trailed down his cheek, slid under his chin. She tilted his chin up. Jack had no choice but to let her. She still had dark circles under her beautiful eyes, and her pretty mouth was drawn down at the corners. "I judge people on what they've done to *me,* Jack. Not what they may or may not have done to someone else. And you've...I mean, I bet it never even crossed your mind to use some of the money from Circle Lightfall for yourself, did it?"

Stunned, he shook his head slightly. He wondered why she was even asking. The double blow of her touch on his chin and her hand in both of his made it impossible for him to pay attention. "No, of course not."

"You haven't been anything but gentle with me—and with Shell, even though he's treated you awfully." She smiled, her eyes lighting up. "What, you thought I didn't notice? Just because I don't say anything doesn't mean I don't notice."

"Anya—"

"When I found Shell, he was living in alleys and eating out of garbage cans. He'd been thrown out of the halfway house he was living in because of budget cuts. And without his medication, he would have fits. He'd hurt a few people, and would have gone to jail if I hadn't taken him in."

Oh, gods. How can I make you understand? He tried again, turning the words over in his head to make them as clear as possible. "You aren't listening. I *killed* them, Anya. Women just like you. I murdered them with no provocation on their part. I hunted them like animals." The guilt weighed the words down, crushed them in his throat. *I gave them to the flames, or I let the Seekers take them, or I killed them with my bare hands. I enjoyed it. I loved my work.*

Anya's sigh brushed the air with gold. "Would you feel better if I hated you?" She ran her finger down his cheek. The touch soothed him, and he would have enjoyed it if the poison hadn't been eating into his heart. "You told me the order—Lupus Dei—was created in the 1500s."

"In the year of our Lord 1491, Innocent signed the bull—extending an earlier papal decree—that gave the Crusade its orders," he recited mechanically, seeing the parchment and the lead seal as if it were yesterday. The smell of incense, blood, and sour excitement rose in his memory. "Circle Lightfall was created in 1532 in response. Givelli received approval for Lupuis Dei in 1533."

"You..." She swallowed, closed her eyes briefly. "I suppose if I can believe in big black toothy things that want to eat me, and if I can believe in magick, and Elise lighting candles with a look, and Theo being able to heal someone just by *thinking* about it, that isn't so much of a stretch. No wonder you're so strange." She paused, but he said nothing. "So...you're a little older than I thought."

Older than you think, piccolo. Older than you know. Just like I'm a little taller, and a little more lethal. "It's the symbiote. It gives a Watcher near-immortality—until the Watcher finds his witch." *This isn't at all how I expected you to react.* "Anya..."

"Just give me a second." She took a deep breath. "I usually don't date older men," she muttered, before she opened her eyes and grinned at him.

The smile threatened to knock him over backward. "Um." This wasn't at *all* how he'd expected this to go. "Anya." He couldn't find any other words.

"What was it like?" Her fingers rested on his cheek. "I mean, back then? You must have seen a lot of history."

You don't want to know. It was a cavalcade of brutality, not to mention filth. His nose wrinkled. "It smelled worse than nowadays. Much worse."

"Really?" She looked interested, her eyes lighting up and her mouth softening.

"The food wasn't all that good, either. I try not to think on it, Anya. I'm one of the oldest Watchers; all the others I knew are either dead or bonded. The new ones don't know what I was—or if they do, they don't show it. I wanted to tell you, but—"

"You must have seen so many things." Curiosity sparkled in her eyes, and she regarded him with actual interest, leaning forward, all the attention he had ever wanted in the world fastened on him.

Has she heard a single word I've said? I'm a murderer, and a sinner, condemned to Hell. "I've been too occupied doing my job." He didn't mean for it to sound harsh, but her face fell. "I wanted to tell you. I couldn't."

She nodded, her beautiful hair sweeping forward. "I understand. No, really, I do. I *stole*, Jack. I'm not proud of it, but I had to. You aren't proud of what you did, but I think I understand why you did it."

Frustration rose inside him again, sharply checked. "I don't think you understand." The thought that she could compare the two of them made him feel slightly sick. She was guilty of nothing more than trying to survive, while he was guilty of a reign of terror and genocide, and all the penance he'd done hadn't eased his conscience one iota.

"Shhh." Her fingers cupped his chin and she leaned forward, her hair brushing his cheek. She kissed his forehead gently. Jack closed his eyes, a sigh forcing its way out through his lips, the never-ending harsh tension trained into his body relaxing for the first time in years. "Come with me."

He automatically rose to his feet, steadying her as she stood. "Ouch." She rubbed at her hip. "I like hardwood floors, but they hurt. Come on. I know what to do."

She led him down the hall and into the kitchen, not letting go of his hand as she reached up to get a glass from the cupboard. "I just read about this in one of Theo's books. It's so bizarre, all of this stuff. I feel as if there's been a curtain over the world that I just pulled back, and now I'm seeing everything for real for the first time."

She turned the tap on, filled the glass, and turned away from the sink, leading him almost absently. Her touch had settled into a warm glow spreading through his entire body, a deep honey haze.

He could find nothing to say.

She led him into the dark living room, empty except for two scavenged bookshelves, the couch he'd had delivered, and a set of blue beanbag chairs from Mari. The gas fireplace was empty and cold, the walls blank. "Anya." It was the only breathless protest he could find the wherewithal to utter.

"Shhh. Kneel down—there." She indicated the spot with the glass of water, and he moved to obey, reluctantly sliding his fingers free of hers. "Now just be still." She set the glass down and closed her eyes. She took a deep breath, and Power started to stir.

"Anya, you should—" If she cast a spell now, she could suffer further backlash.

She shook a warning finger at him, and he swallowed the rest of his protest. *What is she doing? I just told her the worst thing a Watcher can tell a witch. What is she going to do?*

Her lips moved silently, and he smelled jasmine and amber incense. Air stirred against his cheek. The Dark in him woke, growling and watchful in his bones. The clear amber light of her Power rose, sketching a circle inside the room.

You should not do this. Don't waste your magick on me. "Anya, don't. You don't have to."

Her concentration didn't waver.

Anya's eyes opened, and she picked up the glass of water. "*Lustrus,*" she whispered, and gold sparks fell from her delicate fingers into the water. A high, humming note of Power rang through the room, rebounding from the circle of golden light, concentrating in the water. Liquid sunshine strengthened, swirling inside the glass.

She dipped her fingers in the water, bent over him. "*Aedirus chaerae lustrate.*" She touched his forehead with wet fingertips. Power flushed along Jack's skin.

What is she doing? It didn't hurt, but it snapped his nerves taut and slid below the surface of his mind, a clear golden glow.

"In the name of the Lady, I declare you free." Her voice took on a weight of blurring Power. There was something else, too—the silvery light of a Guardian, feeding her from the city's well of energy.

Gods above, she's grown stronger. How is that possible? Her aura was pure incandescent light, a fine network of silver threading through. He looked again, squinting against the brightness, and saw the same silver that accentuated the other three Lightbringers. *She is a Guardian. How? She wasn't here when they cast the initial spell—she's only been in Circle with them once!* The sleeve of Power around him tightened, his breath squeezed out by the sudden stricture. His bones creaked under the pressure, a python's hug.

"Lustrae dominum aeternus Aphroditum cheridum," she breathed, Power rilling through the air sliding chill down Jack's back. His coat crackled, and his own aura compressed close to his skin.

Then she tilted her hand and dumped the entire glass over him.

Jack let out a short surprised yell but stayed where he was. The yellow light faded, the high sustained note of power draining into the ground. The scent of jasmine remained, overwhelming for a few seconds, then fading to a light perfume. The pressure vanished, his ribs flaring as he finally breathed.

Anya sank down to kneel in front of him, her eyes luminous. She set the empty, singing glass aside. "That's a purification ritual. A baptism."

Cold water trickled down his neck. He reached out, his fingertips touching her shoulders. She swayed slightly. "A baptism?" His heart felt strangely light, the familiar song of unconscious pain leaving him for the first time in years. Decades.

He thought he was suffering a cardiac arrest for a few seconds until he realized his pulse was still treading away in his chest—but the gaping, tearing pain of grief and guilt behind the steady beat had eased.

"Usually the person receiving the baptism takes a new name." She blinked. A wide, disbelieving smile spread over her face. "There's so much light...You know, that was my real first spell."

Her first solo spell, especially while she was suffering from backlash, cast for him.

For a murderous wreck of a Watcher.

"Thank you," he managed around the lump in his throat. His hair stuck to his head and water dripped on the floor. The thought that she had cast her very first spell for him—and done it while she was still sick with pain—made his heart feel even stranger. Light, and beating so quickly he was almost afraid it might explode. Cold water sank into the knee of his jeans.

Her disbelieving smile widened. "Elise is right, it *is* better than chocolate." She reached up, leaning forward, and touched his face again, running her fingers lightly down his cheeks, her thumb brushing his mouth. "Do you still want to be Jack Gray? You don't have to be."

"I don't care." He wondered why his eyes were burning with salt water. He hadn't cried since the last Lightbringer he'd killed had forgiven him. He had never thought he might have tears left. "Call me whatever you want."

His hands slid free of her shoulders as she leaned forward. *Is she going to pass out? She's probably going to go deeper into backlash, I should have stopped her.*

As if he could have.

"Hm." Her hands cupped his face. His stubble scraped at her softer skin, and he frantically tried to think of what he was going to do if she fell and he had to catch her.

Her mouth met his.

He took a deep breath flavored with her, their lips and tongues dancing to an old rhythm. Fire slid down his skin, worked into his bones, and he sank into a golden haze. When he surfaced again, he had her in his arms. Her hands had somehow worked another magic and found their way under his shirt. Her skin scorched him, leaving trails of sweet fire behind. He gasped and tried to think.

"Upstairs," she said, and he made it to his feet.

She tripped, and he held her steady, blinking. When they reached the stairs, she halted, turned while she stood on the third stair, and kissed him again. Jack's entire body began to burn.

"Anya. Wait."

"What? I don't think I want to." She kissed his cheek, the corner of his mouth. The smell of jasmine wrapped around him.

"I've...I mean, I never...um—"

She laughed, a sweet throaty sound. "I know. You were a priest, right?"

"Um...Anya, I—" He suddenly couldn't think well enough to finish even half a sentence. He sounded like an idiot.

"Don't worry," she whispered. "I think instinct takes over at a certain point. Come with me." She kissed him again, deeply, her hands cupping his nape and holding him steady. "Unless you don't want to."

He closed his eyes. *I should be checking the perimeter.*

The fading voice of responsibility and duty was drowned out by the swell of sensation. "I don't deserve you," he muttered into her hair.

Thank you, gods. A coherent sentence, in English even. It's a miracle.

"You're a new person now," she said. "Reborn."

He felt it, too, the crushing weight of guilt slid free of his shoulders, the black shame draining away. She had such incredible power. If this was what bonding with a Lightbringer felt like, no wonder the Watchers fought so hard.

No wonder they had *always* fought so hard.

Then her mouth met his again and he was lost, his hands sliding under her sweater, feeling her softness, the light from her aura blazing inside his head. She led him up the stairs, laughing in a low husky tone when he almost tripped. When they reached the door to her room, she reached up and pushed at his coat, trying to slide it free of his shoulders. He helped her, his fingers suddenly clumsy. She kicked the door shut behind them, and he dropped the bulky leather beside her bed, metal clanking and shifting as its weight settled.

Then she pulled him down, her fingers working on the button of his jeans. He pushed her sweater up and found the glorious arches of her ribs, the supple shallow channel of her spine, and the round slopes of her breasts.

"Anya," he whispered against her neck, tasting salt and incense and jasmine. He said it into her hair and her fingers as she brushed them against his lips. When they finally tangled free of their clothing and she slid into his arms, it was a relief. He could think of nothing else.

She was right—at a certain point instinct *did* take over.

***

Anya slept in his arms.

Jack ran his fingers—delicately, so very gently—over the curve of her shoulder. She was exhausted, a sweet flush on her cheeks, breathing deeply and silently, her head on his shoulder. He didn't even mind the painful tingle of nerve-compression running down to his fingers.

What was his arm going to sleep when his entire body hummed with pleasant, languorous voltage, the aftermath of blinding pleasure? Less than nothing.

I don't deserve this. The thought was wondering, reverent instead of weighted with black guilt. *I don't deserve her. I have not paid nearly enough for what I did.*

It was sheer mercy. The biggest trait of the Lightbringers— forgiveness. Why hadn't the gods made all of humanity this way?

Her aura, with the deep peculiar motionlessness that meant

sleep, relaxed into a pool of golden light fringed at the edges with red-black—his own aura, drawn protectively close. All was as it should be. Watcher wards hummed in the walls. Outside, the night was hushed and tranquil. The world held its breath, Anya's spell still working in the air, a spreading ripple of calm and peace threading through the neighborhood and beyond.

She had such incredible power.

The blurring pleasure of her skin against his had turned to a sated glow, soothing every nerve with a weight of honey. Jack shut his eyes, waiting for the reflexive bite of guilt. He was profaning this silence and harmony, even as he was helpless to stop touching, his hand moving unbidden in a caress up her shoulder, the tender hollow of her throat, the silk of her hair.

Guilt came, but it was *different*. He shifted a little, restlessly, and froze as Anya murmured in her sleep. A faint sound of dreaming irritation escaped her lips. She turned away, trapping his arm under her head as she presented her back to him, pulling instinctively on the covers. The house creaked and ticked to itself as she settled back into slumber, and Jack held his breath, cooler air touching his knee where the blankets had been pulled away.

Her window was dark, a sliver of night peeking between the curtains, pressing soft against the glass.

Night, and Dark. He should slide his arm from under her head and get up, get dressed, and go out into the cold. Make *certain* there was nothing hiding in her neighborhood, make absolutely sure no danger was present. It was his duty to slide free of the bed's warmth and patrol the neighborhood. She wouldn't know he was gone.

Hello? he asked the silence inside himself in every language he knew, squeezing his eyes shut until tracers of green and gold flashed under the lids. *Who are you now?*

The answer was stupidly simple. He was Anya's Watcher. He didn't need another name. Whatever she called him, he'd answer to.

He lay in the dark, listening to her quiet breathing, and struggled with himself.

I know what I should do. But gods help me, what I want to do is wake her up and kiss her again.

And not just kiss her. There was a whole world of things he wanted to explore. All of them involved waking up his witch, and plenty of them involved a few fascinating things he hadn't had nearly enough time to do to her.

Well, for the oldest virgin in the world, I think I acquitted myself well. Then again, she's easy to worship. The unfamiliar smile stretched his mouth, and he felt the corners of his eyes crinkling. *It was worth the wait. No wonder the Church calls it a sin. Something like this could make a man stupid. Or less easy to control.*

Much less easy to control.

Anya made another sleepy, irritated sound. Jack curled over onto his side and gathered her into his arms. The mutter turned into air blown through pursed lips, and she relaxed into total boneless sleep, soothed.

It's a miracle. She's *a miracle.*

He buried his face in her mussed hair and inhaled, drawing her down to the bottom of his lungs.

She smelled like home. *His* home.

All the struggling and the penance boiled down to this— here was his witch. He didn't deserve her, true, but that didn't change his responsibility. He was here to protect her, the last line of defense between his witch and the Dark. The black weight of guilt was an indulgence he could no longer afford— her spell had relieved it, to be sure, but he could so very easily turn to torturing himself again.

If he did, it might make him just a fraction less effective. If he was busy brooding over the past, he might make a fatal mistake.

His hand slid down her arm, touched the fragile arches of her ribs, the roundness of her hip. She was so soft, so utterly vulnerable.

A new penance, then. One that balanced everything out, one that might save even a soul as blackened as his.

Penance isn't supposed to feel this good.

The Church had been wrong about everything else. It wasn't too hard to believe they might be wrong about atonement, too. Jack's arms tightened, pulling her closer, and he pulled up the blankets, smoothing the sheet and tucking them both in more securely. He ran warm, a Watcher's metabolism burning fiercely to provide enhanced musculature with strength, but he wanted to be certain she wouldn't be cold.

His conscience gave a sharp twinge. *I should go outside.*

There was nothing out there. The world had stopped. If Dark drifted near her house, he'd go out and fight it off. For right now, he was going to selfishly snatch whatever comfort he could, and keep her in his arms as long as possible.

Morning would come soon enough. Jack relaxed, muscles kept constantly locked in singing alertness loosening, his breathing deepening. If he wanted to, he could slide over the border into the waking trance, or even—maybe—true sleep, human sleep, helped by pleasant exhaustion and the cessation of pain.

I don't want to. I don't want to miss any of this. His lips moved, and after a moment of thought he realized he was— was he?

Actually *praying.*

Gods, whatever God there is, don't let anything happen to her.

Still, gods could only do so much. It was up to a Watcher to make sure, something drilled into every trainee's head from the beginning. Luck, chance, fate, gods, it didn't matter. It was the Watcher's job to do whatever was necessary, whatever it took.

"Anya," he whispered into her hair. "I promise. Whatever it takes."

She made no reply, sleeping the deep dreamless sleep of an innocent. A necessary sleep; she was exhausted. He shifted slightly, wondering if he was going to make up for so much time spent celibate by embarrassing himself.

Down, boy. Let her sleep. She needs it.

The unfamiliar, unwilling smile still lingered around his mouth as Jack tipped over the edge into soft blackness, one small corner of his mind dozing watchfully, ready to wake if any threat presented itself. His breathing deepened, his shoulders relaxed, and for the first time in his life as a Watcher, Jack Gray slept without nightmares.

Twenty-Seven

"Anya?" Shell whispered. A cold wet hand shook her shoulder.

She groaned, Jack's arm tightening around her. It was warm, and comforting, and safe where she was, and she didn't want to wake up.

"Anya!"

Swimming up through dark water. Her head hurt. Not as badly as it had yesterday, but badly enough. "Whaaa'?" She couldn't finish the word.

"Shell." Jack sounded fully awake, his voice clear and cold. "What's going on?"

"The bad things," Shell whispered. "Outside. The phone was ringing."

"Did you answer the phone?" Jack moved, sitting up, his arm sliding from under Anya's head with infinite gentleness. He stroked her hair back from her face, his callused fingers scraping slightly.

"It sounded like the funny radio." Shell's breath whistled through his nose. "And I feel funny."

Anya pushed herself up on her elbows, holding the sheet to her chest. "Jack?" She was still warm from sleep, but a cool bath of dread slid down her back. "What's wrong?"

Jack said something quiet and low. It sounded like a curse. Something clanked, and he levered himself up off the bed. Leather creaked, his coat moving. A breeze smelling of leather and spice touched her cheek. The room was dark, but she could see the ghost of his movements and a faint slice of gray around the edges of the curtains.

She began to wake up.

"You heard the phone?" Anya asked. "Shell, you know you're not supposed to answer the phone."

"It was ringing and ringing. It woked me up."

I was busy sleeping, wasn't I. God knows I wore myself out last night. Anya's entire body glowed. *What's wrong? Something's not right here.*

"I don't feel anything," she whispered, her eyes instinctively turning Jack's direction. He was a tall blot of shadow with luminous eyes. She heard the sound of movement.

"Neither do I. Best to be safe, though. Stay here." Jack

leaned down and kissed her forehead. Anya tangled her fingers in his hair, pulled his mouth to hers and kissed him properly. She was breathing heavily when he finally broke free, and he murmured something she didn't catch, though she suspected it wasn't in English. The meaning was clear enough. *Hold that thought.*

She laughed, and he disappeared. A single stair creaked under him, the front door opened and shut quietly, and she felt him testing the house shields, his attention lingering briefly on her like a caress.

Yum. She sighed and reached over and flicked the bedside lamp on. "Shell."

He blinked at her, sweat standing out on his cheeks. His heavy-lidded eyes were dark and his hair stood up in wild spikes.

His lower lip pooched out. "*He* was in here." It was obvious who he meant.

"He was," Anya agreed. "You answered the phone? Why did you do that?"

"It rang and rang. Then it sounded like the funny radio."

He means static. The dread intensified, prickling gooseflesh up her arms. "Did they say anything?" She was suddenly breathless, as if her lungs had deflated.

Shell looked down, his hands dangling loosely by his sides. He shifted from foot to foot. "Why was *he* in here, Anya?"

Kid, you don't want to know. And I don't want to tell you. It's private. She took a deep breath. "Because I like him, Shell. Don't you? He's kept the bad things away."

"He's mean." Shell's lip pooched out even further. "I don't like him. I wanta go."

"We can't go, buddy." Anya pushed herself up and sat cross-legged, wrapping the sheet and blanket around her. She yawned and pushed a hand back through her tangled hair. She couldn't seem to wipe the smile off her face. "We don't have anywhere left to go. That's why we ended up here."

"We always went before." Shell pouted.

"I had money before, Shell, and a job." She yawned again. "Have you taken your shower yet?"

Best to get him into his normal routine, maybe. I didn't hear the phone ring. I must have been tired. Her head still felt tender, but not nearly as painful as it had been. Her thighs felt sticky, but her entire body glowed. *Jack can't have been a priest. He knows entirely too much about how to use that mouth of his.*

Then again, a few hundred years might teach a man something. Maybe it's the Italian, every girl likes tall dark and handsome with an accent. Though it didn't sound like any Italian I've ever heard, especially with his mouth full.

She returned to herself with a shake, looking up at Shell.

He pouted even further, sticking his lip out and getting the stubborn line between his eyebrows that meant trouble. "Don't wanna take a shower. I wanna *go*, Anya."

I don't feel anything out there. Maybe there is nothing out there.

She examined Shell, her eyes narrowing. "We can't go, buddy. Besides, Theo says she might have a job for me here. You like Theo, don't you? And Elise?"

His face softened a bit. "Nice ladies," he said hopefully. Anya mentally scolded herself for suspecting him. "I like Theo."

"I do too, buddy. You're going to have to get along with Jack somehow. He's staying." She said it firmly enough that Shell dropped his head, looking at his toes. "Do you want to go back to bed? Or are you awake? Do you want to take your shower and have some breakfast?"

He shrugged. "Back ta bed."

"Well, go on, I'll come and tuck you in."

She found her smile widening. *When Jack comes back, I think he'll come back to bed.*

It was an unexpectedly delicious thought. The urge to giggle like a teenager rose and was ruthlessly repressed.

Anya heard the front door close. The wards on the house shivered as Jack tested them. His aura was dark and thoughtful.

Shell lumbered toward the door. Then he stopped, looking at the floor. "Anya? Are you gonna send me away?"

"Of course not. What gave you that idea?" She slid out of bed, wincing as her entire body twinged. She hadn't had a relationship in four years, and it had been even longer since she'd had a man in her bed. "I would never send you away, Shell. You know that." She found her bathrobe and pulled it on, tying the belt tightly.

"What if he told you to?"

"Then I would tell him *no*. Nobody's sending you anywhere, Shell. I promise."

She made it across the floor and reached him, impulsively taking his hand, slipping her fingers through his. He was chilly and damp, cold even though he was sweating. His feet were wet and bare. She was looking down, or she might have missed the grass clinging to his toes. "Shell, were you outside?"

"No." He started toward the hallway again.

Anya followed, turning so she could fit through the door after him and still hold his hand. Floorboards creaked. She heard Jack moving around downstairs. He was making a point of making noise, she sensed, even though she wasn't sure why.

"Nope. No way. Not outside," Shell said.

"Are you sure?" she persisted.

He led her into his room. His Green Bay sweatshirt lay on the floor near the chair, and his window was slightly open, the curtains pushed back. Anya shivered, letting her fingers slip free.

"I wasn't outside, Anya. I promise."

Why is he lying? But that didn't bother her nearly as much as his tone of sincerity. If she hadn't seen the grass clinging to his feet, she might have been convinced.

No, she *would* have been convinced. Shell had never lied to her before—or had he? The thought was troubling.

Very troubling.

She tucked him in, then picked up his sweatshirt and hung it over the chair again. "I wonder how this fell down." Then she crossed the room and closed his window firmly, glancing out. Unless he wanted to drop straight down onto the driveway, he couldn't have climbed out. "Were you too hot? Is that why you had the window open?" She pulled the curtains tight and made sure they were closed, turned back to him. "Shell?"

"Are you gonna send me away?" he asked, the covers up to his chin, his forehead wide and glistening wet. The dark panic in his blue eyes tore at her heart. How could he think she'd desert him?

"Of course not," she said again. "I promise, Shell. I haven't sent you away any other time, why would I do it now? Go back to sleep. It's still early."

She dropped a kiss on his damp forehead. He closed his eyes and pretended to be asleep, his eyelids flickering.

Anya let herself out into the hallway, closing his door instead of leaving it open, and would have padded downstairs. Jack, however, was already in the hall, silent, his hair wildly mussed. She had to hide a smile. Holding a finger to her lips, she tilted her head toward her bedroom. He followed her without a sound.

"Well?" she asked, as soon as she closed her door.

His shrug made leather creak a bit. "The back door was unlocked. Tracks in the grass. But no Dark, not that I could sense."

It was a wonderful feeling to actually have someone to *talk* to about something that bothered her. It was also a good feeling to look up at him and feel so wonderfully, blessedly safe. "Shell's feet had little bits of grass on them. But he swore he wasn't outside."

Jack's eyes turned chill and flat. Anya dropped down on her tumbled bed and regarded him.

"Hm." He offered nothing but a soft sound that might have been inquiry or agreement.

"He asked if I was going to send him away."

"You probably should, Anya. He needs professional care. And he's a Feeder." Jack shoved his hands in his pockets.

"A Feeder?" She shook her head. "Come here and sit down. I don't suppose you want to go back to bed."

He shrugged, then gave her a lopsided smile. "I'd like that." His tone dropped and became so intimate Anya's cheeks flushed. "But I don't want to push my luck."

"Tease." Anya yawned again. "I'm tired. I don't want to think about this."

"Go back to sleep. I'll keep watch."

She hauled herself up to her feet again. "I'm going to go brush my teeth. If you're not in that bed by the time I come back, I'll take it to mean you don't want to be."

He was already sliding his coat off his shoulders as she passed him on her way to the bathroom. The floor creaked under her feet, and she hummed as she flicked the light on. The sudden brightness made her squint. She used the toilet, flushed, and washed her hands and face. Then she picked up her toothbrush.

The shields on the house vibrated uneasily. Anya stopped, holding the toothbrush. Her reflection stared back at her with flushed cheeks and tangled hair, gray eyes wide and strangely soft. She was still smiling, a foolish grin that only widened as she contemplated herself.

Well, we can all tell what I spent last night doing. Elise is going to tease me to no end about this.

She felt the shields reverberate again, more definitely this time.

Anya dropped her toothbrush and opened the bathroom door. "Jack?"

He was already in the hall. "The front door." Even though he didn't have his coat on, he had a gun in his left hand and one of the strange black-bladed knives in his right. Crimson light dappled the blade. "Go check on Shell."

"But—"

He was already gone, ghosting down the stairs. Gooseflesh raced up Anya's back. She heard a car door slam, an engine purring away on the street outside.

It's so quiet. Why is it so quiet?

She touched Shell's door. "Shell?"

The door moved easily on its hinges. It was open.

He probably just opened it a little. He hates having his door closed.

It swung open. The first thing Anya saw was the empty chair, with no Green Bay sweatshirt hanging on it. The next was the empty bed, covers flung back and the sheets touched with grass stains at the foot.

"Shell?" she said, stupidly. *He went downstairs to use the bathroom, please tell me that's what he did.* She ripped the closet door open. "Shell?" Then she fell to her knees and peered frantically under the bed. "*Shell?*"

She was halfway down the stairs before Jack appeared at the bottom. "He's gone." The gun disappeared. "A black van— I didn't see it when I swept earlier."

"Where is he?" Anya's throat closed up. "Jack—oh, God—"

"What did he say to you? What *exactly* did he say?" Jack caught her arms and forced her to stop. She lunged toward the front door, and he pulled her back. "Anya! What did he say?"

"Something ab-b-bout the phone, and s-s-static. Then he asked if I was g-going to s-send him away." Her teeth chattered, chopping the words into meaningless noise. "Jack, we have to go after him, we have to—let *go* of me!"

"Anya." He closed his arms around her and pressed his lips to her forehead. He was warm and solid and real, and she wanted with sudden fiery intensity for him to tell her this was all a dream. "Shh. We have to *think*. Running after them unprepared will only hurt you. They want you badly, more badly than I thought. I suggest we call your Circle and have them—"

"Let *go* of me!" she yelled, struggling. His arms turned to iron. He didn't move even when she kicked at him, trying to throw him off balance. "They'll *hurt* him! He *needs* me!"

"*Listen* to me." Jack spoke softly, but his tone was harsh enough to make the entire house groan, dishes rattling in the kitchen, glass flexing and wobbling in the windows. "He was outside earlier and they didn't hurt him, did they? No. If they hurt him, they lose their chance to manipulate you. He went *of his own volition.* Anya, *piccola, cara mia, dolce,* think about it. *Think.* He knew what he was doing. Why do you think he went out there?"

"He d-d-d—"

"He knew, Anya. He knows far more than you think. He's more intelligent than you think! He's got you wrapped around his little finger. What do you suppose they promised him, huh? Probably something like, *We'll make the big bad Watchers go away,* you think?"

Jack's lips peeled back from his teeth, a mirthless grimace that would have frightened her if she hadn't known him.

Tears trickled down Anya's face. "He's just a little boy. He doesn't understand."

"No, he doesn't." Jack's grip gentled as soon as she stopped struggling. "I know he doesn't. He doesn't comprehend the first thing about these people. If he knew what they really wanted he would have never gone outside. They're using him. But you won't do him any good if you run after him. Let me do my job, *cara.* All right?"

She made one last effort, trying to writhe free, then went limp. The tears were scalding hot on her cheeks, her eyes burning.

Shell lied to me. He'd been outside, and he lied to me. What else has he lied to me about? Then she shook her head. *No. No. He doesn't understand, and this has been so hard on him. He doesn't know.*

"You have to get him back," she whispered around the choking sob caught in her throat. It escaped, a bubble of sound. "You *have* to help him. Please, Jack. *Please.*"

"I will," he said into her hair. Heat spread over her stinging skin from his hands. He thought she was going into shock and was using the Watcher heat-tingle to bring her out. "Of course I will, *cara.* But I'll need the other Watchers. If I go after him alone, that leaves you unprotected. And I can't take you with me. They'll do anything to acquire you."

Shell, her heart moaned. *Oh, Shell, why?* "But...I can't..." Anya buried her face against his chest and tried to swallow the sobs. *I can't. I can't tell them! I can't!* The image of Theo's disappointed frown, Elise's snort of disdain, and Mari's wide blue eyes turning dark with disgust rose up and taunted her. "I can't."

"You have to stay safe, stay under cover. The other Watchers will stand guard while I bring Shell back."

"No." Her hands wrapped around the leather straps of the harness holding his weapons. "Take me with you. I'll help you. *Please*, Jack. He's going to be so frightened."

The phone shrilled. Anya jumped, swallowing half a scream. Jack clapped a hand over her mouth.

"It's all right." He half carried her into the dark kitchen. The faint light from the coffeemaker's clock and the LED display on the stove was overwhelmed by the glow of the motion-sensor light in the back yard. Jack grabbed the receiver and held it to his ear, stroking her shoulder with his other hand. Then he shook his head. "Why did I suspect this? Here, *cara mia*. It's Mari."

Anya, dazed, took the phone.

"What's wrong?" Mari sounded breathless. "I've already called Elise; she's the closest. I heard you say my name not ten minutes ago. What is it? What's happened? Anya?"

She took a deep breath. "They've taken Shell," she heard herself say, with all the stunned calm of an accident victim. "Because of me. I did something bad, and they have proof. Jack says it's the Brotherhood."

"Oh, gods above," Mari breathed, and cursed with an inventiveness that managed to shock Anya back into reality.

She closed her eyes, waiting for the inevitable disappointment. *After all we gave you. Anya, how could you? Then she'll hang up, and I'll—what will I do? Shell. Oh, God, Shell, what will they do to him?*

"I'm on my way," Mari said. "So is Elise. We'll let Theo sleep, she needs her rest. Hand the phone to Jack, Anya. It's going to be all right."

"What?" Anya would have asked more, but Jack took the phone from her.

"Jack." His tone was clipped and chill. "I'm fairly sure it's them. She's very upset. I'll need your Watcher to stand guard while I retrieve the boy." A pause. "Yes, ma'am." He didn't sound pleased. "No, ma'am. Of course not, ma'am." Another long pause. "Yes, ma'am."

He finally hung up, pulled Anya into his arms, and rested his chin on her head. "Well. She just told me that I'm not giving her any orders and we'll see who gets sent where when they get here. Apparently the Brotherhood's still giving Remy and the fire witch some trouble. They've been trying to acquire her for a few months."

"M-months?" Anya's teeth chattered. His skin was warm, almost feverishly warm, and he sent another tingle of heat through her, his hand spread flat on her back over the bathrobe. His other hand, on her shoulder, tightened slightly. "They're doing this to Elise, too?"

"No, they didn't try to blackmail her, just tried to scoop her up with a full squad of kobolds and a very nasty *kalak*. They've grown more cautious, it seems, since Remy and the other Watchers have put a dent in their numbers."

"They? Who are *they*?"

"I told you, the Brotherhood. They acquire Lightbringers and other psychics and brainwash them, sell them to the highest bidder. Elise is valuable because she's a fire witch, and not many of them survive adolescence. She also has a Talisman— that dragon thing she's always wearing. It's the Trifero, the Stone of Destruction."

He stroked her hair, his warmth closing around her. Anya's teeth stopped chattering. It was all so much noise. None of it mattered.

"Shell," she whispered. The entire world narrowed, darkness sliding over her sight for a second. In that one terrible moment, she knew what she had to do.

Jack was still talking. "Where did they tell you to meet them?"

Anya racked her brain, trying to remember. "Some place called Wescorp downtown, on First Street. That's what he said."

That's where I have to go.

"Good. Now listen to me, Anya. Why don't you go get dressed, and I'll make some coffee? When the other Watchers get here, I'll take them aside and we'll figure out what to do." He shook his head, forestalling her protest. "I don't have to tell them *what* the Brotherhood's been blackmailing you with, just that they've frightened you. That's all that needs to be said. Then we'll go get Shell, and take care of the problem."

"But—we have to *go*. We have to go right now. They could be *hurting* him!"

"If they do, they lose a bargaining chip. If they're going to hurt him, he's already dead and I don't want you to join him. *Trust* me, Anya. Please."

The words slammed home. *Oh, my God.* She looked up at him, tilting her head uncomfortably far back. His face was set, his mouth a thin line.

"I should—" She stopped. *He doesn't understand. It's my fault. Shell. Oh, Shell. No.* "Jack...are you sure they won't hurt him?"

He kissed her forehead so gently she almost forgot how scary he looked. "If they do, I will make sure they're repaid at least ten times over. Go get dressed. The Lightbringers will be here soon."

Anya gathered herself, wiping at her cheeks with the back of her hands. She took a deep breath. *I know what I have to do.* The image of Shell's face rose up to accuse her. What could they have told him? Why had he listened? And why, *why* had he gone outside?

Her eyes burned. She looked down at Jack's belt, unwilling to let him see the Power gathering on her face.

"Anya?" He didn't sound nervous or suspicious. His hands were on her shoulders, gentle, his thumbs moving slightly, brushing across her bathrobe. "It will be all right, I promise. I'll make them regret ever coming near him. Or you."

Her throat swelled with a scream, but she sounded almost maniacally calm. "No, Jack." She tilted her head up, catching his eyes. The Persuasion bolted out and wrapped around him, *contact* made. Familiar euphoria bubbled up her spine. It was much stronger now, so much stronger the Power physically shoved Jack a step back toward the wall. "You'll stay here until the others get here. It's me they want. Maybe if they take me they'll leave all of you alone."

She shook her head slightly, wrapping the ends of the Persuasion deftly around him, making a cocoon of sticky-soft compulsion. It was much easier now that she *understood* and could See what she was doing. "You'll stay here until the others come."

He struggled, but it was no use. She'd caught him off-guard, and he was nailed to the floor. Glass spikes of pain slid through Anya's head. *Now I have to go get dressed.* She backed away from him. He strained against the Persuasion, but she had done well. He was stuck there until the others came.

Anya bolted for the stairs, almost tripping on the first one. If Elise and Mari were on their way, she might not have much time.

I'm sorry, Shell, she cried silently as she tore open her closet door. She pulled a sweater over her head, stepped into a pair of jeans and yanked them on. Stopping only for a pair of socks, she grabbed her sneakers and her purse and ran down the stairs, through the kitchen. Jack's eyes shone balefully. She looked away from him, standing like a shadow there in the dark kitchen, his guns gleaming, and ran into the garage, smacking the button to open the door. The door began to rise, and Anya dropped into the driver's seat and jammed her key into the ignition.

I'm so sorry, Shell. I'm coming.

Twenty-Eight

The fury was cold and unremitting, a feeling he'd had only once before in his life—when he'd found out how completely his father had lied to him. The rage burned at the fine, thin threads holding him, working tirelessly at the cocoon of beautifully crafted magick she'd trapped him in.

Anya had caught him off-balance, her mental compulsion strong and unerring, helped along by the recently completed bond between them and the natural inclination plus the harsh training of a Watcher to *obey*. But she obviously didn't know how patient Jack was—or how the Dark in him could tear at Lightbringer magick. While he might fight the Dark, he was still akin to it, naturally resistant and corrosive to a Lightbringer spell. He called on every last erg of Power he possessed to fight the spell she'd lain on him.

One by one, the threads snapped. One by one, he worked them loose, disregarding how others came crowding to take their place. He only needed one weakness, one tiny glitch in the pattern to exploit—and it came sooner than he'd thought. She had been nervous, unsettled, sick with backlash, and upset when she'd *pushed* him. All those things told against the compulsion, made it weaker, even though she had such incredible power at her command. Even though every muscle in his traitorous body strained to obey her.

She's my witch. And she's in danger.

He understood, of course—she was very attached to the boy. Loyal to a fault. She loved Shell, no matter if he manipulated or hurt her. Jack would be happy with just a fraction of that affection. Would be satisfied with only a small crumb from that table.

The break in the pattern widened, cracks in the amber cocoon holding him fast. Jack, patient and deadly, gathered himself. *Flexed* his will.

The cocoon of magick burst, glass rattling in the back door to his left, the phone making a slight tinny sound as stray energy crackled through the air. The electrical outlet down by his boots sparked, a cascade of gold. The faucet popped too. The glass in the window over the sink made a high ringing sound.

Just as he broke free, he sensed the red-black stain of Watcher near the front door. And a crackling red-gold pattern—

that was the fire witch.

"Stay *back*, Elise. The front door's wide open. *Jack!* Are you there?" It was Remy, the Hunter.

"I'm here," Jack forced out, shaking free of the last bits of Power. "Anya put me under a compulsion. *Damn* it."

"Where is she?" The fire witch strode down the hall and burst into the kitchen, a wavering ball of staticky anger roiling around her raised right hand. Remy was right behind her, his guns disappearing into their holsters as he scanned the house and found nothing but Jack. "Is she okay?"

"She put me under a compulsion and left." Jack shook his head. "I've got to go after her."

"They took Shell? Gods damn them to the lowest hell—" Elise stopped, staring at him. "You look *awful*," she said, matter-of factly.

Jack rubbed his cheek, found warm copper blood trickling from his right eye. His upper lip was wet with blood too, from his nose. "She calls it 'the Persuasion.' It's a kind of *push*. She didn't mean to hurt me; she was frightened. She's going after Shell. Thinks she's going to save us all by making the Brotherhood go away."

He pushed past them into the hall, the clear red glow pouring from Elise making his bones start their half-forgotten song of agony. As if barbed wire was being dragged across the nerve endings inch by inch.

Oddly enough, the relief from Anya's touch made the pain somehow more bearable.

They'll torture her, if they don't drug her first. And good luck trying to bring her back—by the time they finish, her mind will be broken, if they can't break the soul they'll take the mind.

His boots echoed on the stairs. He made it to the bedroom and shrugged into his coat, thanking the gods he hadn't unlaced his boots. He had just been sitting down to do that when he'd felt the front door open.

A new thought occurred to him, when he was halfway down the stairs again, pulling slightly on his coat to make it hang properly. She was a Guardian now, tied to the city. If they tried to take her beyond the city limits, would the borders of the city, so recently reinforced, stop them—or would the attempted removal kill her?

Fear slammed through his chest, cold reflex turning it to rage. *Please, gods, no. Don't take her now.*

The water witch had just arrived, tumbling in the front door. "What's wrong? What's happening? Where's Anya?"

"Put him under a compulsion and left," Remy explained. "Jack, what are you going to do?"

"I'm going after her." His voice made both of the other Watchers draw themselves up a little straighter, Remy moving half instinctively in front of Elise, who hissed something at him and pushed at his back.

Hanson's icy blue eyes flicked over Jack once. "You need backup?"

"I don't think so." Jack was already pushing past him. The Dark symbiote wedded to his body gave one tearing flare of pain as he brushed through the fringes of the water witch's aura. "Do some protection work for Anya, if you can. She'll need it."

"Oh, no you don't," Elise said. "We're going to help you."

Jack was already out the front door. He felt the tugging inside his chest telling him which way Anya was and broke into a run, the symbiote gathering every whisper of Power available to him, ready for combat. Early-morning darkness lightened in the east as false dawn crept up on the city, a hush deeper than death. Jack tore through the darkness, not bothering to damp the sound of his footfalls on pavement, running not for his life but for Anya's.

Wescorp building, her voice whispered, teasing him. *On First Street.*

If he hadn't been scanning out of habit, he might have missed the telltale flickers of movement at the very edges of his sensing range. A Brotherhood team, sent to slow him down? Perhaps. Or sent to collect Anya now that they had Shell?

I don't have time for a fight, Jack thought, and put a little more speed on.

Unfortunately the Brotherhood thought differently, and opened fire on him less than thirty seconds later.

Twenty-Nine

Anya parked in a pay-for lot on Fourth Street and rested her head on the steering wheel for a moment. Tears blurred her vision, making it difficult to drive. She was just lucky she hadn't been pulled over.

She took a deep breath.

It had hurt far more than she'd thought to Persuade Jack. As a matter of fact, her head was pounding with a return of yesterday's headache, and exhaustion pulled at her arms and legs. The thought of crawling back into a bed—any bed—and just letting the world go on without her was powerfully tempting.

Shell. She grabbed her purse and opened the car door, letting in a blast of chilly air. She was shivering by the time she locked the car and dropped the keys in her purse. She ducked her head and one arm through the purse strap so she could settle it against her hip. Elise had bought her this cute little bag, yellow sunflowers on canvas, just big enough for a wallet and keys and maybe some lip gloss.

It hurt to think of Elise and Mari. Right now, Jack was probably explaining to them about the Persuasion, that she wasn't one of them, that she was a thief, and that it was her fault Shell had been taken.

Or maybe Jack was simply too angry. He was likely to be furious with her for using the Persuasion on him, especially when he'd asked her to wait.

She couldn't wait. Shell was in terrible danger.

Besides, I've had enough *of waiting. I'm going to* do *something about this.*

She put her head down and started walking, shivering. The pavement was bruisingly hard under her sneakered feet. *I don't know why I thought this city was going to be different,* she thought bitterly, not paying any attention to the closed-up shops and looming skyscrapers. This was in the heart of downtown, oddly still and silent. It felt eerily like walking through a huge movie set.

Her head ached so badly she almost missed the sound. Very faint, the cry came to her as the wind picked up, cutting through her thin gray sweater like a blunt knife.

"*Anya...Anya help...help me...*"

Shell's voice. Sobbing. A thin wild cry.

Gooseflesh rose on Anya's arms and legs. She stopped and cocked her head, straining to hear more clearly.

That was Shell, I know it was. Please, God, gods, Goddess, whoever You are, if You're up there, please let me hear him again.

Nothing.

She finally started walking again, too cold to stay still. At Fourth and Dirickson she turned the wrong way and had to backtrack as she reached Sole Street, figuring out her mistake. She was still a little hazy on downtown geography, despite working so close to the city's heart.

She found Fourth and Aventine, and tried to decide whether she should turn right or left. She chose left, up the hill, and found Fifth Street after a long block that made her calves ache. Shivering, she turned back downhill, her head pounding so hard she almost didn't notice the black van creeping along the street behind her.

If it's the people that have Shell, I wish they'd just kidnap me. At least it would be warm inside the van. She almost stopped and turned to look, but decided instead to just keep walking.

Anya passed Aventine and Fourth again, walking past two coffee shops and more art galleries. One had a huge glass sculpture of a spider in the window, crouched over a small realistically-modeled fly made of wet black steel. In the next window was a black and white canvas—a painting of a man behind a woman, both of them looking in different directions, the man's arm around the woman's chest. It made her think of Jack, and she shivered again. If he was here, he would be walking next to her, perhaps holding her hand.

That thought hurt too much to continue, both in her aching head and her aching heart. She waited for the light at Second and Aventine, a smattering of traffic actually passing by. One man whistled out his window at her, and Anya wished dully for something to throw at him. Then, ashamed of herself, she put her head down and crossed the street.

First and Aventine. She looked around and found the Wescorp building diagonally across the street. It was an office skyscraper, an impressive pile of granite and glass.

Crossing the street meant she had to turn into the wind streaming up from the bay. False dawn was well under way, the eastern sky just beginning to glow with quivering streaks of gold. Real dawn would come soon. Anya crossed her arms over her chest and stood in front of the Wescorp building. The logo—a shark twisted on its own tail—pulsed slightly as her eyes blurred.

Well, I suppose I should try. She noticed the shiny black van parked across the street. Had it been following her? The windows were heavily privacy-tinted, and she couldn't tell.

She walked up to the building and found, with some surprise, that the glass doors were open.

"Well, here goes nothing," she whispered, and went in.

Inside, the lobby soared up, light coming from banks of glass windows. A fountain splashed musically, a granite sculpture of the shark logo twisted back on itself, covered with water cascading down into a pool below. Glimmers of coins showed from the bottom of the pool. There was a bank of elevators, a directory housed in another chunk of smooth polished granite, and a small coffee cart set in a kind of solarium, ferns and other plants gracefully arching over tasteful little tables. A teenage girl whistled a tune that sounded vaguely familiar as she moved behind the cart, getting ready for the day. The rich smell of coffee floated through the other anonymous smells of "office building" and "downtown."

Where do I go now? He said the Wescorp building!

She looked wildly around, shivering, her hands clasped around her elbows. Her entire body felt like an ice cube.

What would Theo do? She probably wouldn't ever be stupid enough to get into this kind of trouble. Besides, she has Dante.

Anya gathered her courage. The floor, checkered blocks of black and white marble, echoed under her sneakers as she crossed to the coffee cart.

"Hi!" the girl said. "What's your poison?"

What? For a moment all Anya could do was stare at her. Then she realized that she was in the normal world—sort of— and she should start *acting* normally before the guys in the little white coats came and she lost all chance of finding Shell.

"Um...coffee. I mean, may I have a hazelnut latte, please?"

"What size?" The girl, blond, perky and freckled, didn't seem to think Anya was out of the ordinary. Or if she did, she didn't show it.

Anya looked down at the chalkboard holding prices. "Sixteen ounces?" Her voice sounded very far away, but she must have sounded natural. At least, she hoped so.

"Right on." The girl ducked back behind the counter and

Anya started digging in her purse for the money.

"That won't be necessary, Ms. Harris," a soft, evil voice said next to her.

Anya froze.

The girl glanced out from behind the espresso machine. "Morning, Mr. Rhodes. Your usual?" Her wide, guileless blue eyes flicked past Anya, who had the sudden horrible thought that the girl's eyeballs looked like balls in a lotto machine, flat and painted-on. And didn't the girl's hair look like straw stuck to her head? The faint shimmer in the air around the girl tried to feed Anya's eyes a lie, and it was easier to just accept it. If the coffee girl wasn't human, Anya didn't want to know.

It was a relief to close off that part of herself. Once she stopped looking under the surface of the world for the energies underneath, her head stopped hurting so much.

"Good morning, Trudy. I'll be paying for the lovely lady's latte, too."

Anya turned slowly, as if caught in the riptide of a nightmare. She had to look slightly up—the man was taller than her, though not as tall as Jack.

Jack. She held grimly to consciousness as her head pounded, black spots dancing in her peripheral vision before she reminded herself to breathe.

The man had slicked-back, conservatively-cut dark hair and wore a tasteful gray suit, a tan trench coat draped over his arm. He even carried a briefcase. His face was even and regular, his hazel eyes cheerful. He smiled slightly as he studied her in return.

"Here you go," Trudy said. "One hazelnut latte and one americano. Eight seventy-five."

He handed her a ten and two ones. "Thank you, Trudy. Keep the change. Would you like a sleeve, Ms. Harris? It might be hot."

She shook her head wordlessly. He picked up his cup and nodded to her. "Come with me, then, please. We'll set everything right."

Anya took her coffee.

"Have a nice day," Trudy chirped, and Anya's stomach revolved.

The man's mirror-shined shoes made crisp sounds as he strode over the slick, hard flooring. "I'm glad you came," he said, as if she were applying for a job or visiting him on business.

"I'm afraid one of our teams went a little overboard. I suppose I must apologize, and I'd like to do so as early as possible. Here, this way."

He led her to the bank of elevators and pressed the "Up" button with the hand holding the briefcase. She noticed he had a folded copy of the *Wall Street Journal* tucked into the coat.

The coffee cup burned Anya's fingers. She found her voice again. "Where's Shell?" The words trembled, bounced off the hard flooring.

The elevator dinged, and he motioned her inside. "Shell? Ah, yes. Mr. Garritson is quite well. Having breakfast, I believe. He requested his toast be cut into quarters. And orange juice."

Scalding relief went through her. They wouldn't know that unless Shell was still alive to tell them, would they? "Why did you kidnap him? What is this? Why are you blackmailing me?"

He actually winced. Inside, the elevator was expensively mirrored, the carpeting plush maroon. Anya changed hands on her coffee cup again, welcome warmth stinging her fingers.

"Like I said, I owe you an apology. Would you be so good as to push the top button there? The one marked 'M'? Thank you. Ms. Harris, the team handling our...negotiations with you has been recalled. Regrettably, we've had some trouble with Circle Lightfall's Watchers, and this team chose the wrong way of approaching you. I am, of course, very sorry."

His voice seemed to crawl into her head. Anya's temples gave an amazing flare of pain, as if a vise was squeezing them. She tried not to sway.

"You're pale," he said. "And I haven't even introduced myself."

The elevator began to ascend, gravity pressing on Anya's entire body.

"I'm Averik Rhodes, procurator-general for Wescorp, which is a division of Fallon International. You will, of course, never have heard of us. Our mission is to provide lucrative employment for those with special talents, such as yourself."

Anya definitely swayed this time, his voice sinking into her head like a fishhook. She stared at the mirrored elevator door's smooth gleam.

The elevator slowed and came to a smooth stop. The doors opened.

"Would you care to step inside? Yes. Thank you. Good morning, Martha, this is Ms. Harris. She'll be visiting for today.

Will you please have Harbins bring his guest up to my office?"
Rhodes addressed this to a stout, gray-haired woman who sat
behind a massive mahogany reception desk with an antique
rotary phone at her elbow. The woman's nails were painted
blood-red, and she wore a thick necklace of gold links strangely
tight on her wide neck. Her lipstick was askew, a slash of bright
red, and for a moment Anya smelled a heavy carrion stink.

The secretary nodded, her muddy dark eyes fastening on
Anya. Then she smiled broadly, showing a row of yellow teeth
that had been filed down.

The blood left Anya's face in one swift rush. *I shouldn't
have come here. Not without Jack.*

The clarity of the thought almost shocked her out of the
half-trance, but the man started to talk again, and she tried to
take a deep breath. Her lungs burned as if she were drowning.

"Will you please follow me, Ms. Harris? I think you might
be more comfortable sitting down."

She had no choice, so she followed him past the desk. The
secretary's gaze was glued to her, and just as she passed, Anya
caught sight of a strange glimmer around the secretary.

She's glamoured. Anya succeeded in biting back a gasp
only by sinking her teeth into her cheek. It wasn't the same as
a Watcher's glamour, which just made people's eyes slide right
over their weapons. No, this was a very powerful, very careful
shell of energy capable of fooling even a witch's eyes. *I wonder
what she looks like under it.*

Anya suddenly realized she didn't want to know. She took
a hurried gulp of her coffee, scalding her mouth. The taste—
bitter and acrid—made her want to gag.

*Oh, God, please tell me that girl just makes really bad coffee
and this isn't something else.*

Rhodes led her down a tastefully appointed hall, and Anya
felt a tremor go through the building. *This high up, I bet you
can feel the wind all the time.*

She caught a glimpse of a meeting room with floor-to-
ceiling glass windows. Through the windows, she could see
dawn coming up on other skyscrapers, none of them quite as
tall as this one. Beyond, the bay was a hard diamond glitter, the
last darkness of night fleeing into the west.

Then the fishhook yanked on her mind again, and she
submerged in a dreamlike stupor. It was all so unreal. This was
a nightmare, and she would wake up soon.

"Martha isn't human," the man suddenly said. "She's rather like Circle Lightfall's Watchers, though of course better-trained. You will have noticed by now that the Watchers are not very...conciliatory. Or careful how they handle themselves. It's regrettable, of course, the magickal process to make them so strong and fast would be quite valuable in the right hands. But then, Circle Lightfall's only interested in one thing."

"What's that?" Her voice didn't shake, and she was hazily proud of herself. But her words were a little slurred. She sounded drunk.

"Why, gathering prime psychic females and breeding them with their Watchers, of course." Rhodes indicated a door with his name engraved on a gold plate.

Anya felt heat rise to her cheeks again. She struggled to *think* through the soupy haze. "I don't think that's strictly true."

"Well, opinions are like noses, everyone's got one." He stepped past a desk with a drift of paper, a computer, and a glass paperweight shaped like a coiled rattlesnake on it, as well as a blinking high-tech phone, and held the door open for her.

She stepped inside and let out an involuntary breath of wonder. It was a corner office, and the glass in the skyscraper opposite was just beginning to catch fire with dawn light. Rhodes turned the lights on, but it didn't detract from the spectacle.

"Beautiful, isn't it?" Rhodes's voice no longer sounded evil. Instead, he sounded firm and professional.

Anya shook herself. The funny draining sensation faded a bit. No matter how polite this man was, she had to remember that his goons had kidnapped Shell.

"I never get tired of seeing that," he continued, hanging his coat up, then setting his briefcase, coffee, and newspaper on the desk. "I think it's why I come to work early."

"Look." Anya's voice made the paper on the desk stir slightly. "I know you're being very polite, but I want to see Shell. And I want to know just what you want out of me. Why are you trying to blackmail me? What have I ever done to you?"

Did he flinch slightly, or was that just her imagination? Anya shook her head, trying to clear it. The headache threatened again, but retreated, snarling, to a back corner of her mind.

Rhodes dropped into an ergonomic chair behind his desk. A framed da Vinci print hung on the wall, and a fake rubber tree perched by the door. A dark, lifeless computer screen sat to his left. *Theo would have a real plant,* she thought, and shuddered.

"You're absolutely right, Ms. Harris. Your case has been handled the wrong way. Please, sit down. I'll explain."

She gingerly lowered herself into a comfortable leather chair, suddenly very aware the office was warm and very sleek, and she was mussed, with unbrushed teeth and uncombed hair, as well as a ratty sweater and sneakers with holes in them.

"I'd like an explanation," she managed, wishing her head would stop pounding. Now that she was sitting down it was better—but she was so tired. So very tired. *Shell. I have to make sure Shell's all right.* She wished the coffee was real. She could have used the caffeine.

The fishhook yanked again, and she fell into another half-trance. *This...isn't quite...right...*

"As I've said, Fallon International is in the business of offering people with special talents very lucrative jobs. I was recruited three years ago and have done quite well for myself. The team originally handling your recruitment saw the Watcher—Jack Gray, I believe? Originally of Italy, recently of Montreal?" At her dazed nod, he beamed as if she'd won a prize. "Well, they panicked. The Watchers are very dangerous, and Mr. Gray is well-respected as an adversary. So some decisions were made that were not quite...correct. I've made sure those responsible will be demoted, and I've decided to handle your case myself. I apologize for calling last night, but I was working on limited information and couldn't be sure that you would even stay on the phone long enough to let me introduce myself. Now, Fallon is prepared to offer you three hundred thousand dollars a year and the location of your choice. With, of course, a paid assistant to help take care of Mr. Garritsen—um, Shell."

The fishhook slipped free. Anya shook her head, sure she hadn't heard him right. "Excuse me?" *What just happened to me?* She'd felt as if she were asleep. What was she doing here?

He leaned forward, tenting his fingers. "Personally, Ms. Harris, I'd hold out for four hundred thou and stock options. The position, of course, comes with full medical and dental. You'll be under a two-year renewable contract, and—"

"Excuse me. I want to see Shell and make sure he's all right." Her voice sliced the air inside the office, and Rhodes seemed to flinch again. Anya watched, fascinated, as a ripple went through him, as if he was made of liquid.

"Certainly. Martha is having him brought up to this very office. But while he's on the way, there's no reason why we can't talk like civilized people, is there?" His smile was very wide and very white.

Too wide, and *too* white. If he smiled any wider, the top of his head would open just like a can.

Oh, my God. My imagination just works too well. Only I'm not sure it's imagination.

Anya strangled the moan rising to her lips. Her head began to pound again, intermittent pain breaking through a blanket of that horrible draining lassitude. He was doing something to her, wasn't he?

He took a dainty sip of his own coffee. "You must realize that your talent, properly trained, is *very* valuable. Why, think of the advantage in international and intercorporate negotiation! You are literally worth millions, Ms. Harris. You could retire in five years, very well-off and able to take care of Mr. Garritsen for the rest of his life."

Dazed, Anya felt the lassitude slip over her again. There didn't seem to be anything to say. "But..." She sounded dazed. "Jack said you use drugs. And torture."

His nose wrinkled. "Certainly *not!*" He sounded properly horrified. "Not our *employees*. And really, why should we, when we can offer our talented employees salary offers in the hundreds of thousands? Would I need to torture anyone to have them work for that much money?"

That depends on what you want them to do. She thought better of saying it at the very last moment.

The vise squeezed her head again, and Anya let out her breath in a sigh. She made the mistake of looking down at the carpet, which was a luxurious blue. *I could just lie down and go to sleep,* she thought longingly.

"I want to see Shell." The pain stalked closer and closer. It was helping, she realized, holding off the weakness so she could stay awake. "And—" Inspiration struck. "Then I can take your business card and go home and think about this. I can let you know in a day or two. This is a bit much."

"Of course!" He sounded jolly and beamed at her, but a fine sheen of sweat lay over his skin. His face looked strange. Pasty. He selected a business card from the silver holder on his mirrored desk and proffered it to her. "Mr. Garritsen should be up any moment now, with my colleague Mr. Harbins."

Anya blinked. She automatically "reached" out past her shields, searching for Shell's familiar pulsing aura. It was a familiar trick, performed so often and so unconsciously it didn't make her head throb.

What she felt instead made her go cold with terror. There was only that thing sitting at the secretary's desk—a thing that felt chilly and Dark, made of cold razor blades in a lipless mouth—and Rhodes, whose own aura glittered with a glamour.

Who, now that she looked at him closely, was definitely sweating. There was nobody else, not for a few floors down. The building might as well have been a ghost town, for all Anya could feel.

Shell was nowhere near.

The fishhook snapped completely free of her mind. Her head hurt, true, but she felt lucid. Awake.

I can't let him know he doesn't have me. The thought was frantically practical. *I should never have come here.*

"Does your colleague have a cell phone?" she waffled, speaking slowly as if she was still under his compulsion. It was a type of *push*, she realized, and a flush of anger dispelled the last of it. He'd been using the Persuasion on her! "If I could just hear Shell's voice..."

Rhodes shook his head. His plastic smile didn't alter, but he dropped the business card on his desk. His fingers were too long, and if she looked closely she could see...claws. "I'm afraid not. He's in a safe place and has probably already left to bring your friend here. He doesn't carry a cell phone."

He's lying. Anya stood up so quickly she almost overbalanced. "I want to see Shell." A particularly strong gust of wind hit the building, rocking it slightly. "Why doesn't this man have a cell phone? What if he needs to contact you?"

"Please sit down, Ms. Harris. No need to get excited." He *was* sweating. Great beads of it stood out on his forehead.

He's stalling me, Anya realized through the incredible headache, the exhaustion of backlash coating her with cold liquid lead. *But why? For what? More of his little friends to get here? Why? I'm not in any shape to do anything to anyone right now.*

Then she felt something else—the familiar red-black of a Watcher, swirling counterclockwise. Anya's shields were thin and raw, so she also felt a flush of rage that scraped along her skin and made her drop down into the chair, her knees giving way. She blinked at Rhodes, whose hazel eyes flashed with liquid crimson.

Anya stared at him. Silence stretched out, thin and delicate as glass, another gust of wind shaking the building.

Maybe he doesn't know Jack's here. Her heart leapt.

Then Rhodes sighed. "I really had hoped to have you sign a contract before anyone else—from their side *or* ours—got here." He shook his head. "That really would have been better. You simply do not realize how much you're worth, Ms. Harris. Alive and cooperative, you're worth more than your weight in gold. But now we'll have to do this the hard way. It's a pity. I liked this suit."

A chill touched the back of her neck. *Jack. He's here. Or one of the other Watchers—no. Jack's here. Of course he's here. He'll be furious. But he's here.*

The pain of the backlash headache faded a little, and she sat up straighter. "What...um, what would my job be?" she asked, playing for time. *Please don't let him see I'm not under the Persuasion anymore,* she prayed. *Please.*

"Your 'job?'" Rhodes wiped the sweat from his forehead with one pale, expensively manicured and long-clawed hand. "Once you pass orientation, you'll be paired with a handler who will give you the specifics of each operation. I'm going to recommend you be given to one of the Skinford brothers. I owe them from our last poker game. You were supposed to come in *tonight*, Ms. Harris. I really should have a talk with the head of Negotiations." He sighed again, heavily, and made a quick motion. Anya stood up again, the chair falling over backward and hitting the carpeted floor with a dull thump. "No, it's orientation for you, my dear. And once they're finished with you, they might even let me have a taste. Don't move."

Anya gasped. Dawn light glowed off the buildings behind him and glittered on the barrel of the gun he produced, pointed at her. Behind her, Anya heard the crash and tinkle of breaking glass.

The sweat ran in runnels down his face, carving lines in the waxen flesh. With the light behind him, she could see the two short, stubby horns protruding from his forehead, and the dark cave of his nose.

Another glamour and a Persuasion. I really am a novice at this, aren't I? And here I thought I was doing so well.

"You're not human." The words died in her throat, fell to the tastefully carpeted floor just as the chair had.

"You're not very bright," Rhodes snarled. "You should have let me move you along. You *should* have come in when I told you. But now that *he's* here, I'm going to have to bring you in the hard way. And you'll be collared and chained before sundown." Cloth ripped as the suit tore, splitting while his body lengthened and changed. "I said *don't move!*" The gun clicked.

She froze and tried to think of something smart to do. Elise or Mari might have had an idea, but she was just Anya, still a novice when it came to magick. Her head pounded with backlash, and she was locked in an office with a stoop-shouldered, horned thing whose eyes began to glow a wicked red.

Thirty

The sword blurred in an arc of steel-silver, and the *vadoakij*'s head hit the ground with a thump. Jack stabbed it again, carving open its spine, and flicked a line of hellfire off his palm at the head, which rolled to a stop and blinked balefully at him, clicking its teeth together. Rage crackled inside his mind as the hellfire met the head and greasy black smoke billowed up. The gold necklace-collar the thing had worn turned into ash, clanking dully and cracking, blowing away on a stray breeze impelled by Power. The body burst into blue flame; the Brotherhood's firecharm used to get rid of the bodies of its operatives. It stank, and the fire might spread.

Anya.

He barely paused, following the insistent buzzing call vibrating through his body. She was close, so close—and *vadoakij* weren't that smart, they were only door guards. This whole place reeked of inhuman flesh. he'd be surprised if anything that worked here was human, unless it was a collared and chained psychic. The Brotherhood used a few diurnal and sunlight-resistant nonhuman species to take care of business in their offices during the day. He was lucky it was dawn, otherwise he might have to face more of them. As it was, the place was deserted, but he'd bet dollars to doughnuts the *vadoakij* had called in reinforcements. He had precious little time.

The call jerked him down a hall, his boots skidding on the carpet, past a secretary's desk to a door that said *Rhodes* on a gold plaque. The lines of Power tangled through this place tingled briefly as he cut through a trap-alarm. He was lighting up the entire goddamn building like a Christmas tree, the place would be crawling with Dark soon.

There, she's in there. He drove his shoulder into the door and spun through as it crashed open, stopping with a jerk as whistling cold air met his skin.

The *apatok*—tall and wiry, dressed in the torn remnants of a three-piece gray Italian wool suit, snarled at him. There, struggling in the thing's primary set of arms, was Anya, her eyes wide and crazed with fear. Alive—and unharmed.

It held a gun to her head, its back to the broken window. "Back off!" it snarled. "Back *off*, Black-knife, or I throw her!"

Jack raised his hands. "That would cut your profit margin,

wouldn't it?" His voice sliced through the whistling wind. "I didn't know the Brotherhood had taken to hiring carrion."

The vulture bared his teeth, his secondary arms fully lifted, exposing the gliding-flaps stretching from its torso all the way down to its knock-knees. Dawn light glowed through the veins on the hairless gray skin. The room stank thickly of magick and glamour, and Anya's pale aura told him she was in backlash and exhausted too.

She was also bleeding golden light through a thin gash in her aura. What had it done to her? Had she followed the thing here, thinking it was human?

Lucky, lucky, luckier than I have any right to be, she's alive. He pushed the relief away. "Let her go, and I won't kill you."

It sneered at him, choking up on Anya, whose gray eyes widened. Her cheeks were paper-pale, strands of her hair blown wildly on the howling wind. This high up it was chill, her breath turning to vapor and the vulture's skin roughening to a pebbly texture.

"You think I believe that? From *you?*" Its snarl widened. "That's rich. How about I shoot you and take her in? You can spend the last few moments of your wasted fucking life thinking about how nice it will be for me to watch them break her."

Jack's lips peeled back from his teeth. "Last chance," he said, and the thing leveled the gun at him.

Anya screamed, struggling, and the vulture's arm tightened across her throat.

"Jack! No! *No!*"

He lunged forward just as the vulture pulled the trigger and flung itself backward. Anya's scream and Jack's rising roar dyeing the air with swirls of crimson and gold.

Move! Move! Pain exploded in Jack's chest. He flung himself out the window, and saw Anya thrashing as she fell, her elbow sinking into the vulture's midsection. It howled, its claws digging through her sweater into her flesh, tearing both.

Anya fell free.

The vulture flapped, but it had lost its hold on her. Jack's hand blurred, cold wind whipping through his hair, his coat making a sound like the sails of a clipper ship pulled taut by a hard breeze.

The thrown *flechettes* tore through one of the vulture's wing-flaps, good solid hits, Power crunched along Jack's bones and he arrowed down, aiming for her. They were both falling, Anya tumbling through empty air and Jack's body reacting with the instinct of long training, arms and legs pulled close to speed his descent and catch up with her.

Dammit, it's not going to end like this.

His hand closed around Anya's wrist. He yanked *hard*, and her elbow smacked him a good one across the cheek. Then he had her, and they were falling, her hair stinging his eyes as it whipped in the roaring wind. *This is going to hurt.*

There was no time. She was still screaming, struggling blindly. Another flare of Power, the laws of physics bending, tearing in his chest, strangely short of breath. The rooftop—*it's a goddamn parking garage, this is going to hurt*—rising up to meet them too fast, too goddamn fast. He curled around her body, trapping her in his arms, hearing a short coughing roar as he threw every erg of available Power into compressing unwilling air into a cushion, ignoring the howl of abused flesh and the sudden scorching of air compressed too quickly, the great bitch called physics taking due revenge on a transgressor.

Impact. His ribs snapped like greenwood, and his arm broke too. The shockwave slammed out along the rooftop, blowing out car windows and scorching the pavement as kinetic force bled away unnaturally, shielding them both from a painful death but not enough, not nearly enough.

Jack screamed, rolling, Anya's breathless yell rising with his. Rolling finally to a stop, he coughed up blood and clear liquid and passed out as steam billowed in the air.

A brief starry moment of merciful unconsciousness was all he was allowed. The *tanak* snapped his ribs back out, melding the breaks together messily, Power roiling like rusted spikes deep in his chest. He curled into a ball, coughing, something lodged deep in his chest. Clear liquid colored with blood gushed from his mouth and nose. The coughs continued, each one a white-hot poker jammed into his chest, until it lodged in the back of his throat and he retched, spitting the hot chunk of metal free. Then came a stinging icy lungful of air, a short howl driven out of him as the *tanak* turned the pain into more Power, feeding on it, using the energy to knit together torn tissues, shocking his heart back into beating. The broken rib protruding out through the skin of his chest jerked back in, crackling. Jack convulsed, his eyes rolling back in his head.

Anya, he thought between the bursts of agony. *Did...she...get...hurt?*

One more walloping burst of excruciating pain, then the symbiote settled into a deep song of agony, the pain turned into Power turned into rage turned into more Power. Jack rolled instinctively and brought himself up to hands and knees. Veils of steam drifted, and hairline cracks graced the concrete underneath him.

"—*jack*—" Her voice was small after the roar of wind, the shockwave of the air-cushion breaking their fall, and the immense pipe-organ of pain playing in his flesh. "—*ohgod, jack*—"

"Here," he rasped, his fingers finding the hard lump he'd coughed up. It was the bullet, flattened and distorted, almost red-hot. Jack shoved it in a pocket. "I'm here." He realized he'd spoken in his native tongue and repeated it in English for good measure.

He blinked. Steam roiled. There was a perfect double-ring of scorch on the concrete, the painted stripes for parking spaces blistered up. Jack's face felt raw; he'd be lucky if he escaped third-degree burns. Burns were the worst, all the pain concentrated into a short space of time while the symbiote forced the flesh to heal.

"Got to get you out of here," he said.

Her fingers met his face. She had crawled to him. Her face was slick and shiny with damp and tears, spattered blood on her forehead and cheek. The instant wallop of honey-spiced pleasure slamming through his entire body from her touch almost made his arms collapse.

"Oh, God," she whispered. "I thought we were going to die."

Not while I have enough time to remember basic physics theory. "No." His hand came up as he crawled forward, closing over hers, clamping her fingers to his face. "Anya. *Anya.*"

She inhaled, a deep sobbing breath, flinching. Jack closed his eyes, for one brief second abdicating all control, just *feeling* her skin against his. She was alive. *Alive.*

"I thought we were dead," she whispered again. "Jack."

If I wasn't so old, we might well be dead. A younger Watcher couldn't have taken that kind of fall, even with a Lightbringer to protect. I'm not even sure I survived it.

Die later, Jack. Take care of business now. "Are you hurt?" His eyes snapped open. He shook the fog out of his head and looked around at the steam billowing in great puffs. The air was strangely warm, and the smell of scorched concrete tortured the back of his throat. The shoal of agony retreated, leaving a ringing awful sense of being ripped apart and put back together the wrong way in its wake. "Anya? Are you hurt?"

"I don't know. My arm. My side..." She tried to tug her hand free of his face, but his fingers tightened, holding it there. "You—we..." She looked back over her shoulder, craning her neck. Paper fluttered from the top of the Wescorp skyscraper, barely visible through the rapidly thinning steam. "We fell from *up there?*" Disbelief tainted her husky, beautiful voice.

"I never want to do that again." He shook his head and reluctantly let go of her fingers. His shirt stuck to his chest, coated with blood and lung-fluid. He took a deep breath in, coughed again, and spat to the side.

Sirens began to wail.

Jack returned to full consciousness of danger with a jolt, scanning the top of the parking structure. He'd made a lot of noise and just cracked what looked like a fairly intense Brotherhood lair. "I've got to get you out of here." He looked down at Anya, whose head was still craned back, looking up at the sixty-story building.

"We were up at the top," she said, dreamily, and Jack saw her pupils were dilated so large her eyes looked as black as Dante's.

She's in shock.

The only good thing about that kind of pain was that it gave him plenty of Power when the agony retreated. He grabbed her shoulders, sent heat and Power roaring through her. "Anya!" His voice was sharp, made the car sitting four spaces away rock back on its springs, broken glass skittering and crunching along the concrete. "*Look* at me."

She did, and flinched. "My arm." She dipped her chin toward her left arm—the one she hadn't touched him with.

"Oh, no." He could tell the humerus was broken by the way her arm hung, limply, with a funny bend in the upper half. His stomach contracted, sick fear sliding up his spine. "Anya—"

"I'll be fine," she said, colorlessly. "We have to find Shell. They'll do something to him—Jack, we *have* to find him."

He made it to his feet. The sirens were getting closer. He scanned for the *apatok,* found nothing. If the thing survived the drop after Jack's thrown *flechettes* tore its wing, it would never fly again. Fury rose inside Jack's bones, he savagely repressed it. The only thing that mattered right now was making sure Anya was safe.

"I'm going to patch this." He knelt at her side, closing one hand over her left shoulder. "It won't be perfect, but we'll get you to the healer and she'll take care of it. All right?"

"Shell," she whispered, blinking up at him. "Jack. You came for me."

"You're *my witch*." He managed to unfreeze his jaw by sheer force of will, his other hand cupping her elbow. "Of *course* I came for you. What did you think I'd do? *Never* do that again, Anya. You could have been..." He bit back the last part of the sentence. "Forgive me. This is going to hurt."

She looked up at him, her face flushed with the heat he'd just fed into her system. "It's all right." She bit her lip, her chin lifting with weary bravery. "Do it."

He closed his eyes, *feeling* for the break, and let out a controlled burst of Power, forcing it down the bone. She didn't scream, but it was close—she made a low hoarse sound that might have been a swallowed cry. Jack sealed the break, setting the rest of the Power deep inside the bone's slim cylinder, where it would leak out and bolster the healing.

"It's the best I can do," he muttered. "Got to get you out of here."

She looked around. A thin trickle of blood slid down her chin—she'd bitten her lip savagely. That trickle—and her broken arm—concerned him far more than his own injuries. He rose, bringing her with him by the simple expedient of sliding his hand under her shoulders and carrying her up. "Let's go."

"God," she whispered, looking at the scorch-ring and the thinning steam. "What was that?"

That was physics theory turned into practical experience in a way I never want to see happen again. "Bending the laws of physics a little; Feynman was the best damn thing to happen to combat magick in centuries. Now come on, Anya. I don't have much time to get you somewhere safe."

Blood dripped. He swore. The vulture's claws had torn into her ribs, and her sweater hung in flapping sodden rags at her side.

She pushed his hands away. "I'm fine." Her voice sounded more natural now, without the dreaminess of shock. "Let's go. We have to find Shell, Jack. They have him, and they'll do something terrible to him."

He spread his hand along her side, almost flinching as her blood touched his skin. "Gods above," he said hoarsely. The sirens were even closer, and the Brotherhood wouldn't be far behind. "Anya."

He tried to be gentle, but she still let out a short yell of pain. When he took his hand away, her skin was whole under the mask of blood, just a few angry-looking long pink scars, flushing as she shivered. She swayed, and he caught her, picked her up by simply bending and leaning forward so she ended up over his shoulder.

"Jack!"

"Where are you parked?"

"Fourth Street, a lot with a big white sign. *Jack,* put me down. Please. I can walk."

"Hang on." He took a quick glance around to orient himself. Shattered cars, pebbled safety glass. The shockwave had caused quite a bit of damage. The drop from the parking garage was five stories, and he was flush with Power from the Dark he'd killed—and from the agony that even now tore at him.

Pain to Power to rage to pain to Power, a vicious cycle. One he was glad of, if it let him get her *out* of here in one piece.

She screamed when he gathered himself and leapt. When he landed in the alley below, her head bounced against his back.

"—*Ouch!*" she finished. "Put me *down!*"

He complied, steadying her as her knees buckled. The alley was dark and close, but sheltered from the wind. He checked her again. No more wounds. Even though she flinched when she moved her left arm, she was whole. He'd done the best he could.

"Stay close to me." He kept his arm over her shoulder. "Very close. We may get out of this without a fight. If I have to fight, you *stay where I put you,* all right?"

"Jack." She looked up at him, her eyes glowing. "You came for me."

Why did she keep repeating that? "Of course I did. You're my witch." *What about this do you not understand? It's perfectly simple.* "Promise me, *piccola.* If I have to fight, I need you to stay where I put you. *Ci?*"

She nodded. "All right." She swayed. Between the backlash and her injuries, it was a miracle she was still conscious. Then she reached up, curled her fingers around a leather strap of his rig, and pulled him down.

Jack, his entire body aching with the reverberations of landing on the parking garage roof and relief at finding her alive, didn't resist. Her mouth met his. It was a short kiss, but it miraculously cured most of his aches by the time she moved her fingers on his cheek, gently pushing him away.

"Jack?"

"What?" He checked the street. Reasonably clear. On the other side of the parking garage the street would be crawling with emergency vehicles by now. Jack glanced up. He could see a slice of the top of the Wescorp building above the line of the parking garage roof. Black smoke billowed out. The Brotherhood would help it along, of course—destroying records. They didn't know if he'd managed to snatch anything, and once a bolt-hole of theirs was compromised, they couldn't afford to stay. A hard, delighted grin touched his lips. He pulled Anya closer into the shelter of his body, his aura staining the fringes of her clear light. Then he guided her out onto the pavement with him, a slight glamour glittering into existence around them. Anyone who looked would see a pair of young lovers out for a morning walk, not an exhausted shell-shocked witch and her Watcher.

He dropped his head slightly, scanning the street, and murmured to her. "Do you have your car keys?"

She reached down with her right hand, patting her hip. Her purse was still there. "I th-think so. Jack, I'm sorry, I—"

"Don't worry. Later. For right now, *never* do that again. I would have come with you, Anya. Never *ever* do that again. Please."

"Oh, I won't." She rested her head on his shoulder and brought out her car keys in one trembling hand. He took them in one bloody fist. "I'm tired, Jack."

For the first time since he'd left the house, he began to relax slightly. He'd had to take down two full Brotherhood teams, saved at the last minute by the other Watchers arriving. He'd left them fighting while he ran for Anya. Now that he had a moment to catch his breath, he wondered how the other Watchers had fared. "I know you're tired. We'll get you to the healer. She can help you better than I could."

"Shell," Anya said. "We have to find Shell. I *heard* him."

The pavement rolled away under their feet. Anya stumbled, and he held her up. "Don't worry. As long as they think there's a chance they can use him to bring you in, they'll keep him alive."

I'm lying. The boy was probably dead by now, with enough personal information extracted from him to string her along and provide proper psychological bait. *I'm sorry, Anya, but I can't tell you that, not now.*

She tripped again, her legs tangling, He held her up, half carrying her and wishing he didn't need his hands free in case of attack. He wanted to hold her so badly it hurt, one more pain to add to the symphony of twinges and aches in the rest of his body.

Then her head came up. "Shell?" She took a deep breath, her aura suddenly strengthening. "Did you hear that? Jack, he's alive. We have to help him!"

Nothing in his long life as a Watcher had ever prepared him for this. "Anya—" How could he tell her that the boy was most likely dead? That if she heard him, it was a decoy or her own wishful thinking?

"That way." She pointed. Jack did some rapid mental calculations. Southwest. She was pointing toward the docks, just where the Brotherhood would possibly hide a hostage. Anya looked up at him, her eyes suddenly shining with hope. "Jack, I can hear him. We have to hurry."

"It could be a trap." He wished he could find some other way to dissuade her. "The best thing to do is go back to the healer, have her tend to you, and wait for the Brotherhood to make another move."

"I don't care. Please, Jack. I know you don't like Shell, but *please*, Jack!"

His entire body ached, he was covered in blood, and if she expended any more Power she ran the risk of passing out cold until her body could recharge itself with more sleep and food.

"It's dangerous, *cara*." He sped up a little. If he could get her into the car, he could have her away from this zone in short order. He glanced down.

Her eyes fluttered closed, and she went almost limp. "He's close. *Very* close. Jack, please. Do I have to beg you?"

That managed to pinch his conscience. *Hard.* Jack cursed internally. He was about to do something stupid. "Anya, if we go after them like this, they'll kill us and Shell too. I'm tired, you're exhausted, and this whole sector will be crawling with Brotherhood teams, as soon as they figure out the fall didn't kill me."

His skin turned momentarily cold and the *tanak* growled, jacking his adrenaline balance. *Could have died. Should have died. If I wasn't so old we would have died. Gods, God, whatever—thank you. Thank you.*

She shook her head. "He's so close, Jack. I can *hear* him. Please help me. Please. I'm begging you, please help me."

He swore, his free hand reaching down to touch a knife hilt's smooth solidity. "I can't."

"Jack." The voice came from his left, a deep alley covered in shadow. Jack whirled, the gun coming up, and he recognized Hanson with a jolt. "Hey. Don't go that way. Crawling with Brotherhood. This way."

I'm too tired, I shouldn't have let him sneak up on me. Jack dragged Anya into the shelter of the alley. "Nice to see you."

Hanson's ice-blue eyes flicked over him. "You look like hell." He looked down at Anya. "Hello, ma'am. Are you all right?"

"How did you find me?" Jack glanced back over his shoulder. Clear. He'd gotten Anya free. Relief tore at him, almost made him stagger.

"Just followed the sirens." Remy appeared out of the deeper shadows, golden eyes glimmering. Jack suppressed another flare of relief at seeing them. He had always worked alone; it was new to have other Watchers to cooperate with. "The other Guardians are with Dante, safely under cover at the shop—best shields in the whole damn city. You know, you're *loud*. I heard it all the way across downtown."

Anya pulled away from him. "We have to find him, Jack! *Please.*"

"The boy?" Hanson glanced past him. "*Damn.* He's probably close."

"I can hear him." Tears glimmered, streaking a clear path through blood and dust down Anya's cheeks. "Won't any of you help him?"

Jack took a deep breath. It took every ounce of self-discipline to hand Anya over to Hanson, who didn't flinch or grimace, though the clear light from her skin must have hurt him. "Get her under cover. I'll go get the boy."

"That's fucking *suicide*, Jack!" Hanson hissed.

"I'll go with him," Remy volunteered. "Where's her car?"

"I found it in a pay-for lot on Fourth, the one run by that

Chinese guy," Hanson supplied helpfully. "You can't mean it, Jack. Look at you."

She gave me a new life. Where else should I spend it? "My witch asks it, so shall it be." Jack turned on his heel, his tattered coat flaring sharply. "I've got to find him."

"They've probably killed him by now," Remy said, low and urgent.

Anya gasped, looking up at him, as if begging him to disagree.

"Keep her safe," Jack said over his shoulder.

Hanson nodded and pulled Anya away. She stumbled again, almost falling. Every fiber of Jack's body wanted to lunge to catch her. But he had something else to do.

Remy fell into step behind him. "Got a score of my own to settle with the Brotherhood." His accent made the words slow and even. "Didn't know they had a nest down here."

"I think I can find the boy," Jack said. "But I'll need you to watch my back."

"Already done, *homme*," the golden-eyed man replied. "Find the boy so we can get out of here. I have a breakfast date with my witch this morning."

Thirty-One

Anya drifted in a velvety unconsciousness, only barely surfacing when familiar green-glowing Power bathed her. Another long period of darkness, then another green glow washing through her. It was welcome oblivion.

She heard confused murmurs—Jack's deep voice, no longer flat but terribly weary, Theo's husky clear tones. Hanson, saying something very softly. Mari whispering, someone stroking Anya's forehead with warm fingers. Elise, then, uncharacteristically quiet, her voice turned to satin warmth.

The green light came again, and Anya gratefully fell into deep velvet blackness.

A pale glow lit up the edges of the universe for a long time before she realized her eyes were half open. She opened them the rest of the way, slowly, drinking in the cloudy light coming from the rain-spattered window. The room was beautiful, with bookcases along one wall. Spider plants and ferns hung from pretty brass hooks. There was a painting of a rose garden under summer sunshine, a single monarch butterfly pausing on one of the white roses; a comfortable-looking chair sat in front of the window. A big cherrywood dresser and a full-length antique oval mirror in a dark wooden frame looked well-loved and polished. A cherub's face was carved into the frame over the mirror, wings delicately feathered on either side of its chubby smiling cheeks. The mirror itself was clear and flawless.

The smell of green growing things and pure delicate Power told her she was in Theo's house. She heard murmurs downstairs. Her entire body felt heavy, sinking into the bed.

How did I get here? The last thing she remembered was falling into the passenger seat of her car as Hanson swore softly, telling her they had to hurry.

The sound of rain whispering on the roof came next. Anya closed her eyes briefly. When she opened them again, the light was different, late afternoon instead of late morning. She was thirsty, but she felt a little better.

It took a few moments for her to prop herself up on her elbows. She looked at the small bedside table, covered with a fall of green silk. There was a glass of water there, and a lamp.

Two tries got the glass in her hand, and a long struggle lifted it to her mouth. She drank, then had to face the difficult problem of getting the glass back on the table. She managed, and flopped back onto the pillows, listening.

The murmurs stopped. There were light footsteps on the stairs, followed by a heavier tread. Theo pushed the door open quietly and stepped into the room.

She nodded as soon as she saw Anya was awake. "Hello there," she said, smiling. Her eyes, though, didn't smile.

Her eyes were dark green depths of deep sadness.

Behind her, hanging back, was Jack. He wore the same threadbare black shirt and torn jeans. He looked awful. His face was gaunt, huge circles under his eyes, and his hair was more desperately disarranged than ever. It looked like he'd taken a weed-whacker to it.

Her heart soared with hope. If Jack was here, everything was all right.

"Shell?" Anya whispered with dry lips.

"Just relax," Theo approached the bed, sank down to sit next to Anya, and took her hand.

The green light returned, swirling around the corners of Anya's vision. Now that she was awake she could see the depth and strength of Theo's gift, and was humbled by it. Anya's left arm twinged a little, but the green light sank in and coated the ache, sealed it away.

Finally, it was done. Theo smiled, but her eyes were still sad. "That's better." She stood up with a sigh. One hand slipped down to rub her rounded belly protectively. "Anya...there isn't an easy way to say this."

Anya's eyes filled with tears. "Shell?" She looked past Theo to Jack.

"I'll tell her." His eyes were pale and lifeless. He took two steps forward and stood at what Anya could only describe as "attention," his hands behind his back, his chin level. The dark stubble on his cheeks made his gauntness seem even more marked. "Anya, Shell's alive."

Relief, sharp as a nail, pierced Anya's chest. "Oh." Her voice was a dried up croak. Then she looked up at him again. "Alive, but...?"

His mouth turned down at the corners. "He's catatonic, Anya. They used the same process on him that they would use on another psychic. Even Mari can't reach him."

"Even *I* can't." Theo sighed again. "Anya, I'm so sorry."

Anya believed it. She stared at Jack, who didn't quite meet

her gaze. He coughed slightly, shifting his weight from one foot to the other.

Just like Shell used to, she thought, dimly.

"I've made a few calls to Circle Lightfall," he continued. "They've pulled a few strings. He's in a hospital, a private one. Theo examined the place; the nurses are good and the care is excellent. It's the best we could do."

"Them," she said. "The...the Brotherhood."

"We took out the team holding him. But with only four Watchers it's nearly impossible. To drive them out of the city completely we'd need more." Jack's chin dropped. He looked at the floor.

"We didn't want Circle Lightfall inside the city," Theo said. "It's our fault, Anya. If we'd let them in, the Brotherhood would have been driven out sooner, and you and Shell would never have had to suffer like this."

The ludicrousness of this being anyone's fault but her own made a thin bitter laugh tear its way out of Anya's throat.

"It's not your fault, Theo," she forced out through her burning throat. "It's mine. They wanted to blackmail me because I stole from a bank—used the Persuasion."

"We know." Tears glimmered in Theo's dark eyes. "They—the Brotherhood, or whatever we're supposed to call them—sent us a packet with papers and pictures and lies. Trying to make us doubt you, I suppose. Thinking we would throw you out or something. I don't know. Elise burned them, furious that someone would say such awful things about you. Anya, it doesn't matter. Jack explained. We know you were desperate and trying to take care of Shell. It's *not* your fault."

"If it's a question of fault," Jack broke in, "it's mine. I didn't reach him soon enough, Anya. If I'd been faster, this wouldn't have happened. The failing is mine."

Anya stared at Theo. "You mean you *knew?*"

"Of course." Theo crossed her arms. "And it didn't matter. We knew you would never steal unless you were desperate, Anya. You're one of us."

"But—" Her eyes flicked back over to Jack. He dropped his gaze, refusing to even look at her. It hurt so much to talk; her throat was on fire. "What else?"

"He thinks you're going to send him back to Circle Lightfall in disgrace, or something of the sort," Theo said. "Make him see reason, Anya. There's just one thing."

Anya held her breath, waiting.

Theo's shoulders came up. It was a familiar movement, though Anya couldn't think of quite why. The healer lifted her chin just a little, her eyes terribly sad but just as terribly determined. "We—Elise and Mari and I—voted to keep Circle Lightfall out of the city. To let them in, the vote has to be unanimous. Elise has changed her mind. Now that we know Circle Lightfall can get rid of these people—and that they can help care for Lightbringers like you who have been driven from their homes—well, she's changed her vote. But it has to be unanimous."

There was a long silence. Anya's eyes flicked over to Jack and back to Theo. None of it made any sense. "What?"

"Your vote. You don't have to vote right away. You've been unconscious for three days. But I—we—want you to know that you're one of us, and you have a vote." Theo nodded sharply. "I'm so sorry, Anya. It's our fault. If we'd been less shortsighted, we would have...oh, we'd have done it all differently. I'm so very sorry."

She turned away, her long sandalwood hair glowing in the late-afternoon light. More rain tapped at the window. "I think I'll excuse myself now." Her voice was strangely thick. It looked as if Theo was actually *crying.*

"Oh, Theo," Anya began, but the healer left the room in a hurry, the door closing behind her with a click.

That left Jack staring at the floor and Anya lying in the bed, trying to figure this out. She felt dry and desiccated, thirsty again, and her heart hurt.

Shell. "He's in a coma?" she finally husked.

Jack stirred slightly. "Catatonic. He'll respond to some orders; he'll eat if they prompt him. But other than that...he's empty, Anya. They broke him. We don't know how to reverse it. If he was a witch, we'd have a better chance. And if Circle Lightfall is allowed into the city, some of the Mindhealers and Rescuers might be able to help. But..." His shoulders slumped. "I failed you."

It sounded as if he wanted to say more, but he closed his mouth with a snap and stared at the floor.

"They did that to him?" *Why doesn't he come here? Why is he still standing there?* "Jack, what *happened?*"

He shrugged. "They had flamethrowers. Remy escaped most of it, I got clipped. Had to trim the burned parts out of my hair. But we got Shell out and exterminated the team holding him." He took a deep breath. "Anya, when the new Watchers arrive, I'll go. Until then, your safety—"

"You're leaving?" She thought her heart couldn't crack any further, but perhaps that was wrong. She could almost hear each new break, like the crackles of ice melting in a rapid thaw.

"I wasn't fast enough," he said stiffly. "I didn't bring Shell back, not all of him. If I'd—"

"You want to leave?" She swallowed the hard, sharp lump in her throat again. "If you want to, I can't stop you. You're an adult."

She sank back into the pillows. *Theo knows where Shell is. I can go to the hospital and try...what? Try to bring him back. What did they do to him?*

"I don't *want* to leave."

"You can if you want." She closed her eyes. The pillows were soft. Her entire body felt as if it could sink into the bed and never return. She gathered her strength and forced out the words. "I can't stop you, Jack. I wish you wouldn't. Besides, it's my fault. If I'd listened to you, maybe you and the others could have found him quicker and we would all be safe now." Tears trickled hotly down her temples into her hair, and her voice sank to a painful, thready whisper. "How soon can I get out of bed? I want to go to this hospital. Maybe I can reach him."

"Theo says it will be another couple of days. I'm under strict orders to keep you in bed unless it's *absolutely* necessary you be moved. Anya, I wish I could have saved him. I truly do. I tried."

"I know you did. It's not your fault, Jack. It's mine." The painful whisper turned into a croak. She forced her heavy eyelids open enough to see him.

He stood, shoulders slumped and head dropped forward, the picture of weariness. Gray light clung to the folds of his battered coat, outlined a widening hole in the left knee of his jeans, and showed his scuffed boots and tangled, chopped-up hair.

Then he raised his head slightly, and in that moment she saw his true age reflected in his eyes. How long had he gone from place to place, solitary and hurting? Completely alone, carrying the festering, crippling weight of guilt that wasn't even his? If Anya lived to be a hundred, she would never forget that look—and the way her heart twisted, seeing that pain.

She patted the bed. It took more concentration than she would have believed possible to make that slight movement. "Come here."

He looked up. "I don't think I should."

"Come *here*."

He obeyed. "I don't ask you to forgive me."

"Shut the hell up, Jack." A tired, bitter laugh wrung its way out of her. She coughed, hacking, and her voice eased a little. "You came for me. You jumped off the top of a skyscraper after me." Her eyelids drifted closed. "I'm not going to ask you again. You want to stay, come here. You don't, it's all right—but don't ask me to act happy about it."

The speech took most of her waning strength and made her cough again, her throat raw and torn.

The bed groaned as he rested his knee on it. Then his hand, most of his weight balanced easily. He dropped down beside her, his leather coat creaking, and there was a moment or two of confusion while he rearranged himself. Then he ended up stretched on the edge of the bed.

Anya was hard-put not to laugh again. "Could have taken your coat off," she pointed out, as he slid his arm under her shoulders and hugged her, no doubt trying to be gentle but driving all the breath from her lungs.

"Shell..." she said, and Jack kissed her forehead. Again. And again, as if he couldn't help himself.

"I'm so sorry, Anya," he whispered into her hair, and she believed him.

"At least he's alive." Her eyes welded themselves shut. "If he's alive we can try to reach him."

"Anything you like." Delicious, drowsy heat rolled through her, easing the cold knot of dread she hadn't realized was living under her breastbone. "Anya?"

"You're alive." She slid back down into the well of sleep. But this time, Jack was next to her, and the comfort of his presence somehow followed her into unconsciousness.

Thirty-Two

Three months later

Jack waited in the hall until the last wave of students flooded out the door. He towered at least head and shoulders over most of them, but they paid no attention to him. His glamour was solid. He was just part of the furniture, and besides, they were too busy yammering about important stuff, like cars and boyfriends and girlfriends and dates and tests and the impending wonders of Spring Break.

This was a private school. Uniforms were the rule, but the students each tried to flaunt the rule in their own way. The Catullus Academy, being a private school for the children of the rich and intellectual, did not try to enforce the dress or conduct codes with draconian discipline; the students in turn didn't rebel too badly. This leniency was also extended to the staff—if the teacher was intellectually gifted enough, an occasional eccentricity was tactfully ignored. Since Circle Lightfall had made a most generous grant, if the English teacher—delicately hinted to have some sort of nervous medical condition—sometimes bolted away with no warning, it was overlooked. The students received a free class period, the teacher was gifted enough to make up for it, and the Academy received generous funding. Everybody was happy.

As soon as Jack could, he slid through the door, feeling the wards Anya had set in the walls of her classroom spark, greeting him.

She's made tremendous progress, he thought, his attention briefly moving over the perimeter of the room. The Academy had taken over an old Catholic seminary, so the walls were half plaster, half dark wooden wainscoting, and all the floors were ancient mellow hardwood burnished by students' feet.

Anya leaned on her desk, nodding as a young girl confided something in rapid whispers. The girl shifted, one loafer rubbing against her opposite calf, polishing the leather against her knee-high stocking. She wore two long blond ponytails and smelled like bubblegum and the slight glow of Power. A young Lightbringer. Thankfully, she didn't notice Jack.

Since the Guardians had allowed Circle Lightfall into the city, things had moved quickly. The Watchers had swept the

Brotherhood out, and the regular Circle infrastructure had been built up. The Guardians had been surprised at the amount of respect and awe accorded them, and finding out about the benefits available to Lightbringers had made Elise cheerfully announce that she was going back to college for an art history degree, if the Circle would fund it.

Anya had said very little, but she had asked Jack afterwards if perhaps she would be able to buy a house. A week later, Circle Lightfall's agent had closed on the quiet little pseudo-Victorian they'd been renting.

In every decision about the city, of course, the Guardians were deferred to. After all, they were the first Lightbringers to successfully cast the Guardian spell in something like four centuries. There were two safehouses being built now, and Jack thought privately that the streets were much safer since more Watchers had mostly driven out even the deep-seated Dark nests on the docks. Jack had missed most of that, between Anya's new job, daily trips to the hospital, and the serious magickal work the Guardians now practiced two or three times a week, aided by Teachers from the Circle.

Anya was beginning to relax, but Jack often saw her staring into the distance, a line deepening between her eyebrows, sometimes rubbing at her left arm as if it still pained her, even though her recovery—helped along by Theo's attentions—had been rapid. And her nightmares were still frequent, terrible dreams of burning houses and her brush with the vulture. But after every nightmare, Jack was there, and even though he cherished comforting her, he hated the way the dreams robbed her of peace and sleep.

He surfaced from his reverie as Anya's gray eyes met his, her long sheaf of glossy black hair braided back. She murmured a few words of explanation to the girl, who laughed, chirped a thank you, and swung out the door, trailing a bright scarf of golden Power.

She should have a Watcher. I should ask Anya to report that.

"Hello, teacher," Jack said. "I've been in the library all day. Did you know I missed the Enlightenment while I was in China?"

"China?" The smile she gave him was worth the entire day he'd divided between prowling the halls unnoticed and being cramped in the Library, alert for any sign of danger while breathing in the smell of paper and dust. She shuffled papers on her desk. Behind her, the blackboard boasted four lines of a Shakespeare sonnet, written in Anya's firm clear hand. "What were you doing there?" She picked up her leather briefcase, scooping up a stack of tests to be graded as well.

"Putting together a Watcher infrastructure and exporting some combat-training techniques. I have to tell you, Watching a teacher is a most enlightening experience."

He pushed a seat back in under a desk, straightened another desk, picked up a piece of wadded paper and tossed it in the trashcan. The room was tall and pleasant, radiators under a bank of windows that showed rolling green lawns outside, the walls just beginning to display marks of Anya's personality—a print of the Mona Lisa, a poster about English and its debt to Latin, a humorous poster of a bust of Shakespeare with a pink brassiere draped over his head. A lectern stood to one side, a small office visible through a door behind her desk. An antique globe made of brass stood on a slim stand in the back of the room. And, of course, the smell of jasmine that followed Anya everywhere was beginning to sink into the floor and walls and pressed-tin ceiling.

She made a good-natured grimace, a pair of couth pearl earrings contrasting with her hair. She dressed a little primly, knee-length skirts and proper blouses, sweaters and blazers, understated jewelry—he had never before seen the beauty of a woman so cool and contained.

Anya stood, sweeping a few more papers into her briefcase. "I'll be ready in a moment."

"Take your time." He smiled, the expression feeling a little less odd and mechanical now. A little more natural. He had even been able to spend a lunch hour with her in the teacher's lounge, watching as she bolted a sandwich and graded pop quizzes.

Anya paused, her head cocked as if listening. Jack tensed slightly. Last week she'd had another compulsion, leaving the school's quiet green grounds in the middle of the day and leading Jack to a carjacking-in-progress. Thankfully, it seemed that she only responded to crimes being committed within about a mile radius—or at least, none of the crimes she'd been compelled toward had been farther away than that. And they were mercifully not very often.

"Anya?"

"Nothing." She shook her head, snapping her briefcase closed.

She picked up her camel coat from the back of her chair, and Jack found himself across the room, holding it for her. She smiled a thank you, her eyes lighting up for a moment, and Jack didn't try to stop himself. He leaned forward and pressed his lips to her forehead, a gentle kiss. The familiar, intense pleasure of her skin against his wrapped around him, roared through his nerves.

"Just thinking," she said. "You want to drive?"

She settled her purse strap over her shoulder and picked up her briefcase. He would have taken it for her, but she preferred to carry it.

"Of course." *Standard procedure, witch. Besides, I've seen the way you drive. Enough to give me a heart attack.* He followed her to the door, stepped out into the hall and scanned while she turned off the lights.

She locked the classroom and they both set off. Anya's heels made crisp sounds against the worn wooden flooring. More students milled around. The few people that saw him at the school assumed he was Anya's eccentric boyfriend or husband. He was always careful to keep a stronger glamour while on the grounds.

"There weren't any phone calls?" She glanced up at him, hope written on her face.

Jack paused. "None from the hospital. I'm sorry, *piccola.* Theo called, she has Lamaze tonight; there's no pressing work. She did say the baby's dropped, whatever that means. Mari wanted to know if you could help her with some old Petrarch texts."

Her face fell, but she reached down and slipped her fingers through his. "Well, maybe we'll see something tonight. Of course I'll help Mari. Shell might like being read to."

He nodded. Her name was called and people waved—she was quite popular already, staff and students attracted to her glow. She smiled, tipped her chin, and was actually humming as they took the staircase down to the east hall, then out a set of double doors and down more steps.

Outside, the air was crisp and cool, full of late-afternoon sunlight and the promise of spring. Tiny green buds were lengthening on the trees, all the ice had melted. The nights were generally balmier now, too.

"It smells like spring," she said as he unlocked the passenger door of the blue Taurus for her.

"I was just thinking that." His hand brushed hers as she dropped into the car. The jolt of pleasure made him shut his eyes and inhale—and, once again, send up a brief prayer of thanksgiving that he was allowed to be so close to her. His witch.

It was a fifteen-minute drive to the hospital—part of why Anya had accepted this job. She was unusually quiet, and he didn't want to disturb her, so he concentrated on driving.

The familiar brick bulk of the Summerline Home rose up, the psychic atmosphere of the building full of the cloudiness of grief and the random sparks of what most people would call insanity. For all that, it was a high-quality institution, and its patients were given the best of care.

She blinked against the westering sunlight as he offered his hand, accepting his help out of the car. A smiled nervously as she smoothed her dark blue knee-length skirt. "I really think he's getting better," she said tentatively.

Jack locked the door and pushed it shut, keeping her hand. "I think so too." He was rewarded with a grateful smile.

She glanced around the parking lot, fringed by juniper bushes and bare-branched trees just beginning to show some green. "Jack?"

"Hm?" He scanned the area, found no danger, and looked down at her. The sunlight brought out blue highlights in her hair, speckles of gold on her pale skin, and made her eyes glow. Jack's entire body tightened.

"What if he doesn't get any better?" She whispered it, as if they might be overheard.

Jack set his shoulders. "We'll come back every day." He dared to touch the curve of her cheek, his callused fingertips scraping. "As long as it takes, *piccola.*"

"You don't mind?"

Oh, so that's it. "Anya, if every day of my life is like this from now on, I will consider myself lucky. If we come here every day for years, I don't mind. Being near you is all I want." He pulled his fingers away from her skin with an effort and brushed the tear from her soft cheek. "You gave me a new life. Where else should I spend it?"

"You really mean that?" Her lower lip trembled slightly.

"We'd better get inside." He smiled and pressed a kiss to

her forehead. "I'm your Watcher, Anya. This is what a Watcher lives for."

"You live for cooling your heels in a library all day and coming to a mental hospital with an insane English teacher?" She adjusted her purse's strap over her shoulder, the tear-track still glimmering on her cheek.

"Sounds like heaven to me."

She examined his face. "You're sure?"

"I was sure the moment I saw you." *Maybe not that very moment, but so close it doesn't matter.* "You're my witch, Anya."

Anya still watched his face. He suffered it, standing very still, wondering if perhaps she was searching for a way to tell him she had changed her mind. That she wanted him to leave. That now that she'd seen what Circle Lightfall was, she wanted a different Watcher—one less grim, one untainted by the Crusade, maybe a Watcher who could ease the crushing burden of grief that kept her coming back to this place day after day.

The strange feeling of impending disaster returned. Four Guardian witches, four Watchers, and a city only newly-freed from the Dark. Jack didn't trust the recent calm, and the other Watchers, even the unbonded ones, privately agreed with him. There was an uncomfortable storm-feeling of some catastrophe approaching.

I can't leave you. He looked down at Anya's now familiar but still surprisingly beautiful face. It stopped his heart and breath every time her eyes met his. *I won't make you suffer my presence, cara mia, but I'm too selfish to leave you alone. Ask for another Watcher if you want—I'm ready to guard you no matter what it takes.*

"Jack?" She reached up and rested her fingertips against his cheek. It was a habitual gesture, and a sweet one. He leaned into her touch.

"What?"

"You're absolutely sure?"

"Of course I am." *If you only knew how sure.*

She nodded, her eyebrows drawing together. "For how long? I'm a Guardian, they tell me. That means I can't leave the city. I don't mind—I've moved around so much that all I want to do is settle down. But you might...I don't know. Get bored."

"No." How could he even begin to tell her that watching the way the light touched her face was all he needed? *A man could watch you for hours and not get bored.* He was amazed that more people didn't stop and stare when Anya walked by. Then again, if they did, Jack might have more difficulty than even he could handle. The thought was almost amusing. "I don't want to go anywhere else."

"If—*when* Shell wakes up, he'll need constant care. And he's not likely to be any easier to deal with. You might not want to be saddled with that."

"Anya." He said it as gently as he could, trapping her hand against his cheek, the feel of her skin sending fire through his veins. "When Shell wakes up, I'll help you any way I can. We'll take him home. His room's still ready and waiting for him." He glanced up, scanning the parking lot. "It's getting chilly out here. Shall we go inside?"

She must have found what she was looking for in his face. Jack watched, fascinated, as a faint blush rose to her cheeks. "I guess so." She went on tiptoe to kiss his cheek. "Let's go, then."

He slid his arm over her shoulders as they set off through the parking lot. "After all, if today's the day he wakes up, we don't want to miss it."

Her smile was enough to reward him, and together, Watcher and witch, they walked toward the hospital.

Author's Note

The invocations in this book were created specifically for this work of fiction. They are not taken from any book, movie, song, or other work; but they may sound familiar due to the standard form of pagan invocation of the elements.

CPSIA information can be obtained at www.ICGtesting.com
Printed in the USA
LVOW041629100812

293846LV00003B/92/A

9 781933 417189